Simon Kernick is forty, lives near London and has two young children.

The research for his novels is what makes them so authentic. His extensive list of contacts in the police force has been built up over more than a decade. It includes long-serving officers in Special Branch, the National Crime Squad (now SOCA), and the Anti-Terrorist Branch, all of whom have plenty of tales to tell.

Severed

SIMON KERNICK

BANTAM PRESS

LONDON • TORONTO • SYDNEY • AUCKLAND • JOHANNESBURG

TRANSWORLD PUBLISHERS
61–63 Uxbridge Road, London W5 5SA
A Random House Group Company
www.booksattransworld.co.uk

First published in Great Britain
in 2007 by Bantam Press
a division of Transworld Publishers

A CIP catalogue record for this book
is available from the British Library.

ISBN 9780593054734 (cased)
ISBN 9780593054727 (tpb)

Addresses for Random House Group Ltd companies outside the UK
can be found at: www.randomhouse.co.uk
The Random House Group Ltd Reg. No. 954009

The Random House Group Ltd makes every effort to ensure that the papers used in its books are made
from trees that have been legally sourced from well-managed and credibly certified forests. Our paper
procurement policy can be found at: www.randomhouse.co.uk/paper.htm

Typeset in 11/16pt Times by
Falcon Oast Graphic Art Ltd.

Printed and bound in Great Britain by
CPI Mackays, Chatham, ME5 8TD

2 4 6 8 10 9 7 5 3 1

Severed

Spin a coin, spin a coin; all fall down.
Queen Nefertiti stalks through the town.
Children's rhyme (anonymous)

Friday

1

From the moment I open my eyes, I know it's going to be a bad day. The room's stifling hot; my head feels like a dwarf on speed's dancing a jig on it; and the blood ... Well, the blood's everywhere. I can feel its clamminess where my cheek's resting on the pillow, and under my casually outstretched arm. For the first few seconds my vision's blurred, but I can see that it's daylight: thin shafts of sunlight are flickering round the edges of the chintzy, flower-patterned curtains covering the room's only window.

This place is totally unfamiliar. I have no idea where I am.

Slowly, I roll over in the bed. It's a massive effort. Every part of my body seems to ache, my head especially. Even in the dim half-light and at the angle I'm lying, I can see that the pillows and crisp white sheets are all drenched crimson. I focus on my arm, the one that feels clammy with blood. It looks as if it's been dipped to the elbow in dark paint, with a few stray splashes further up.

Shock hits me then. I sit bolt upright and my vision blurs for a second time. I stare down at the bed and try to make some sort of sense of what's going on. There's a lump beneath the sheets, completely obscured. It's worryingly human-shaped. The blood seems to have emanated from its top half. I feel dizzy and nauseous. For a moment, I try to remember the previous night, searching for a clue that'll tell me what I'm doing in a blood-soaked bed in a strange room I have no recollection of entering. But nothing presents itself. Nothing at all.

The previous day is a complete blank.

A panic-stricken thought flashes across my mind. How much of my memory have I lost? Am I going to be one of those poor bastards whose whole past's disappeared on them, who can't even remember his own name? But no, I know exactly who I am. My name is Tyler. I'm a car salesman by trade, a high-class one too. I own a BMW franchise. I was in the army for a long time. I am a veteran of Northern Ireland, the first Gulf War, Bosnia and Sierra Leone. And I am in a lot of trouble. This much I know immediately.

I flick my eyes from the lump to the clock radio and back again. The LCD display tells me it's 9.51 a.m. Very late for me. I'm usually an early riser. I switch on the bedside lamp, the brightness making me squint sharply.

My mouth is bone dry and I feel like shit. I really don't want to look under the covers, but I know I'm going to have to.

Clambering unsteadily out of the bed, I reach over with hands that I notice are shaking a little and touch the top of the sheets, recoiling against the dampness, wondering what it is under there, then pull them back in one swift movement.

Oh, Jesus.

Retching, gasping for breath, I stumble backwards, banging into the wall. I can't believe what I'm seeing. The shock is blinding, terrifying . . .

A naked young woman with very pale skin lies stiff and lifeless on her back. Her body is lithe and athletic, if a little on the skinny side. Underneath a silver belly-button ring, the faded tattoo of a butterfly sits on her waxed skin, next to a thin, perfectly straight strip of very short dark pubic hair. Her fingernails are varnished a sky blue colour, and she has rings with Celtic symbols on the middle and index fingers of her right hand.

But what scares and revolts me the most is the simple, inescapable fact that her head is missing. The neck is a jagged, raw stump where the head has been either hacked or sawn off, and the blood surrounds it like a huge crimson halo. It is the only obvious injury to the body.

For some seconds – it may be as few as three, it may be as many as twenty – I simply stare at the corpse, and although I can remember nothing of the previous night, I know without a doubt that there is no way I am responsible for what's happened here. You see, I recognize this girl, even without her head.

Her name was Leah Torness, and I was in love with her.

I can't believe this is happening. Yesterday, she was a smiling, chatty young woman with everything to live for. Today, she is a butchered corpse, as pale and lifeless as an alabaster statue. My head spins with the confusion of what I'm witnessing. I feel like I have a terrible hangover, and the nausea rises through me in bitter, debilitating waves. I've seen sudden death before, on the battlefield. It's always a terrifying sight, but this is worse. Far worse. On the battlefield, you are psyched up for death; as a soldier you are constantly preparing for it. But I have been a civilian now for three years, and the memories of blood and cordite are fading. And as for the woman lying in front of me, she never fought in any battle, never put herself in the firing line. She was a twenty-five-year-old nanny enjoying life in the big city. She was innocent. Why kill her?

Why?

I can't look at her any more. If I do, I think I might break down. It's an obscene sight and yet, somehow, brutally compelling. But I tear my gaze away and look round the room, trying to find something familiar to hang on to, something that may explain how I got here. Apart from the bed, which is drenched in Leah's blood, the room is neatly decorated and furnished in a distinctly feminine but old-fashioned style with cheap reprints of still-life and classical oil paintings dotting the pastel-coloured walls. The furniture – a huge double wardrobe, a chest of drawers, and a dressing table with oval mirror – is all antique pine and matching. It reminds me of the inside of a kid's dolls house. Except that in the corner there's a TV on a metallic black stand with a DVD player in the space beneath. A folded cardboard sign sits on top of the DVD player and it grabs my attention immediately. It's handwritten in black marker pen, the words in neat block capitals. Still shaking, I take a couple of steps towards it.

And curse.

The top line says, simply, TYLER, and then beneath it PRESS PLAY.

For a moment, I'm too shell-shocked to figure out what it's trying to say, but then the realization hits.

TYLER.

Someone else knows I'm here.

I take a step back, shut my eyes, and attempt to take stock of what's going on. Outside the window, I can hear the sound of birds singing, which tells me I am a fair way from home. No-one ever hears birdsong in central London. I don't even know whether or not I came here voluntarily. I know nothing – that is the huge and insurmountable problem I face at the moment. I am in a strange room next to the headless corpse of the woman I still love, with a sign telling me to press play on the DVD player. I feel a sudden burst of panic, which I have to fight down ruthlessly. I need to hold myself together. Different emotions – revulsion, shock, grief at the loss of a loved one – come at me with the force of explosions, but I was a soldier for fifteen years and I'm trained to remain calm in tense situations, and to deal with events rationally.

I take a series of deep breaths, trying to clear my head. I need to remember how we got here, and why we came.

Think.

I think so hard it hurts. I concentrate like a contestant on a game show one answer away from a million with the answer on the tip of my tongue, the effort draining what little strength I have. But still nothing comes back. My last memory is watching a documentary about global warming on the TV with a takeaway Chinese meal: squid in black bean sauce with egg fried rice. It had tasted greasy, and I didn't finish it. I was alone. I seem to recall that Leah was seeing friends that night. As an ex-soldier, I tend to like routine, and I almost always have takeaways on a Wednesday, so I'm guessing this was when it was. But it doesn't help a lot, because I don't know what day it is today.

I feel the back of my head. There's no tenderness on the skin, no tell-tale lumps, so I haven't been hit over the head. This means I've been drugged, and with something powerful enough that I wouldn't bat an eyelid while Leah, who was a fit young woman, was slaughtered only inches away from me.

I shut my eyes, fighting off another wave of nausea. When I open them again, I find my gaze returning to Leah's body. The blood on her neck wound has coagulated, and the thick patches on the sheets are also drying. She died some time ago, then, two or three hours at least, probably longer, and for the first time I notice the smell in the room, the vague sour odour of faeces and decay that lingers round the recently dead like a humiliating farewell.

Standing there in the dim, leaden silence, it feels as if I've stepped into the middle of someone else's nightmare.

But I'm wrong. As I crouch down and press the play button, I am about to find out that this is my nightmare. And it's only just beginning.

2

I can hear my heart thumping as I sit on the edge of the bed and wait. For several seconds the screen remains blank before wobbling slightly with interference. Then the film starts.

It opens with a static shot of the room I am now in, taken at roughly chest height and facing towards the top of the bed. The bedside lights are on and it's night. Although the focus is very slightly blurred, like a bad home video, it's easy enough to make out Leah lying spread-eagled on the sheets, very much alive. Her wrists and ankles are tied to each of the small wooden posts at the head and foot of the bed, and she is naked. The expression on her face is one of lust. The sight catches me out. In the few short weeks I've known her, Leah and I had a healthy and enjoyable sex life, but it never involved bondage. I suddenly feel uncomfortable, like some kind of voyeur, unearthing secrets that are best left alone.

Her full pink lips quiver and form a lazy half-smile, and her eyes are half-shut. It is obvious she's enjoying her confinement; that she's viewing the situation as part of some kind of sex game. The pale contours of her soft young skin ripple with life, her hips snaking as she tries to rub herself against the sheets. She looks good, too – just as I remember her from our first meeting. Her hennaed hair is cut short and stylish, spiky at the top, and her face is a perfect oval, with prominent cheekbones that are dotted with a scattering of freckles. She has mischievous brown eyes that sparkle with the vibrancy of youth, and a model's aquiline nose, with an emerald stud in its left side.

Seeing her alive on the screen is like a hammer blow, and I feel my jaw tighten.

As I watch, there's the sound of the bedroom door opening off camera and someone coming in. Leah turns her head in the direction of the newcomer and her expression changes perceptibly, the lust replaced by a flicker of confusion. 'Tyler,' she says, addressing the person off camera, 'what are you doing? Why are you wearing that mask?' Her words are distorted on the film and sound tinny. There's a mumbled reply that I can't make out, then Leah's expression changes again, this time the confusion being replaced by a wide-eyed fear. 'What's that?' she asks, panicky now. 'Why have you got a knife? Tyler, tell me.'

I feel my head throbbing painfully as the person she's talking to finally appears, moving round the foot of the bed in profile to the camera. He's naked as well, but his head is completely covered by a black rubber bondage mask, and in his right hand he holds a long, wicked-looking, wide-bladed butcher's knife.

Leah is speaking again, but I can no longer see her, as the man with the knife is in the way. 'Tyler, if this is a game, stop it now. Please. You're scaring the shit out of me.'

I know the guy isn't me – I would never do anything like this – but I have an extremely serious problem. He is roughly my height and build, and given the poor quality of the recording, it's not that easy to tell one way or another. So a court of law might see things differently. Especially with the way Leah is talking.

Either she's a damn fine actress or she genuinely believes it's me standing there behind the mask. And I don't think you can act as fearful as she's sounding. Her fear comes right from her bones, and it is easy to see why.

The man pretending to be me slowly advances round the front of the bed towards her side, taking his time and enjoying each step, lifting the knife higher so that Leah can see it more easily. The blade glints threateningly in the lamp light as he raises it above his head. Beyond him, I can see her struggling vainly on the bed, but the knots that bind her hold easily. She's helpless.

And then, as the guy turns his back to the camera, the trouble I'm in increases tenfold. You see, there's one way to tell without any doubt whatsoever whether or not the man with the knife, the one Leah is calling Tyler, is me. Ten years ago, I suffered a number of shrapnel injuries in a bomb attack, and I still carry the scars. Most are deep but small puncture marks, but three are noticeable from a distance. They are all on my upper back. One is like a pink birthmark, about three inches across, near the right shoulder blade. The other two are deep, thick lacerations that run down either side of my spine, almost symmetrically. The man with the knife has those three scars. They aren't that clear in the film, but if you know what you're looking for, you'll see them. And I know. I stare at them grimly, my teeth clenched tight. They are in the right place on his back, there's no doubt about that. The man in the shot may not be me, but the way things are looking, I could well end up in a minority of one holding that opinion.

Leah cries out again, her voice loud and full of confused desperation as she continues to struggle uselessly against the bonds. 'Tyler, please! Don't do this! Please!' This last word seems to stretch out for seconds, ending in a terrified, unintelligible sob. It is the sound of someone whose world has suddenly and inexplicably fallen apart, who cannot come to terms with the simple, cold fact that she is about to die.

He stops by the bed, raising the knife high.

And that's it. I can't watch any more. Not another second. I scramble to my feet, grab the TV in both hands and tear it from its wiring, hurling it against the wall. It lands heavily on the floor and something inside shatters.

The room descends into a heavy, tomb-like silence. The smell of death is so thick it feels like I could almost reach out and touch it. I stand naked and alone, staring at the wall, trying to control the nausea that's rising up in me.

Slowly, very slowly, I turn round and face the bed where Leah's body lies. The sheets are bloodstained almost black. The absolute stillness is virtually impossible to bear.

'Oh God, Leah,' I whisper. 'I'm so sorry I wasn't here for you.'

As I speak, I sink to my knees, my eyes squeezed shut against the tears that are forming. My head aches ferociously and my mouth is bone dry. In those few moments, I honestly feel like I want to die, and the question that keeps running through my mind is 'Why?' Why has someone inflicted this savagery on an innocent young woman like Leah, and left me alive in here with her?

I have to get out of here. The cloying atmosphere is beginning to envelop me, but I can't leave her behind. Not alone, in this place. It would be an act of cowardice, something I could never forgive myself for, because God knows what will be done with her after I'm gone. The least she deserves is a proper resting place.

My mind's a maelstrom as I try to work out how I can take her with me, in broad daylight, and I hardly hear the movement behind me, the soft scrape of a shoe on carpet.

But hear it I eventually do, and my eyes fly open. I turn round fast, just in time to feel the ferocious electric shock that surges right through me from my toes to my skull. I jangle on the floor, helpless and wild, rolling and writhing, unable to focus on who's doing this to me. The seconds seem to last for ever as my body spasms uncontrollably, and my vision fuzzes and mists.

The current stops as quickly as it began. I'm lying on my back, staring upwards into nothingness. Through the gloom and fog I can make out a blurred, dark figure, almost like a shadow. He grows larger as he leans in close to me.

And then I feel a light sting on my upper arm, and everything goes black.

3

Tinny music penetrates my subconscious, a familiar tune mangled into a mobile phone jingle. It seems to go on for a long time, and in my head I hum along to it, trying to remember what it's called.

Then my eyes open and I am awake once again. The first thing I see through the car's windscreen is pine trees. Lots of them, rising up on each side of the track my car is parked on. This is my BMW 7-Series – I recognize the leather interior. The music is coming from an unfamiliar mobile phone on the seat next to me. Beside the phone, standing upright, is an equally unfamiliar black leather briefcase. There is also a litre bottle of Evian with the seal intact. I reach over and pull off the lid, gulping the water down until my raging thirst passes.

The memory of what happened to Leah comes flooding back, and I experience another wave of grief. I hurriedly look round the car, but there's no sign of her and I realize, with a sense of shame, that I've left her behind, all alone in that stinking little room. I am dressed now in the clothes I'm assuming I was wearing last night: a long-sleeved cotton shirt, jeans and a pair of sand-coloured Timberland boots.

The phone is still ringing. I recognize the tune now: it's 'the Funeral March'. Someone, somewhere, has a macabre sense of humour, and it's clear that whoever it is knows I'm here and wants to speak to me.

I hunt around in my pockets for my own phone, but it's gone, which I suppose is no surprise. I look at my watch again. It's 10.41. I've just lost the best part of another hour of my life, but then that's a lot better than Leah, who's lost maybe fifty years of hers.

I pick up and press the answer button. 'Hello,' I say wearily.

'Mr Tyler. I'm glad you're awake.' The voice is deep and artificial, disguised by a voice suppressor.

I don't say anything. I don't have to. I can tell from the confidence in the tone that the person addressing me knows my situation.

'I'm guessing you slept well,' the voice continues. 'I'm not surprised. It must have taken it out of you, slicing the girl's head off.'

I feel a long slow shiver go from the small of my back to the nape of my neck. Still I don't speak.

'You don't have to say anything, Mr Tyler. As long as you do what you're told, this whole unfortunate matter can be tidied up, and you can avoid spending the rest of your days in prison.'

'You've got the wrong man,' I say at last, trying to stop my voice from shaking. 'I don't know any Mr Tyler, and I haven't cut anybody's head off.'

'I thought you might not remember the actual event, not after all the drugs you've been taking. A nasty mixture of rohypnol, dimethyltryptamine and a trace of amphetamine sulphate. Very good for losing your inhibitions. Not so good for the memory. That's why I made the film, which I understand you've already watched. Let me lay things on the line for you, Mr Tyler, just so there are no misunderstandings. The DVD you watched is a copy. I have the original. I also have possession of the murder weapon. The fingerprints on it are yours and yours only. I can release both these things to the police at any time, and if I do, there'll be no court in the country that could fail to convict you of murder. Do as I say, however, and all the evidence connecting you to this brutal crime will be destroyed, and you will never hear from me again.'

'What is it you want?' I ask, knowing that I'm speaking to the man – and I'm guessing by the tone beneath the suppressor that it is a man – who murdered my lover, and that for the moment at least I have no choice but to co-operate with him.

'On the seat next to you is a briefcase,' he answers. 'The lock code is one-four-one. Open it.'

Keeping the phone to my ear, I place the case on my lap, key in the combination, and click open the twin catches. I exhale when I see what's inside. At least a hundred thousand pounds in bundled fifty-pound notes are staring back up at me, probably more. I work in a business where I'm used to seeing large sums of cash, but never this amount in one go. Sitting on top of the bundles of notes is a silver pistol which I recognize instantly as a Glock 19. I pick it up and eject the magazine. It is fully loaded with live nine-millimetre ammunition. Shoving the magazine back in, I return the pistol to the case and shut it.

'I'm not going to shoot anyone,' I say into the mobile.

'It's your choice, Mr Tyler, but you have a task to perform, and the gun may come in useful. When I end this call, I am going to text an address in east London to the phone you're now hold-ing. You are to go to that address and tell the person who answers the door that your name is Bone and that you have what he's asking for. Your job is then to take delivery of a briefcase from him.'

'What's in it?'

'You don't need to know that. What you need to know is this: under no circumstances are you to leave the address until you have ownership of that briefcase. If you do, then our arrangement is finished and I will hand over the evidence I have against you to the police immediately. Do I make myself clear?'

I know right then that by following his instructions I am heading into extremely dangerous territory, but in the end, I figure I have no choice. This guy, whoever he is, holds all the cards. I, on the other hand, have no idea of his identity. But make no mistake, I'm going to find him. And when I do, he's a dead man. First of all though, I need to buy time, and the only way I can do that is by following his instructions. Once I have the briefcase he wants, then maybe I can move forward.

'All right,' I tell him, 'I understand. But what are you going to do with Leah?'

'Don't worry about the girl. No-one's going to find her body. And no-one except you and I knows that the place where you awoke this morning exists.'

His coldness is sickening. 'That's not what I meant,' I say. 'I want to make sure she's properly buried.'

'You have no choice in this matter,' he answers, and I think again about what I'm going to do to this bastard when I find him.

But for now, it's going to have to wait. 'Where the hell am I now?' I ask, looking round at the trees.

'Drive to the end of the track and turn right. Eventually, you will get to a road. Turn right again. By that time, your GPS navigation system should be working. It won't work where you are now because of the extensive tree cover. Then all you need to do is type in the address. You're about an hour away from the northern edge of London and you are expected at the east London address at twelve thirty.'

'One last question. What day is it?'

'It's Friday,' he replies, not missing a beat. 'Now get moving, Mr Tyler. The clock's ticking.'

He cuts the connection and leaves me sitting there with the phone to my ear, still trying to think where Thursday went. I know little about memory loss, whether or not it's permanent, or whether at some point it'll all come flooding back to me. It's hugely frustrating, given the position I'm in. This bastard has me bang to rights, there's no doubt about it, and I realize now that Leah's murder has definitley been carried out in order to set me up. The question is why. Why have I been chosen, and what exactly have I been chosen for? You see, all the evidence the man on the other end of the phone has pointing to my involvement in the crime, from the way he lured me in to the positioning of the scars on my back, tells me one very important and very disturbing thing.

He knows me. To set me up so perfectly, he has to.

And if he knows me, I must know him.

4

We crashed trolleys in the Italian supermarket two hundred yards from where I live in north London. That's how we met. It was early one Saturday evening three weeks back, not long before closing. I was turning into the booze aisle, looking for some decent Chianti, and she was coming the other way. Our trolleys hit each other head-on, and she apologized with a wide smile that seemed to light up her whole face. She was very petite and very pretty, with short, spiky, hennaed hair and big brown doe eyes. I had her down for mid-twenties, but there was something almost childishly mischievous in her manner that made me think she might be younger. She was wearing a tight-fitting pink T-shirt which accentuated the curves of her small pointed breasts, and a pair of low-slung blue jeans. The T-shirt said 'I'm the girl your mother warned you about' in bold, sky blue lettering. I could believe it.

'I'm sorry,' she said in a light Home Counties accent, smiling over at me like a cheeky kid. 'I think I was speeding.'

I smiled back. 'And I think I've got whiplash. I might have to consider suing.'

Neither of us made any move to reverse our trolleys. Instead we continued looking at each other. It was a moment straight out of a romantic comedy. Quite pathetic really, and totally unexpected. I had no idea what else to say, but she solved the problem for me.

'My name's Leah. Who are you?'

'I'm Tyler,' I answered, putting out a hand, which she took, giving it a firm shake. 'Pleased to meet you.'

'Likewise. Do you live round here, Tyler?'

'Just round the corner.'

'Planning a boozy night in, were you?' she said, looking down at the Chianti in my trolley.

'Just stocking up. You never know when you're going to be needing it. And you? Are you local?'

She shook her head. 'No. South of the river. Richmond. I was on my way home and I thought I'd stock up as well.'

The silence came again and once more I was left racking my brain for something to say that would keep this conversation going. I liked this girl. It might even have been love at first sight. There was a real vivaciousness about her, an energy that had been missing in my life for a while.

'Well,' she said, 'I think I'd better get on. As you can see, I haven't got very far.' Which was true. Her trolley was empty.

I knew I was going to have to strike while the iron was hot. After all, I told myself, I had nothing to lose, and I wasn't going to get too many chances like this one in my life. I'm not a bad-looking guy, but it's never easy to meet people in the big city.

'Do you want to go for a drink?' I asked quickly.

'What, now?' She gave me a playfully coy look and I noticed for the first time that she had a cute line of freckles running across the bridge of her nose and on to both cheeks.

I smiled. 'Sure. Unless you've got something else planned.'

Outwardly I was calm, but all the while I was praying she didn't, because I really didn't want her walking out of there, and out of my life. I was smitten. It had been that quick.

'No, I've got nothing planned. But you haven't finished your shopping, have you?'

I shrugged. 'It can wait.'

I know the supermarket's owner, a big Italian guy in his fifties. Not by name, but we always have a chat when I'm in there, and I've been a regular for a couple of years now, so I got him to put a bag containing my shopping behind the counter, telling him I'd come back and pay for it tomorrow. Seeing me with Leah, he winked and gave me a sly, knowing smile. 'Have a good evening, eh?' he called out as we left the shop.

'So, what brings you to these parts?' I asked as we walked down the street.

'I stayed with a friend last night. I was on my way home and she said I should try this shop, that the food's excellent.'

'It is. They've got the best parma ham outside Parma.'

She grinned. 'And because of you, I've missed out on it.'

'You can always come back.'

She gave me that playfully coy look again. 'Maybe I will.'

We went to the local All Bar One just down the road. She drank Bacardi and Cokes (doubles) while I quaffed Peroni. She could really put it away. I was impressed. We got on well, and conversation was easy. After a couple of rounds, I asked her if she wanted to get something to eat. 'I'd love to,' she said, and by the way her eyes lit up I could tell that there was something happening here. Sometimes, I think you just know, and I knew then.

We ate at a Thai place further up the street, and carried on our conversation. It turned out that Leah came originally from a village in Dorset, and had come to London about three years ago. She was, she told me, a nanny for the three young daughters of a wealthy professional couple in Richmond. They paid her well: three hundred pounds a week and the use of a Saab convertible. It made me think I was in the wrong job. We talked about her life and her travels. She'd learned to dive as a teenager in the waters off Portland and had spent a year backpacking and diving round South and Central America.

As the waitress cleared the plates away, I asked her if she'd ever got to Belize.

'Second biggest barrier reef in the world,' she answered, smiling. 'How could I miss it?'

'I know, it's a beautiful place, isn't it? I was stationed there for six months once.'

'Are you a soldier, then?'

'I was, for my sins. Not any more.'

'Where did you serve?'

'I was in the army for fifteen years, I served everywhere. Northern Ireland, Iraq in the first Gulf War, Bosnia, Sierra Leone, Afghanistan. I've seen them all, although some of them I'd prefer not to have seen.'

'It must have been a really interesting job, though,' she said, looking right into my eyes as she spoke. They say that some women are very good at making the men they're talking to feel hugely important. If so, Leah had it down to an art form.

I gazed back at her over my wine glass. 'It had its moments, no doubt about that.'

'Why did you leave?'

'My wife persuaded me. She got sick of me disappearing away for weeks, sometimes months, on end.'

'Your wife? You're not still married, are you?' She glanced over in the direction of my left hand. 'I don't see a ring.'

'That's because there isn't one. No, we split up a couple of years back. Not long after I left the army, as it happens.' I smiled. 'I guess when it came down to it, she preferred me being away to being home.'

Leah asked me if I missed the military life.

'Sometimes,' I answered, thinking about her question, 'but not enough to want to go back now. The older you get, the less you crave the excitement. I'm happy enough being a civilian.'

'I don't believe you,' she said playfully. 'You look to me like you love the action.' As she spoke, she lowered her glass of wine and leaned forward so that her face was only inches from mine. I could feel her breath on my face. It smelled minty. 'Am I right?' she whispered breathily, and this time there was an underlying intensity in her tone. Under the table, a hand moved up my thigh.

I'll be honest, all resistance crumbled, if it had ever been there in the first place, which I have to admit I doubt. We finished our drinks quickly and I paid the bill. 'Let's go to my place,' I said, reluctantly extricating my thigh from her hand.

As we walked back together, I put my hand through hers. It was a warm, balmy night and music drifted through the air from the various open windows we passed. I felt truly happy. I'd been living on my own for several years and I think, even with a reasonably active social life, I'd been getting lonely. And now, suddenly, I'd met a beautiful girl. Just like that. Sometimes Lady Luck can smile on you. That's what I was thinking at the time. It never occurred to me that she could just as easily take it all away again.

When we got back to my place, I opened the door for Leah, followed her inside and shut the door. As I switched on the hall light, she reached up and pulled me close to her.

The kiss was electric, the intimacy incredible. Our hands ran across each other's bodies with an urgency that seemed to come out of nowhere, as if we both knew that very soon our time would run out. Clothes were ripped off and strewn across the room as casually as confetti. I kissed her neck, her pert round breasts, kneeling as I moved my lips down across her washboard-flat stomach, breathing in her warmth, revelling in her tight gasps of pleasure.

We finally made it to the bedroom where we made love with a furious intensity that I think surprised us both, and when we were finished, and temporarily sated, we lay there naked in each other's arms, talking and kissing, before the passion took us once again.

When we were resting a second time, she asked me if I minded if she smoked and I said, no problem, so she rolled a thick, three-Rizla joint which we shared. It was my first dope since Afghanistan, and although it wasn't quite as potent as the stuff we got hold of then, it was enough to get me in one of those moods where the whole world's treating you right, and everything you say and do, and everything the person you're with says and does, is uproariously funny. We laughed, we made love, and the night went by all too fast, disappearing with the remorseless inevitability of grains of sand through an egg timer.

Some time towards dawn, just before we slipped into the sleep of the satisfied and exhausted, I kissed her forehead and ran a finger along the pale skin of her jawline, and she smiled that beautiful cherubic smile at me. In that instant I knew, with a blissful sense of terror, that I was falling for this girl in a big, big way.

The next day we stayed in bed until midday, and when we finally did rise, Leah made me take her back to the shop where we'd met. She wanted a picnic, so we bought salami, olives, stuffed peppers, ciabatta bread, Taleggio cheese and, of course, parma ham, and took it with us to Hampstead Heath, where we sat and ate it in the sunshine, washed down with a bottle of Chianti, before finally she said it was time to head back to her place in Richmond.

'I need to freshen up before tomorrow and get an early night,' she told me.

'Can I see you again?' I asked, and I knew that if she said no, I'd be heartbroken.

But she didn't. Of course she didn't.

If she had, then she'd still be alive.

Instead, she leaned over and kissed me gently on the lips. 'I'd love to.'

I drove her back to Richmond, and almost as soon as she'd said goodbye and walked away I felt that hollow emptiness all new lovers experience when they're forced to part, even if it's only temporarily. Thankfully, I didn't have to wait long for our next meeting. I called her the next morning from the BMW showroom I own, and we arranged to go out that evening.

And that was the beginning of a relationship that for the past three weeks had been growing progressively more serious. We might have lived a fair distance apart in travelling time, but we saw each other at least every other night, and in the last few days I'd been thinking that we were going places. I was in love. I wanted her to move in with me. I hadn't said as much – I was going to leave it another couple of weeks because I didn't want to scare her away – but I genuinely wanted to commit.

The last time I remember seeing Leah was early Wednesday morning when she left my house to go back to her family in Richmond, having arranged to meet friends that night. But at some point yesterday we must have seen each other, with fatal consequences. Where did we go? What did we do? And how the hell did we end up out here in the middle of the country, at the slaughterhouse where she met her bloody end?

5

The address I've been given is in a part of east London that has so far resisted the steady process of gentrification that's been a feature of so much of the East End since the late 1980s. The main drag is tired and litter-strewn with a windswept, forgotten feel about it. Running along both sides are cheap takeaways with bags of uncollected rubbish outside; discount shops offering all kinds of useless paraphernalia for under a pound; and, most common of all, empty, boarded-up units, blackened by smoke or covered in graffiti and fly posters. At one intersection there is even a roofless, jagged shell of a building that looks like it might have been bombed back in World War Two and is still waiting for its turn to be repaired. The house I want is on a quiet residential road, lined with mature beech trees. It must have been quite a grand road once, but its tired-looking Georgian town-houses have long ago fallen into disrepair, their white paint now, for the most part, a dirty, stained grey.

I drive past number 33 – not much different from the others, with an ancient Ford Sierra taking up the tiny carport – and keep on going, watching for any suspicious activity, anything that may suggest that this is some sort of trap.

When you've been a soldier exposed to guerrilla warfare, especially the hate-filled maelstrom of Northern Ireland, you learn to be paranoid. You develop antennae that can spot trouble in a way ordinary civilians can't. They're twitching now, telling me that the street's too quiet, almost dead. I don't like it. The Glock feels comforting against the small of my back, as does the Kevlar vest I picked up from home on the way here. I bought it a year ago after another car dealer I know vaguely in Tottenham was shot in the leg while trying to stop a masked gang stealing his two prize Mercedes. I'd intended to wear it whenever I was working late and on my own, but in the end it was never going to be practical, and even though I shelled out three hundred quid on it, it's been gathering dust ever since. Until now, that is.

I continue driving, keeping my eye on the rear-view mirror and the cars parked on either side of the road to see if they contain anyone who may be noting my presence. But there's nothing.

I find a parking spot in one of the adjoining roads several hundred yards away, between a battered old combi van and a skip that is overflowing with household junk, including, bizarrely, a huge African woodcarving of a long, narrow face that has a big crack running through it. The face seems to be giving me the evil eye, and I feel like telling him not to bother. The evil eye's been placed on me already.

It's just short of 12.15, and it's strange, but the fact that I'm on the move and at least temporarily in control of events again has helped to dissipate the grief and shock that almost incapacitated me earlier. I try to push thoughts of Leah from my mind. There'll be time to think of her later, when I'm alone and through this. But for the moment I need to concentrate on survival.

There's a navy blue New York Yankees baseball cap on the seat next to me – something else I picked up from home – and I put it on now. There are bound to be council-run CCTV cameras monitoring this area, and I don't much want them getting a good look at me. I pull the brim low over my face and get out of the car. The space is metered so I put a couple of quid in, knowing that the last thing I need is to return to the car and find it clamped or, worse still, towed away. Once again, I wonder what it is I'm collecting. The most obvious thing would be drugs. I don't like to generalize too much, but it would fit with the area. It's going to have to be some truly high-grade gear though, given how much effort has been made, including committing a murder, simply to ensure that I come here to pick it up. And that's what makes me think it may be something else, something hugely valuable but also dangerous. Because whoever wants this case won't risk coming here himself. It also bolsters my earlier suspicion that I know the person or people I'm doing this for: they would know that, with my training and experience only a little out of date, I have a better chance than most of emerging in one piece from a difficult situation.

As I walk back the way I've come, I pass a grimy-looking take-away called Ace Fried Chicken. At least I assume it's Ace: the 'c' is missing on the garish orange sign, as is the 'h' in the chicken. A gang of half a dozen teenagers, all wearing the delinquent's uniform of pulled-up hoodie and big trainers, congregate on the pavement outside. The day is hot and bright, the temperature probably close to eighty already, but these guys are protecting their IDs, which means they're probably up to no good. A couple of them are on mountain bikes, and they are laughing and fooling about as they devour their greasy fare. I catch the eye of one of them – probably no more than sixteen, but big for his age – and he appraises me from the shadows beneath the hood, a predator sizing up potential prey. I meet his gaze with blank disinterest and give it a long second before turning away, at the same time slowing my pace a little so he knows I'm not intimidated. Body language tells the people watching you everything. Keep your poise and your movements assured, and just the right side of casual, and people will know you're not scared and will, almost without exception, leave you alone. This guy and his friends are no different. They ignore me, going back to their food and banter. There are plenty of easier victims out there.

I stop on the street outside number 33. All the windows are closed, and it looks deserted. As I approach the door, the honk of a car horn startles me. I turn round and see a short, wizened-looking white guy in the driver's seat of the ancient Sierra. He beckons me over with a bony arm.

I walk up and crouch down by the open car window.

'Who are you?' he asks in a voice that somehow manages to be high-pitched and gravelly at the same time, as if it belongs to a chain-smoking twelve-year-old. To add to the mix, the accent is pure 'cor blimey' cockney, making the end result a very strange sound.

'I'm Bone,' I answer, remembering that this is what I've been instructed to call myself. 'I'm here to pick up a briefcase.'

He looks me up and down carefully yet dispassionately through pale, bloodshot eyes. I stare back at him, thinking he is one of the strangest-looking guys I've seen for a while. His face, partially obscured by long, lank, mousey hair that exposes blotches of pink scalp, is thin and deeply lined, yet some-how the end result gives the impression of agelessness. This guy could be anything between forty and sixty, although nothing about him looks well kept. He is dressed in a cheap brown suit that smells of mothballs, underneath which is a faded Iron

Maiden T-shirt that was once black but has now turned the same off-grey pallor as his skin.

'You've come to the wrong place,' he tells me.

I notice then that he isn't sweating, even though a steady wave of cloying heat is emanating from the interior of the car.

'Are you going to tell me where the right one is, then?'

His eyes dart down. 'What's in the case?'

'Have you got the one I'm here to collect?' I ask him.

His face contorts into an unpleasant smile, revealing a plaque-stained jumble of teeth that come straight out of the 'before' posters on a dentist's wall. 'Is it the money?'

'Have you got the case I'm here to collect or not?'

He shakes his head ever so slowly. 'No,' he says at last, 'someone else has. I'll take you to him.'

I step out of the way as he opens the door and slowly climbs out.

'You got a name?' I ask him.

'You can call me Sellman,' he says, turning and beckoning for me to follow him.

At full height, he stands no more than five five, and when he starts walking I see that his right foot drags. All in all, he's not the finest figure of a man you're ever likely to see, but I spot the telltale bulge in the back of his suit that tells me he's armed, and I guess he's the kind of guy who enjoys being underestimated.

We walk up the street in silence while his eyes move back and forth, taking in everything. It is obvious that he trusts me as much as I trust him. Two Asian kids in Islamic clothes and prayer caps are coming down the pavement in our direction. They talk animatedly and ignore us as they pass, but Sellman's eyes still drift back to them, just to make sure they are nothing more than bona fide passers-by. 'You can't be too careful,' he says, more to himself than me. I don't bother to reply.

After we've gone about fifty yards, we stop at a corner house that's in an even greater state of disrepair than the others. The paintwork is peeling away, and the ancient windows are hanging loose in their wooden frames. A dusty skip filled with household junk and bags of foul-smelling rubbish sits in the middle of the carport, while the area around it is unkempt and overgrown with weeds and stinging nettles.

'Here we are,' says Sellman, pulling a phone from his pocket and motioning me towards the house's decrepit front door. I watch as he speed-dials a number and starts speaking into the phone. He tells whoever is on the other end that we've arrived and that I've come alone, but as the door buzzes and he pushes it open, ushering me through, he checks the street one last time.

'This way,' he says, leading me through a dingy hallway with a huge burn mark splashed against one wall, and up two flights of uneven, carpetless stairs.

'Nice place you've got here,' I say as my boot catches a nail sticking out of the bare wood.

'It does the job we need it for,' he answers in that strange high-pitched voice of his.

The building has been split into separate apartments, both of which appear to be empty. At the top of the stairs, a narrow walkway leads to a single door. Sellman steps up to it, knocks on it three times, pauses, then knocks three more times. A second later comes the sound of two locks being released and the door slowly opens about six inches. An immense shaven head belonging to what appears to be a similarly immense body glowers at me over Sellman's shoulder from behind a thick metal chain, then the chain is released and the door opens just far enough for us to walk in.

Sellman steps to one side and I find myself in a large, cluttered living room. The blinds are pulled down on all the windows, and the only light is provided by a TV in the corner which is showing one of those daytime property programmes with the volume turned down so low it's almost mute. Three desk fans whirr away at different points round the room, but they do little to banish the stuffiness.

To my right stands the shaven-headed man who's just let us in. He must be six feet five and isn't far off being of similar width. He's dressed in jeans and a tight-fitting T-shirt and is carrying a gun in a shoulder holster, American cop-style. He glares at me. I ignore him.

To my immediate left stands Sellman, and then beyond him, in front of a partially open door that leads through to the rest of the apartment, is a third man. Intimidating without being particularly big, he watches me with a professional malevolence. He has shoulder-length brown hair, cut in a style I remember being popular with soccer hooligans circa 1985, and unpopular ever since then with pretty much anyone who cares about fashion, and is wearing a baggy purple suit and white shirt unbuttoned at least two buttons too far. A thick gold chain round his neck and thick tufts of chest hair poking out of the gap in the shirt top off his retro appearance, making him look like a gangster straight off the set of *Miami Vice*.

There's a fourth man at the end of the room. He's sitting behind a table facing the door, next to one of the fans, his face a silhouette in the near darkness. Straight off, I can tell that he's the boss, and he confirms this by snapping an order for Sellman and his shaven-headed colleague to search me.

Sellman produces a sawn-off, single-barrelled shotgun from the back of his cheap suit and points it at my midriff. I clutch the briefcase but don't resist as Shaven Head comes forward and gives me a rough search, quickly locating the Glock. I let him remove it, and he holds it up in the air for his boss to see.

'Pass it over here,' says the fourth man.

Shaven Head checks the internal safety mechanism and chucks the gun over to his boss, who catches it one-handed by the barrel, his hand shooting out like a snake's. 'Ah,' he says admiringly, 'a Glock Nineteen. Very nice.' He turns it over in his hands, giving it a once-over, then places it on the coffee table.

I look at him as he speaks, and I'm almost unable to believe my ears. Unless I'm very much mistaken – and I'm damn sure I'm not – I know the man in front of me. I recognize the voice. A clear, slightly West Country brogue with a confidence in it that hangs very close to arrogance. He served in the same battalion of the Parachute Regiment as me. He was a captain. I didn't know him well – I can't even remember his last name – but we were soldiers together, and that will always count for something.

'Hello, Iain,' I say.

He tenses in his seat, then reaches over and switches on a lamp, which is when I get my confirmation. This is definitely the man from the battalion. He's looking thinner than I remember, and he's bleached his hair blond and added a thin beard-like strip of hair, which is also bleached and runs from his bottom lip to his chin, but it's still him. Beneath the look of surprise, his face is etched with knots of tension. I don't know whether to feel relieved or mightily pissed off. In the end, I plump for both.

He squints at me. 'It's Tyler, isn't it?' he says in a way that tells me he knows exactly who I am. 'Jesus, what the hell are you doing here?'

'You know exactly why I'm here,' I answer.

Like everyone else, Sellman looks surprised. 'You know him, chief?'

'Yeah, we know each other,' I say.

The captain shakes his head. 'I didn't think someone like you would be in with them, to be honest.'

42

'I'm not in with anyone,' I tell him. I glance at his three body-guards. I don't want to say too much in front of them. 'Is there anywhere we can talk?'

He looks at me distrustfully. 'You're not a cop, are you, Tyler?'

'Of course I'm not. You know that.'

'You might be working with them.'

'I'm not working with anyone.'

'But you've got what I want, right? The money?'

There's a glint in his eyes as he speaks, and I remember a story that once did the rounds that he was something of a gambler and used to lose a lot of money on the horses. The military isn't the kind of career that can sustain heavy financial losses. Considering that one of the job hazards is sudden and violent death, it's actually very poorly paid. I'm guessing that this is why the captain's started a new career, and from the amount of money I'm about to hand over to him, whatever it is is pretty lucrative.

'Have you got what I'm here for?' I ask him.

He ignores the question and addresses Shaven Head. 'Check if he's got any mobile phones on him.'

Shaven Head silently continues his pat-down where he left off, and pulls out the one I was supplied with.

I put a hand on his wrist. 'You don't need that,' I tell him, meeting his eye.

I'm trying to be as reasonable as possible, but I'm not going to let these people take the piss out of me, and I have to hang on to this phone. At the moment, it's my lifeline. Shaven Head and I glare at each other and I tense my body, ready to strike out. If it comes to it, I'll use my free hand to take him in the pressure point just below his left ear, swing him round while he's weakened, and smash my knee into the small of his back. He's a big guy, no question, but anyone can be beaten if you know what you're doing, and I've always known what I was doing, even if, at the moment, I'm not exactly feeling my best.

'Be careful of Tyler,' the captain tells Shaven Head, with just a hint of amusement in his voice. 'He's a dangerous man when aroused. We just need the thing turned off, Tyler. For security reasons. They can do anything with mobile phones these days. Even turn them into recordable microphones. I don't want anyone listening in.'

'I told you. I'm not a cop.'

'It's not just them who can listen in,' he answers cryptically.

At this point, Shaven Head interrupts. 'Let go of my wrist,' he tells me, his tone one of barely suppressed rage, 'or I'll break your arm.' I notice then that he has an Eastern European accent.

'Let him turn it off,' says the captain, 'then you can have it back. OK?'

I release my grip on Shaven Head's wrist, knowing there's no point in forcing a confrontation. He turns off the phone and smacks it down in my hand, and I put it back in my jeans pocket.

The captain looks over at me, and I think I see confusion in his eyes. 'You actually want it, do you? What's inside this case?' He leans down behind the table and produces a burgundy briefcase smaller than the one I'm carrying, and carefully places it on the table in front of him.

'What I want is to talk to you,' I say.

'What's there to talk about?'

'Has he got the money or not?' demands Sellman. 'We need paying, chief.'

'You'll get your money, Sellman,' the captain tells him.

'I just want five minutes alone with you, that's all. I'm in trouble, sir. All right? So, for old times' sake, do me this favour.'

He doesn't say anything for a couple of seconds, and if I'm honest, he doesn't really owe me anything. We're not great

44

mates. Christ, I still can't even remember his last name. But then he nods slowly and gets to his feet, picking up the Glock and the burgundy briefcase. 'We'll go through to the kitchen.'

'Are you sure you want to do this, chief?' demands Sellman. 'It could be a trick.'

'He's unarmed. Just keep an eye on the front door, and make sure no one comes in.'

The captain motions me to follow him through the door the man from *Miami Vice* is guarding. Miami Vice himself, who's remained utterly impassive throughout the conversation, moves aside as we pass.

As the captain switches on the overhead strip light, shutting the door behind him, I see that the kitchen is cramped and ancient, with holes and gashes in the linoleum flooring. There's a small table with two chairs squeezed into one corner, and we sit down opposite each other. I put my briefcase down by my side, and he does the same thing. Up close, I notice he isn't looking so well. His skin is pink and blotchy, and his cotton shirt is so heavily sweat-stained that parts of it are clinging to him. It's clear he's under a lot of strain.

I wipe sweat from my own forehead. The kitchen is windowless and stuffy, and the overhead light is making an annoying buzzing sound.

'So, what's there to talk about, Tyler?' he asks.

'I need your help,' I tell him. 'My girlfriend's been murdered and I've been set up for it.'

'I'm sorry to hear that.'

'I need to find out who's behind it.'

He shakes his head. 'I can't help you.'

'What's in the case you're selling?'

His expression changes, as if a shadow is passing across his face. 'Something you don't ever want to see, I promise you.'

'I know I don't want to see it. I just want to know what it is.'

He sighs. 'Listen, Tyler, I always liked you,' he begins, although I don't think he ever did particularly, 'but I'm in a lot of trouble too, and I don't know who it is who's setting you up. All I was told was that somebody would be coming here today to pick up this case, and they'd have a hundred and fifty grand in cash. Have you got that?'

'You're not helping me, Iain.'

'I told you, I can't.'

'If you're in trouble, maybe I can help you.'

He smiles, but it comes out looking close to a sneer. 'No, mate, you can't help me. No-one can. That's why I need that money. I'm finished here, completely. And I'm a marked man.'

'What have you done?'

He crosses and uncrosses his hands on the table in front of him. Drops of sweat run down his cheek, and there is a hint of something painful – is it shame? – in his expression. 'I've got something on someone,' he says quietly, his eyes moving about but not quite settling on anything. 'Something bad. Something that'll ruin him. Rather than ruin his life, I've thrown him a lifeline. In exchange for some money, he can have that something back.'

'You're blackmailing him?'

He pulls a pack of Marlboro out of the pocket of his cotton shirt and lights a cigarette with hands that aren't quite steady. 'You could call it that.'

'That's what I am calling it. Who is he?'

'A businessman. Someone who won't have been involved in your girlfriend's death. He's not that type of person. He's the sort who keeps well away from the dirty work.'

'How can you be so sure?'

He takes two short, angry drags on the cigarette. 'Because

I am, all right? Listen, you remember Maxwell and Spann?'

I nod. They were members of my platoon before moving eventually into the shadowy world of security work. Everyone remembered Maxwell and Spann.

'You heard what happened to them?'

'They got killed doing some bodyguard op, didn't they?'

'That's right. Three years back, in a Paris hotel. They were guarding some big-shot Russian mafia man in the penthouse suite. He was only meant to be in the country for a couple of days to sign some contracts, but he was the kind of guy who made a lot of enemies, and word was that one of them had put a contract out on him. The idea was that it was better to hit him in Europe because he'd have less security here than he'd have in Moscow, but because word got out, the guy panicked and made sure he had security to the hilt. He travelled to his meetings in a bombproof car with a police escort, and the hotel was sewn up tighter than a drum. Him and his entourage had the whole of the top floor, with cameras in every lift and stairway, and the local gendarmerie all over the building. There was no way a hitman could get through.'

'But someone did.'

'That's right. The next morning, the cleaner found the Russian dead in bed with his throat slit from ear to ear. Outside his bed-room door, they found Spann. He'd had his throat cut as well, the wound so deep it almost severed his head. His gun was still in his hand. It hadn't been fired. Maxwell was out in the hall-way. Also armed, also killed the same way. No sign of a struggle from any of them. They'd been taken completely by surprise, one by one, and it seemed the first each of them knew about it was when the knife was crossing their throats.' He pauses and takes another short, urgent drag on the cigarette. 'And Maxwell and Spann . . . well, they were pros.'

'I know,' I say, recalling them as a pair of hardnosed bastards who wouldn't easily have been caught off guard.

'The thing about the Russian killing', the captain continues, 'was that the hitman didn't leave a single clue. Nothing. He spirits into the place and right back out again, past all the security and the surveillance cameras, and no-one hears or sees a thing. So, you know what? They start calling him the Vampire in police circles, because it's almost as if he's got some sort of super-natural powers. Apparently, they've linked him to contract killings all over Europe, and his modus operandi's almost always the same: cuts his victims' throats from ear to ear. He even got hired by the Iranians a year or so back to kill an Israeli diplomat and his family, as revenge for an Israeli air raid in Lebanon that killed a couple of their Revolutionary Guards. He cut the throats of all of them, even the kids. Nobody knows who the Vampire is, or what he looks like. He's invisible. Like something out of a nightmare.'

I'm beginning to lose patience. His story reminds me of Leah and the butchery that was done to her in that stifling, blood-drenched room with the chintz curtains.

'Why the hell are you telling me this?' I demand.

'Because I'm hearing that this guy I'm selling the briefcase to . . .' He pauses a moment, and our eyes meet through the smoke. His are grey and haunted, and I know what he's going to say even before he says it. 'I'm hearing he's hired the Vampire to come after me.'

6

'Well,' I say at last, 'I'm no vampire.'

He leans over and grabs an ashtray from the sideboard, stubbing his cigarette out in it. 'I know you're not him. At least, I'm pretty sure you're not. But sooner or later he's going to come knocking. That's why I've got an insurance policy.'

'What's that?'

He picks up the burgundy briefcase and lays it on the table so that the handle's facing me. 'If anyone tries to get into this thing without the right code, it'll blow into a million pieces. Same if anyone tries to force it open. There's a nice big lump of PETN plastic explosive wired up to the case's locking mechanism on the inside. See this?' He points to a tiny flashing red light attached to a thumbnail-sized black stand next to the lock. 'This tells you that the bomb's armed. Now, I'm not going to phone the guy I'm dealing with and give him the access code until half past two, so I figure I've got' – he looks at his watch – 'about two hours to get the hell out of here. After that I'm the walking dead.'

'Whatever it contains must be very valuable.'

'It is to him. Something else, too. Something that I'm only telling you because we go back.'

'Forgive me if I don't kiss your feet in gratitude.'

His eyes narrow, and it's obvious I've annoyed him. 'Fuck you, Tyler. I don't have to help you. Now, listen carefully. At two thirty this afternoon, make sure you're not standing in the vicinity of this briefcase, and that goes for anyone you care about too. Because this thing can be detonated by mobile phone, so as soon as my client has the number, he can blow the case remotely.'

I lean forward angrily, grabbing his arm. It's wet to the touch. 'What's the client's name, captain? I need to know his name.'

'I told you, I can't tell you. It's more than my life's worth. Now, let go of me or I'll call in the three stooges.'

I assess my options, but the reality is I don't really have any, so I do as he says.

He reaches into his shirt pocket for another cigarette. 'Have you got the money, Tyler?'

I nod slowly, put my own case on the table and click open the locks, then swivel it round so the handle faces him. A smile creases his features and the tension in them eases a little as he opens the case and regards the money sitting there in front of him. He picks up a bundle of notes and stares at it close up with something approaching awe. Consequently, he doesn't hear the kitchen door open.

I do, though, and I turn to see Sellman's misshapen head emerge through the gap like a toad breaking water. His eyes go straight to the money, and a lustful expression not that far removed from the one the captain's wearing crosses his face before disappearing as quickly as it arrived. There is a great deal of greed in this room, and as far as I'm concerned, that usually spells trouble.

'Everything all right, chief?' asks Sellman, trying to make it sound like a routine question.

The captain glares at him, closing the case. 'Don't interrupt, Sellman. If I need you, I'll call.'

Sellman nods once, and the head slips back through the gap.

'Who the hell are those guys?' I ask.

'Security.'

'And they're the best you could get?'

'I don't want to involve anyone I used to know. So, yeah, they're the best I could get.'

'Watch them. I think they want your money.'

'Don't worry,' he says, getting to his feet, 'I'm watching everybody.' He picks up the briefcase with the money and motions to the one on the table. 'That's yours now, Tyler. Whatever you do, be careful with it, and don't let your curiosity get the better of you and try to open the damn thing. That bomb's perfectly constructed. And remember: by two thirty, be at least a hundred feet away from it.'

'I won't forget,' I say, standing up as well.

'Well . . . good luck.'

His words are awkward. He wants to feel sorry for me but in the end he's a lot more interested in saving his own skin. In the army, we were taught to be team players, but it's a lesson the captain seems to have long forgotten. Right now, we are both men operating entirely on our own.

'Can I have my gun back?' I ask him.

He looks uncertain for a moment, then he reaches into the waistband of his jeans and hands it over.

This could have been a mistake. I could have turned it on him, shoved the barrel against his temple and explained in cold, quiet tones that if he didn't tell me the name of his client in the next five seconds his brains would be all over the grimy kitchen work surface. But I know he won't talk, and he knows I know it too. More importantly, he knows I can't pull the trigger. We served together. We may not have known each other that well, but we were still brothers in arms, and we were trained never to kill in cold blood.

The problem is, I'm convinced his client is the person who murdered Leah and set me up for it. And I need to know who he is. At the moment, nothing else matters.

'Do me one favour,' I say to him as he starts towards the kitchen door.

'What?' he asks, without turning round.

'Phone me after two thirty and give me your client's name. That way it won't affect you. You'll be gone. But it'll help me one hell of a lot.'

Still, he doesn't turn round. 'What's your number?'

I give him the name and location of the showroom. He makes no move to write it down. Instead, he simply answers, 'OK.'

'Thanks,' I say, knowing I have no choice but to trust him to do it.

He doesn't speak as he leads the way out of the kitchen, at least not until he opens the door. Then he curses, and stops dead.

The lamp has been switched off, as have all the fans, and the room is once again in hot, stifling semi-darkness. Near the apartment's front entrance, Sellman lies on his side in the fetal position, not moving. To the right, Miami Vice sits against the wall, arms by his side, his head slumped forward, while to the left, Shaven Head lies face down on one of the sofas, only his legs visible as they jut over the edge.

The silence is ringing in my ears. My grip on the Glock tightens. The apartment's front door is a few inches ajar.

'Oh, Christ,' the captain repeats, his voice cracking. 'He's come for me. He's here, Tyler.' He reaches into his jacket, scrabbling round for his gun.

I can hear my heart thumping away in my chest and I have to will myself to remain calm. One of the most important things I learned in the army was how to channel my fear and turn it into pure concentration. The world of the combat soldier is a wildly unpredictable place where you have to react coolly to whatever is thrown at you. Although I'm now thinking it's a lesson that was lost on the captain, who's looking close to panic.

I raise the Glock, my eyes becoming accustomed to the gloom as they slowly circle the room. Searching for an unseen enemy.

And then I notice it.

There's no blood.

'It's a trap!' I yell.

But Sellman's too fast. He swivels round on the floor, revealing the sawn-off shotgun tucked in close to his belly, and without a moment's hesitation pulls the trigger.

The noise in the room is deafening as the captain takes the full force of the blast. It lifts him off his feet and sends him crashing into the sofa. The case of money flies from his hand and lands on the floor. I don't think he even managed to get hold of his gun, because I don't hear or see it fall. Sellman pulls the trigger a second time and the captain's head snaps back as he clatters to the floor.

Miami Vice is fast too, but not fast enough. I am already swinging the gun in his direction, guessing that he will be the one to target me, and as he lifts his head and his gun, his eyes wide with the adrenalin of battle, I shoot him twice in the face.

I turn and aim at Sellman. At the same time I see Shaven Head out of the corner of my eye as he rises up on the sofa, the pistol from his shoulder holster clutched firmly in both hands. Sellman is smiling triumphantly, knowing he has the half-second advantage. He doesn't look under pressure at all. Even in the semi-darkness I can see the calmness in his leathery features, the absolute knowledge that this is a confrontation he's going to win. He's right too. In the tiny gap of time before he pulls the trigger, I know I'm too late.

The noise reverberates off the walls as he fires, and I feel a tremendous pain somewhere in my solar plexus as the force of the shot drives me backwards into the kitchen. The case I'm holding flies off and hits one of the cupboards and my legs go from under me. I go down with all the agility of a lead weight and slam into the cracked linoleum, shoulder blades first, before rolling onto my side, the Glock falling uselessly from my hand. I gasp for breath but can't seem to get any, and my vision blurs and swims. I'm thinking of Leah, alive and laughing, as my eyes close and my body slumps in defeat.

7

'Right, let's move it,' hisses Sellman, limping over to the case containing the money. 'Before someone calls the cops.'

'How much is in there?' asks Shaven Head, getting up from behind the sofa and replacing the pistol in his shoulder holster.

'A hundred and fifty K. Not bad for a couple of days' work.'

'Seventy-five apiece. That'll do. What are we going to do about Ivanov?'

'Not much we can do, my boy. He's a goner.' Sellman picks up the case. 'Check whether he's carrying any ID on him. If he is, take it. We don't want anyone linking him to us.'

Shaven Head nods and crouches down beside his fallen comrade, searching through the pockets of his cheap purple suit. 'Strange plan, lying down like that,' he says, concentrating on his task.

'It worked though, didn't it?' answers Sellman, leaning over and blowing Shaven Head's brains out of the front of his skull. 'Sucker,' he cackles, putting the sawn-off away. 'All fucking suckers. Even you, chief. Didn't your mother ever tell you, there's no such thing as vampires?'

He limps over to the corpse of the man he's addressing. Except he isn't quite a corpse yet. The captain's still breathing shallowly, and his eyes are open. Blood leaks slowly from the corner of his lip.

'Ah, I see you're not quite dead. Were you pretending so that I wouldn't see you? Oh, you're a naughty boy, chief. Very crafty indeed. But I'm afraid I'm an extremely thorough man, and the last person I want to leave alive is you.'

'Fuck you,' gasps his victim.

'Now, now, no need to be rude.' Sellman chuckles, enjoying the power he's wielding as he reloads the shotgun. 'Now, this might hurt a little,' he says. He slams the stock shut and takes aim.

'Not as much as this,' I announce, sitting up with the Glock in both hands.

He whirls round to face me, a hunted expression on his wizened features as he realizes the tables have been turned. In the darkness, his eyes flicker with an animal cunning, and I know that he'll react quickly, so I open fire, shooting him twice in the forehead.

For a long second, he stands absolutely still, staring right into my eyes, before crumpling onto the threadbare carpet and lying there in an ungainly heap.

Slowly, I get to my feet. The flak jacket I'm wearing might have taken the impact of the shot, but it hasn't been a painless process and my chest feels like someone has been hammering nails into it. I walk over to the captain, giving Sellman a kick en route, just to check he is actually dead, and crouch down beside him. He's been hit twice – once in the gut, once in the chest – and his shirt's already drenched in blood. His face is as white as a sheet and his breathing is becoming progressively more laboured. His eyes, though, remain alert.

He looks up at me. 'Oh God, Tyler, I fucked up.'

'It's OK. I'm going to get you an ambulance.'

'It's too late,' he gasps, his words echoing my thoughts.

He coughs, and more blood pours out of his mouth. Then his body jack-knifes and he rolls over onto his front, still coughing. I can see two melon-sized exit wounds, exposing organs and bone, in his back. It's clear he's beyond help.

But I'm not. 'The client,' I say, leaning closer. 'What's the name of the client?'

He tries to roll back but can't quite manage it, so I take his shoulders and gently help him onto his side. His eyes are no longer focusing, and his mouth is hanging open.

'Tell me the name of the client. And the code for the case. Can you do that?'

When he speaks, his words are slurred and final. 'God forgive me.'

Then his head goes limp.

I feel for a pulse. There isn't one. In desperation, I pump his chest. Nothing happens.

Finally, I accept the inevitable. He's gone. I exhale deeply and stand up. The room, already heavy with the heat, is now beginning to fill with the smell of death. I look round at the four corpses, all positioned unnaturally. Shaven Head is on his knees, leaning forward into Miami Vice as if he's kissing him. One hand is still in the other man's inside jacket pocket, where he was hunting for ID. I can hear the blood dripping heavily from what is left of his forehead as it splatters into his friend's lap. It is the only sound in the room.

Four people dead, all for a measly one hundred and fifty grand. You can't even buy a shed for that in London these days. I shake my head at the futility of it all as I look down at the briefcase containing the money. I could pick it up and take it, and I'd be leaving here one hell of a lot richer, but what's the point? It's blood money, and with Leah gone, I wouldn't even know what to spend it on. The other case, the one I'm here to collect, is far more important, because that'll lead me to the person behind this.

But as I turn round to go to pick it up, events take yet another turn for the worse. Before I've even taken a step, there's a huge crash downstairs and I realize that the front door to the house has just been smashed from its hinges. A second later come the urgent shouts I'm dreading.

'Armed police! Do not move!'

Their footfalls are heavy on the bare, carpetless floor, and I can hear them coming up the stairs. They are moving fast, which tells me that they know exactly where they're going.

And, worse still, who they're looking for.

8

As the footfalls get louder on the stairs, I make a rapid calculation. There is no way I'm going out the front of the building, so that leaves only one alternative: the back. I run into the kitchen, scooping up the burgundy case with its mysterious contents. It leads into a short hallway, and I hurry through and into a bedroom that appears to be missing a bed as well as furniture. A set of ancient French windows with peeling paint running down the frames leads out on to an equally decrepit balcony with a less than attractive view to the rear of the houses on the next street. I try the handles but they're locked, and there's no sign of any keys. Behind me, I can hear the shouts of the advancing coppers. It sounds like they're only seconds behind me. Only a few minutes have passed since the outbreak of gunfire and I don't know how they got here so fast.

Taking a step back, I karate-kick the midsection of the French windows. The lock breaks and the doors fly open. I run through, clambering onto the balcony's wooden balustrade. Below me, I can see two plainclothes cops with police-issue caps and MP5 carbines strapped to their shoulders climbing over the boundary wall. At least two cop cars are parked out on the adjoining road, and I can hear the sound of sirens converging from several different points in the distance. The balustrade makes a worrying cracking noise as I scramble down the other side of it and hang from the bottom rail by one arm before jumping the final dozen or so feet to the patio below. I hit the ground with knees bent to absorb the impact, and roll to one side – a typical parachutist's landing. A bolt of pain shoots like a bullet from my ankles to my calves, and my shoulder bumps hard against the stone. But I'm uninjured and back on my feet in a second, running for the fence that separates the garden from the rear of the neighbour's property.

'Stop or I'll fire!' yells one of the armed cops behind me.

Harsh words, definitely, but I'm calculating that he won't shoot me in the back. The British police have some of the toughest regulations in the world governing the use of firearms and can only pull the trigger if there is an immediate threat to life. And there isn't. At least not yet. Although maybe I'm being a little over-confident, given that these are days of paranoia, with men being held down and pumped full of head shots on the Underground. Everyone's a little bit more trigger-happy these days. But I was a soldier a long time and I'm used to taking risks. And today of all days, I'm not stopping for anyone.

I vault the fence, crash through the trellis running along the top, and land in a grubby backyard full of kids' toys. I run straight across it, vault the next fence, land in the flowerbed of a better-kept garden, then do a rapid left turn and charge through an unlocked gate at the end, which leads into the alleyway providing rear access to the properties. I sprint along it for about twenty yards, try a couple of locked gates, finally find one that isn't, and disappear through that. At no time do I look back or listen out for the pursuing cops, preferring to focus every ounce of my energy on putting as much distance as possible between me and the apartment where four men have just died, two of them by my own hand.

I run down a garden path towards a particularly attractive young woman who's sunbathing on a lounger, stark naked and glistening with tanning oil. She shoots up in her seat, putting one arm across her ample chest and the other down below, and stares at me from behind oversized sunglasses, like I'm the one with no clothes on, not her. The back door to her house is open, so I run past her and through the gap, emerging into a kitchen with a ton of washing to do in the sink. I jump over a binbag full of rubbish and continue into the hallway.

A muscular black guy in a string vest pokes his head out of one of the doors. 'Oy, you! Come here!' he barks angrily. He steps into the hallway to confront me, which is the moment when I tug the Glock free from the back of my jeans and aim it straight at him, all without slowing down.

'Out the way!'

He doesn't need asking twice, diving back inside the door and out of my line of fire with an impressive athleticism.

Replacing the gun, I pull open the front door and run down the steps. The sirens are almost on top of me now, seemingly coming from all directions. I can see the flashing lights of one cop car roaring down the street towards me and I know I have seconds rather than minutes to get out of here. I charge into the road and straight into the path of the cop car.

There's an angry screech of tyres as the driver brakes violently in a desperate effort to avoid me. He almost loses control, but somehow manages to stop about six feet in front of me without hitting any of the parked cars.

He's the only occupant of the car, and I'm guessing he hasn't been given much of a description of the suspect he's meant to be apprehending, because he looks more angry than anything else.

'What the hell do you think you're doing?' he yells, sticking his head out of the window.

'Stealing your car,' I tell him, producing the Glock once again, running up to the driver's side door and pulling it open. I shove the barrel against his temple, grab him by the shirt and haul him out of the car.

'You can't do this,' he splutters, but like most regular British cops he's unarmed, so it's perfectly obvious to both of us that I can.

I knee him in the groin to relieve him of any excess enthusiasm he may have, and shove him onto the pavement.

Another cop car has just turned into the street behind this one and is bearing down on us fast, so I don't hang around. Jumping into the driver's seat and flinging the Glock and the briefcase onto the passenger seat, I shove it into first and I'm off again. Unfortunately, I'm also going back in roughly the direction I've come, towards the murder scene; but it's a narrow road, and with the second cop car behind me, I don't have a lot of choice. Speed is my weapon here. Not much more than a minute has passed since they kicked in the door, so I'm thinking that the bulk of the arriving cops will still be concentrating on the house, not me. I change up into second gear, then third, accelerating towards the junction.

Meanwhile, the cop I've just evicted from his vehicle is signalling to his colleagues and they come to a halt, realize what's happened, and speed up again, sirens blaring. By this time I'm at the junction and I don't slow down. Instead, I put my foot flat on the floor and go straight across, glimpsing as I do a couple of armed officers on foot taking aim at the car's tyres.

I'm through and out of sight before a shot's fired, but time's not on my side. There are three police helicopters on permanent standby for the London area. They're based at Lippitt's Hill Air Base, not much more than three minutes' flying time from where I am now, and as soon as one of them joins the pursuit, I'm effectively finished. There's no escape from the flying eye and, unfortunately, the cop car behind me is catching up fast. He comes up right behind me until he's so close I can see the hairs up the driver's nose, and I can't help thinking that it's just my luck to have Stirling Moss on my tail. By the number of occupants, I'm guessing it's an ARV – an armed response vehicle – and that I'm going to have to get rid of these guys pronto if I don't want to end up in the cells, or the morgue. So as I come to another junction I change down to second and take a hard left that sees me almost wipe out a parked car on the corner. I swerve like a drunk at closing time, straighten up like a Methodist on Sunday, and my foot hits the floor again.

But the ARV's still with me, and it's time for more radical action. We're still in a residential area, but the road's a little wider now and as I come round a bend, a car appears ahead of me, travelling in the same direction and crawling along so slowly he'd be better off walking. There's another car coming towards me, and it's slowing down as it sees me approach with my lights flashing and sirens wailing. The gap between them is narrow to say the least, and narrowing all the time, but beggars can't be choosers, so I change down to third gear, slam my foot to the floor and pull out onto the wrong side of the road, heading straight at the oncoming car and sucking up the distance like it's a thread of spaghetti.

Thirty yards, twenty yards, ten . . . I pull in just before I hit it head-on, still flooring the accelerator and almost losing control of the car as I fight to straighten it up. Almost, but not quite, and I've bought myself precious seconds as the ARV gets held up further back.

There's a T-junction with traffic lights, which leads back to the main road. The lights are on red and there are four cars lined up in a queue, so I veer once again onto the wrong side of the road, passing them like they're not there. I'm braking a little by this time, and it's a good thing, because a minibus is turning into my path. Thankfully the driver sees my lights and slams on his brakes, giving me enough of a gap to drive straight through.

I am still doing forty when I shoot out onto the main road, causing cars to skid and horns to blare, but somehow I don't hit anyone and my momentum keeps me going onto the other side of the road where I do a hard right and join the traffic, weaving in and out of the cars. It's an exhilarating feeling, I have to admit, being king of the road. You have a real sense of power, and the more dangerous your manoeuvres the more confident you become. If I wasn't so desperate, I'd be really enjoying this.

I snatch a glance in the rear-view mirror. The ARV is twenty yards back but has taken advantage of the fact that all the traffic stopped to accelerate out onto the main road, and is already making up the distance between us. It's police procedure to terminate high-speed pursuits when they become too dangerous, but it looks like the rule book's been thrown out of the window today. But then I suppose I am leaving the scene of four violent deaths in a hurry, so I can see why they're keen to keep me in their sights.

I come to another set of lights, and once again they're on red. This time, however, there's no obvious way through. I slow a little, pull on the seatbelt, and as the ARV races up behind me, I do an emergency stop. The ARV hits me right up the arse, shunting me forward several feet, but I was expecting the impact and they weren't, so they now have a couple of seconds of shock in which their reactions are slowed to almost nothing. My head hits the windscreen, but as I bounce back into my seat I shove the car into first, pull into the nearside lane and, like the worst kind of joyriding delinquent from one of the 'Eye in the Sky' police pursuit programmes every channel seems to love, I mount the pavement and drive along it, blasting away on my horn and scattering confused and occasionally angry pedestrians in all directions. I drive off again on the other side, having passed the junction now, then turn the wheel hard left, merging with the passing traffic and aggressively forcing it out of my way as I at last put some space between myself and my pursuers.

After about twenty seconds and a quarter of a mile, I see a Sainsbury's superstore looming up like an architectural monstrosity on my right-hand side. Behind me, the ARV is nowhere to be seen. Neither is any other sign of pursuit, so I veer across the central reservation, drive down the wrong side of the road for twenty yards, once again making everything in my path come to a screeching halt, then park up half on and half off the pavement. I've lost the cap I was wearing when I arrived at the apartment, so I keep my head down as I shove the Glock back in my jeans and pick up the briefcase.

Ignoring the looks I'm getting from other drivers, I walk rapidly into the superstore car park. I move along the lines of cars, going slower now so that I don't attract attention, and keeping as far away from the main entrance as possible. I'm looking for a suitably old car that won't have a sophisticated alarm system, and since this isn't the poshest end of town, it doesn't take long to locate a couple of likely candidates. There are plenty of people around, mainly in the process of loading up their shopping, and I use them as cover as I hear the first telltale whirr of rotor blades. It seems the airborne cavalry have arrived.

But the problem with all these real-life cop shows is that you learn how the cavalry operates and can therefore always second-guess them. For instance, they're already circling the area, so it's obvious they're talking to the guys on the ground, which means they haven't picked me up on their infra-red cameras yet. And the yodel-like shriek of emergency service sirens is such a part of London life that no-one takes a blind bit of notice as I stroll along, trying the doors on the cars I've singled out as potential theft material.

The first two are locked, but in my experience there are always people around who are careless about security, and the door on the third opens when I try the handle. I don't bother to check whether an eagle-eyed member of the public has spotted me. If you act casually enough and cut out the furtive looks over the shoulder, most people will assume you're bona fide. I clamber inside and shut the door, putting the case down on the passenger seat.

Now that I'm out of view I can move a bit faster. Bending down low, I put the gearstick into neutral and remove the steering column's plastic sheath, exposing the maze of wires beneath. I locate the two I need, touch the ends together, and the engine kicks into life. Just like that. Working in the used car trade has its compensations, I think, as I put the shitheap I've picked into reverse and back out.

There's a second entrance to the car park on the other side of the superstore, and as I follow the road round and join the line of traffic slowly filtering out of it, I can hear the sirens continuing to approach from all sides. My heart's beating like a hammer drill and beads of sweat are running down my face, but I wait my turn patiently, and within a few seconds it comes and I'm out on the road heading east with no sign of any flashing lights showing in my rear-view mirror.

It seems I've made it.

9

It's another ten minutes before I feel I can breathe again. I'm still driving east, not a hundred per cent sure what I should be doing other than putting as much distance as possible between myself and the police. I turn the phone my blackmailer supplied me with back on, but there are no messages.

I'm hungry and exhausted. I take some deep breaths as the traffic ahead slows at lights, knowing that my situation's now taken a serious turn for the worse, while my memory of yesterday remains a steady, stubborn blank. Before I continue my search for Leah's killer, I need to stop somewhere and take stock of what's happening. And I need food. I desperately need food.

The phone starts playing 'the Funeral March' and I pull up onto the pavement to take the call.

'Have you got the case?' demands the robotic voice.

'Yeah, but I only just made it out,' I tell him. 'Things went wrong and now the place is crawling with police.'

'What do you mean, things went wrong?'

'The guy I was picking the case up from had some very dodgy

security. They decided they wanted his money. There was some shooting and the police got called.'

'But he's all right, is he? The man who gave you the case?'

'No. He's dead. So's his security.'

'If you had anything to do with his death—'

'I didn't. I knew the guy.'

'What?'

Straight off, I know I've made a mistake. I should have kept my mouth shut.

'I've met the guy before,' I say, trying to sound casual.

'Where?'

'That's my business.'

'What did he tell you about the case?'

'Nothing.'

'He was supposed to provide us with a code that would open it.'

'Well, I'm afraid he's no longer in a position to help you there.'

'He said the case would be booby-trapped. Is it?'

'It is, and it looks like it's been professionally done as well.'

There's a long silence down the other end of the phone. I imagine him trying to work out how to deal with this unforeseen and most unwelcome eventuality. I find myself enjoying his discomfort, even though it could very easily be deflected on to me.

'You'd better not be lying, Tyler.'

'I'm not,' I answer firmly. 'Check out the TV. It'll be on the news pretty soon. There are four people dead.'

'Where are you now?'

'A couple of miles east of the address you sent me to.'

'All right,' he says, sounding like he's come to a decision. 'I'm going to text you an address in King's Cross. You're to bring the case there in an hour's time, at a quarter to two.' The speed of his voice slows down and becomes calmer as he assesses the situation. 'When you arrive, knock on the door slowly four times. You'll be asked to identify yourself. Give your name, and say you have an urgent delivery that needs signing for. When you get inside, hand over the case to the man who lets you in, and in return he will give you a plastic evidence bag containing the murder weapon from last night, and the master copy of the DVD which shows you killing the girl.'

'I didn't kill her,' I snap. 'I didn't kill Leah.'

He ignores my protest. It's irrelevant to him. 'When I have confirmation that we have the case, her corpse will be disposed of, along with any further forensic evidence linking you to the crime, and you won't hear from us again.'

I feel a rage building. It's the way she's being described. Like some product that has malfunctioned and needs discarding. I fight to keep it down. Anger won't help me now. I'm almost certain I'm being sent into a trap, but once again I have no choice but to appear to co-operate.

'OK,' I say tightly, 'I'm on my way.'

'And, Mr Tyler?'

'Yeah?'

'Don't be tempted to try anything clever. I know exactly the type, dimensions and distinguishing features of the briefcase you collected. If you don't hand over the right one, you'll have to answer to the authorities for the girl's murder and mutilation.'

'You'll get the right one,' I tell him, but the bastard's already cut the connection.

I replace the phone in my pocket and look down at the case beside me on the passenger seat. So far, five people have died for whatever it contains, and I'm determined not to be number six.

It's time, I think, for some back-up.

10

I remember the day so vividly, and always will.

June the nineteenth 1996, a warm if cloudy summer's morning on the back roads of South Armagh, a mile from the town of Crossmaglen, and a few hundred yards from the Irish Republic. There were eight of us travelling in the Saracen armoured personnel carrier and we were responding to reports of suspicious movements at a minor border crossing. Because of the dangers of operating in that area, and the risk of ambush, a second APC containing a further eight members of the platoon was following a short distance behind, while a Lynx helicopter was providing aerial reconnaissance.

You were always a little nervy on any form of op in the bandit country of South Armagh, because this really was the IRA's home territory, but at the same time there was nothing to suggest that this day would be different from any other, and the mood in the back, where I was sitting, was even quite jovial. I remember that we were talking about the football. Euro 96 was on and England had beaten Holland 4–1 in their group match the previous night, which was, to put it bluntly, a surprise result.

We'd wanted to paint the scoreline on the side of the APC, just to annoy the locals who we knew would have been rooting desperately for Holland, but this had been vetoed by our OC, Major Ryan, who knew it would be seen as unduly provocative, and would do little to bolster the 'hearts and minds' approach that was now being fostered by the British government in its efforts to get the IRA to declare a second ceasefire.

I was still smoking in those days and I'd just lit a cigarette and was about to add to the debate on England's chances of winning the competition when bang, it happened. Just like that. There was a deafeningly loud roar that seemed to engulf everything around us, followed by a sound like an aluminium can being crumpled, and the APC was lifted into the air before being slammed down on to its side. All six of us in the back were flung around the enclosed space like puppets. We were wearing berets rather than helmets, and I remember smacking my head hard against the ceiling before coming to rest in a twisted heap with someone on top of me.

Thoroughly disorientated, for the first few seconds I wasn't even sure whether I was alive or dead. Everything was utterly still, utterly silent. It's difficult to describe adequately, but it felt like I was unconscious, yet somehow aware of my surroundings. Then my ears began to buzz loudly, and I could just about make out the groans of my comrades, although it sounded like they were coming from a long way away. My eyes had squeezed shut instinctively, and when I opened them I saw that the interior light had gone out and I was in semi-darkness. Acrid-smelling smoke was filling the cab and it was difficult to see. The APC's armour plating was buckled and cracked, and flames licked at a thin jagged tear that ran down the side opposite me; but it had done its job and largely withstood the force of the blast that had knocked it upside down.

The smoke was making me choke and stinging my eyes, while the heat from the flames was burning the soles of my feet, and I felt a burst of claustrophobic panic as I realized that at any moment the fuel tank might blow, burning us all alive in this cramped, dark tomb. I had to get out of there.

The man on top of me was my best mate, Martin 'Lucas' Lukersson, who'd been sitting across from me in the back. As I struggled to get him off me, his eyes opened and he coughed loudly. I didn't ask him if he was all right. In those few seconds, he didn't even cross my mind. Instead, I silently thanked God that of all the people in the back of the APC, I was in the best position – on the opposite side from the bomb and nearest the rear doors.

My hand fumbled desperately for the handle as I breathed in another mouthful of thick smoke, and I yanked it down hard. It wouldn't budge. I yanked again. Still nothing happened. I remember how frightened I was at that point. As the prospect of cremation came just that bit closer.

Someone cried out from further inside the cab. The words were 'help me' and there was a pitying desperation in the voice, as if he knew already that all was lost. Though it was faint, I recognized it as belonging to Jimmy McCabe, a lance corporal from Dunfermline and the only man in the APC pissed off about the fact that England had won the football the previous night. He cried out again, and I'm ashamed to admit that at that moment I didn't give him a second's thought either. Survival was everything.

The flames were growing bigger now as they danced through the gap in the armour. They were the only things I could see through the smoke, although I could hear and feel movement as other men crawled towards the rear doors.

I yanked the handle again, then felt another hand grab it.

'Wrong fucking way,' I heard Lucas gasp, before I realized that everything was upside down, and that's why it wouldn't open.

We pulled it together, and the first of the double doors flew open. I scrambled out, knocking open the other door with my desperate momentum, and rolled over on the tarmac. As I turned back towards the stricken APC, Lucas emerged on his hands and knees through the billowing smoke, followed by a third man I recognized as Private Rob Forbes. I staggered to my feet, keeping hold of my assault rifle, and helped Lucas to his. He looked concussed, but I didn't have time to worry about that now. There were other people to help. I grabbed Rob and managed to get him upright, and then a hand appeared in the gap in the double doors. I got a grip on it and pulled its owner free, dragging him well clear. It was Ben 'Snowy' Mason, another private, so-called because of his prematurely white hair. The back of his flak jacket was on fire, and he was crying out in pain. I hurriedly pulled it off him and threw it to one side while Snowy rolled over, choking.

By now, I was managing to take stock of the scene. We'd been hit by an extremely powerful roadside bomb that had created a deep, wide crater on the grassy bank at the side of the road, and demolished much of the low flint wall bordering a sheep field, behind which the bomb had obviously been hidden. A huge fire was burning, its heat so close and intense that I could feel it blistering my skin. The gouting flames were already setting light to the branches of some oak trees and a huge black plume of smoke stretched up into the sky, obscuring the Lynx helicopter as it circled impotently overhead. At the front of the APC, I could see the top half of Lieutenant Neil Byron as he clambered out of the passenger side of the cab, which was now upright, his face smoke-stained and bloodied. Our eyes met, and his were wide with shock.

And then I found out why. As he lifted his right arm, I saw that it ended in a blackened stump at the elbow, the wound already cauterized. He waved it uselessly in the breeze, staring at it now, unable to comprehend that it was gone, and that for the rest of his life he would be disabled.

I've got to admit that the knowledge that at any moment the APC could blow, killing us all, was at the forefront of my mind. But in those kinds of situations you simply don't dwell on the dangers involved. You've got to get everyone out before you can even think about retreating.

I could tell the lieutenant needed help, and I started towards him, which was when the dull, ringing silence was broken by a single burst of heavy machine-gun fire. The lieutenant's body jerked ferociously and it looked like he was being attacked from below by a shark, then two thick, winding lines of blood flew out of his chest and splattered onto the tarmac, leaving behind two exit holes the size of oranges in his flak jacket.

He didn't make a sound. Not even a peep. He simply slid back into the cab and out of sight, and I never saw him again. That's the nature of violence – its utter suddenness. It can be over in seconds, yet so great is the damage it wreaks that the ramifications often last for ever.

I dived to the ground, alongside Snowy, grabbing Lucas as I did so and dragging him down with me. Rob Forbes, a few feet away, wasn't so lucky. I can't remember if he even moved. We were all still in shock, our reactions slower than usual, and as the next burst of machine-gun fire shattered the silence, I watched as he was lifted off his feet and driven backwards through the air, his rifle clattering to the ground.

The bastards had set a clever trap. They would have known that even a powerful bomb would not destroy an APC completely and that some, if not all, the men inside would be able to evacuate it. But by placing a machine-gun crew nearby with a good view of the ambush point, they could simply pick off the survivors. The brazenness of it was incredible considering that there was a helicopter flying overhead and reinforcements would be on the scene very quickly. It wouldn't have worked if we hadn't been so close to the Irish border, but with barely a few hundred yards to travel before they crossed it and were out of our reach, and with the knowledge that the helicopter was unarmed and therefore unable to fire on them, our attackers obviously considered it a risk worth taking. And Lucas and I were now totally exposed to their fire.

A drainage ditch ran along the other side of the road, and the two of us were facing it. It represented our best chance of cover.

A third burst rang out, the heavy .5-calibre rounds kicking up chippings of tarmac only inches away from where we lay.

'Go! Go! Go!' I howled, leaping to my feet, my hand still gripping Lucas's flak jacket.

I gave him a huge shove and together we charged across the road, limbs flailing, adrenalin pumping through me so fast I felt like I was almost flying. We launched ourselves headlong into the ditch, landing in a foot of muddy, foul-smelling water. I rolled over in it and got to my feet, while Lucas remained on his hands and knees, coughing and spitting out phlegm. The back of his head was bloody and there was a deep gash at the base of his skull. He'd lost his rifle, but I still had mine. I moved over to the edge of the gully and took up a firing stance, trying to pinpoint the machine gunner's position through the assault rifle's sights.

There was a bend in the road about thirty yards up ahead, and a tree-covered slope running up behind it. I thought I caught a glint of metal in there somewhere, but such was the thickness of the tree cover that I couldn't be a hundred per cent sure. The rules of engagement in Northern Ireland were strict: only shoot if you're being directly threatened, and use the minimum force required to neutralize the threat. But the potent combination of adrenalin and the frustration of being attacked by an unseen enemy meant I wasn't really thinking about that. I cracked off half a dozen shots in the direction of where I thought I'd seen the glint of metal, then stopped, my finger tensed on the trigger. There was no return fire. The world was silent once again, save for the angry crackle of the fire across the road.

Meanwhile, Snowy was getting to his feet, using the back of the APC as cover. He had a deep gash on his forehead and he was wiping the blood from his eyes as another of the men, a recently recruited Fijian called Rafo, climbed out of the smoking double doors.

I shouted for the two of them to make a run for the ditch in case the fuel tank ignited.

At that moment, the second APC finally roared into view. I doubt if even a minute had passed since the initial blast, but it felt like hours. The APC drove past us and turned sharply in the road some twenty yards further on, so that it acted as a buffer between the stricken APC and the hostile machine-gun fire.

A second later, the doors flew open and the men inside were disgorged onto the tarmac. The first one I saw was our OC, Major Leo Ryan. He was striding towards me, shouting into a radio and barking orders at the rest of the men, half of whom were following him while the other half took up positions by their own APC, facing in the direction the heavy machine-gun fire had been coming from.

Just the sight of the major filled me with a sense of confidence. You need leaders who inspire you in adverse circumstances, and there were few men better at it than Leo Ryan. He was a tough little bastard with a prematurely silver Bart Simpson-style buzz cut and a pockmarked, scarred face that looked like it had been hewn out of rock by a blind man – the result of some serious grenade shrapnel injuries he'd received as a young lieutenant in the Falklands conflict, during the battle of Goose Green. Even though the grenade blast temporarily blinded him, he still managed to get two of his more seriously wounded men to safety under heavy enemy fire, before rejoining the fighting and making three confirmed enemy kills. He later got the Military Cross for his bravery.

Even with the first APC on fire, and one of his men clearly dead in the road, the major's expression remained utterly calm. His eyes met mine and he yelled something at me. Something that chilled the blood in my veins.

'Out of there! Secondary device!'

Secondary device. The classic terrorist tactic of planting a second bomb that could be detonated while members of the security forces dealt with the first. They'd done that down the road in Warrenpoint in August 1979 in a dual attack that had killed eighteen paratroopers – the biggest single military loss of life during the Troubles. It's easy and effective. And what better place to plant it than in the soft earth of a flooded ditch where survivors of the attack were bound to take shelter?

My heart jumped. Was something down there beneath the water? A mine? A few pounds of Semtex? If there was, in all likelihood it would be detonated by remote control rather than a timer in order to maximize casualties, and with the ambush pretty much at an end and the enemy thinking of making good their escape, that meant any second now.

I flung the assault rifle over my shoulder and turned round fast. Lucas was still on his hands and knees, so I grabbed him by the shoulders and pulled him out of the muddy water.

'Secondary device,' I snapped. 'We've got to move.'

He stumbled into the ditch wall and I could see that his eyes weren't focusing properly. All my instincts told me just to jump out and get the hell out of there, that in situations like this it's every man for himself, but I couldn't leave him. He was my mate. So I bent down, put a hand between his legs and pushed him up and over the edge. Lucas seemed to realize the urgency of the situation and managed to get to his feet and stagger blindly in the direction of the other APC, while I clambered out after him.

One of the other men came forward to grab him while Major Ryan and the others rushed over to the back of our vehicle. The men took hold of Snowy and Rafo while the major leaned in the double doors, trying to help out whoever was still inside. I started to run over to them, remembering that I hadn't seen Jimmy McCabe come out of there.

Which was the moment there was a loud bang behind me, like a very old car backfiring, and I was sent hurtling forward, crashing and somersaulting over the tarmac like a rag doll, every part of my body feeling like it was on fire. I just had time to think that the major was dead right, there had been a secondary device, before I lost consciousness.

That day was ten years ago, but I will never forget it. I sustained sixteen separate shrapnel injuries, spent three weeks in a military hospital in Belfast, and had to take two months off work. It cost four other men their lives, and gave the IRA a tremendous propaganda victory. Their Active Service Unit – the men who'd attacked us – did indeed escape over the border and for months afterwards the following graffiti appeared round the villages of South Armagh: IRA 4 – 0 Brits.

The conflict's long finished now, and already it's turning into ancient history. But one thing hasn't changed: I saved Lucas's life. Without me, he almost certainly would have died.

Which means he owes me. In normal circumstances, I would never hold him to his debt. I like him too much for that. But circumstances are no longer anything close to normal, so today I'm going to call it in.

11

I've known Lucas since we entered the army together nineteen long years ago, when we were seventeen apiece. He lasted nine years, but left not long after the Crossmaglen ambush. Although his own injuries were superficial, he told me he took what happened as a warning from God to change careers, and when his service was up, he didn't renew it. I don't think the life ever suited him like it did me, but somehow we've always stayed in touch in a way I've never really managed with the rest of the men I served with. We just hit it off, I suppose. There's not much more you can say about it than that. Lucas is a funny guy, always has been. He's got charisma, and charm too. The ladies have always loved him. He's half Swedish, and he's inherited the blond hair and irritatingly golden skin that you associate with the Swedes, if not their passive neutrality. Add to that the strong jaw and high chiselled cheekbones, and you've got the sort of guy who in his younger days could have been a model.

These days he works for himself as a private detective. He's been doing it for six years now and claims that he'll take on any job if the money's right, although most of his work involves divorce cases. Those and missing persons. He's good, though, and he's done work for me on three occasions, hunting down people who owed me money through the car business but decided to skip town rather than pay up. Every time he's found them, and every time the two of us have got the debtor to cough up the money. I trust Lucas. I haven't seen him in close to three months, but that doesn't matter. He's one of my best friends, possibly *the* best, and I know that when things are bad, he'll be there.

And they don't get much worse than they have been today.

I've abandoned the stolen car on a back street on the borders of Whitechapel and Aldgate and I'm walking along Commercial Street in the direction of Liverpool Street tube station, the brief-case in one hand, just one person among the hordes of short-sleeved office workers on their lunch breaks who are out enjoying the early afternoon sunshine. Lucas's offices are above a Bangladeshi textile wholesalers just south of Spitalfields Market, about two minutes' walk from where I am now. It's already 1.30, so I use the phone I've been supplied with to dial his office number.

'Martin Lukersson Associates,' he states confidently, his voice deep and fearless, making him sound every inch the kind of guy you can rely on in times of trouble. 'How can I help?'

'I've got a problem,' I tell him, not bothering with introductions.

'I know,' he answers.

That throws me. 'How do you know?'

'Because you phoned me about it.'

'When?' I ask, surprised.

Now it's his turn to sound surprised. 'Yesterday,' he says impatiently. 'You called me yesterday.'

'What did I want?'

'Don't you remember? Christ, Tyler, what's wrong with you?

Have ravenous women been spiking your drink again so they can get you into bed when your defences are down?'

'It's a long story,' I tell him, thinking he may not actually be that far from the truth.

'Care to explain?'

'Tell me what I wanted first.'

'You asked me to find some information on a young lady you've met.'

'Leah Torness,' I say, having no recollection of this conversation whatsoever.

'That's her.'

I'm having difficulty getting my head round this. 'What information did I want?'

He sounds aghast. 'You really can't remember?'

'No.'

'You wanted an address.'

'But I've already got an address. She's a nanny for a couple in Richmond. I dropped her off there the other week.'

'You said the address was false. That she didn't actually live there.'

His words hit me like hammer blows, and I have to stop walking. So confused do they make me that I even wonder if this could be some kind of wind-up.

'Are you sure about this, Lucas?' I ask cautiously. 'Because if this is—'

'I'm positive, Tyler, and if you really can't remember what we talked about, then I think we'd better get you to a doctor.'

'There's no time for that now. Did you find an address?'

'No, and I've hunted everywhere for her. Her name doesn't appear on any database. She's not on the electoral register, she doesn't own a credit card, and the mobile number you gave for her is a pay-as-you-go not registered to anyone. So I got Snowy to have a look as well. You know what he's like. The guy's a ferret. If there's information there, he'll find it.'

Snowy, the other guy I pulled free from our stricken APC that day in Crossmaglen, has been a junior partner in Martin Lukersson Associates for the past two years, and he's also proved to be an excellent private detective, maybe even better than Lucas himself. It was Snowy who located two of my bad debtors, one of whom had changed his name and moved to Germany, so he knows what he's doing.

'And he didn't find out anything either?' I ask, more in hope than expectation.

'Oh yeah, he found something out all right.'

I feel a small burst of excitement. 'What?'

'He found out that the name's an anagram. Mix the letters up and guess what you come up with?'

'Lucas, I can't even do the *Sun* crossword.'

'She's not real.'

'What do you mean?'

'Jumble the letters and that's what it spells: *she's not real*. Leah Torness equals "she's not real",' he adds, just in case I've some-how failed to get the message. 'Someone's fucking you around, Tyler.'

I'm silent for several seconds. I can hear my heart beating in my chest. This has got be some coincidence, surely. If it isn't, then . . . Then what? I push the thought to the back of my mind. I don't want to go there.

'So, what the hell's going on?' asks Lucas at last.

I take a deep breath. 'I've got a serious problem,' I tell him, 'and I need your help. Right now.'

'All right,' he answers, and I'm wondering if he's remembering that day back in Crossmaglen. 'What do you need me to do?'

I stop outside the Bangladeshi wholesalers and press the buzzer for Martin Lukersson Associates. 'Let me in and I'll tell you.'

12

It's just turned two o'clock and I'm standing alone with the brief-case in my hand. I'm on the other side of the road from the address I've been given in King's Cross, looking at an empty, three-storey redbrick building dotted with broken windows and graffiti. It's at the end of a street consisting of tired-looking council blocks, many of which also look empty, about half a mile behind the station. A low mesh fence adorned with banners advertising the brand-new two- and three-bedroom apartments that will soon be here surrounds the building, and there's a condemned notice on the unlocked gate.

The area is quiet; only the sounds of construction work from the huge building site that runs north towards Camden Town puncture the silence. It's strange to think that I'm in the middle of a bustling city, yet this street reminds me somehow of the burnt-out, war-ravaged villages we used to pass through during our tour of Bosnia in the 1990s. It's far more intact than they ever were, of course, and without the smell of death and decay, but there is still that dull air of neglect and abandonment, and I'm thinking that, like them, this place would be a perfect location for an ambush. No witnesses, no potential for inter-ruption, and a ready-made resting place for the corpse among the rubble the bulldozers are going to create any day now. It's unlikely that my body'll be found for days, or even weeks.

I watch the place for a couple of seconds. I can't see anyone inside, but then, that's the point. Someone will have slipped in there, quiet and unseen, and he's waiting for me now. If I walk in the door, I know there's little chance of me coming out, and for some reason I feel a sense of betrayal. I've kept my side of the bargain, but the man who in all probability killed Leah doesn't seem to have kept his. Well, fuck him. I don't have to play by his rules any more. I've got what he wants, and he won't dare give me up to the cops until he's got it. So I turn away and start walking, the briefcase in my hand.

I'm thinking about Leah, and what Lucas told me about her name being an anagram. I keep telling myself it must be a coincidence, but if that's the case, why couldn't he track her down, and why did I ask him to look into her in the first place? It's worrying me. If Leah isn't her real name, then it means she lied to me. And if she lied to me about that, it's possible she lied about other things as well. Again, I push the thought from my mind. I don't want to besmirch her memory.

I think back to Wednesday night, to that takeaway meal of squid in black bean sauce. I watched a documentary about the Brazilian rainforest on National Geographic, followed by the news. Then I went to bed. That was it. Nothing exciting at all; a typical weekday evening on my own. Except I don't remember anything else until this morning.

Lucas told me we spoke yesterday afternoon, and that I sounded like I had something on my mind. He asked if I was OK and I replied that I was fine, everything was all right, and he hadn't pursued the matter. The only thing I can think of is that I found out something about Leah that caused me some concern.

The frustration of losing such an important day is intense. It makes me want to bang my head against the nearest wall, as if this might help to jog something. I'm also thinking that if this single patch is indeed going to be permanent, then it begs an important question. If I'm never going to get that memory back, why bother killing me? You see, in my current state, I have absolutely no clue as to the identity of the man behind this, so it's going to be extremely difficult for me to find him. So, either the guy wants to kill me because he's got some kind of personal grudge, or because eventually my memory *is* going to come back, and when it does, it's going to lead me straight to him. Either way it's a none-too-attractive scenario, because the end result is that someone wants me dead, and that person seems to have the ruthlessness and the resources to ensure it happens.

But I have the briefcase. That, for the moment, is my trump card.

I'm on the Caledonian Road, heading in the direction of Pentonville Road, when I pass a café called Rudy's. The door's open and the smell from inside is surprisingly pleasant, with a hint of fresh herbs. Times may be difficult for me, but I haven't eaten for a long time. I go inside and order today's special: grilled chicken escalope topped with melted mozzarella on toasted ciabatta, with iceberg lettuce and tomato, washed down with a glass of freshly squeezed orange juice and a large mug of black coffee.

The interior of the café is empty, and I take a table in the corner as far away from the door as possible. The owner, a smiling Greek guy with very hairy eyebrows and a shiny white apron, brings over the juice and the coffee, and tells me that the chicken will be a few minutes because he likes to cook it fresh. I tell him that's fine, and as I take a long drink of the juice, reeling a little against the sharpness of the taste, the mobile breaks into the sombre strains of the 'Funeral March'. I look at my watch. It's 2.15.

'Where the hell are you?' demands the voice.

The menacing robotic tone no longer unnerves me. 'I didn't like your choice of drop-off point,' I tell him.

'I don't care what you thought of it. Get over there now.'

'No, there's been a change of plan.' He tries to interrupt but I don't give him the opportunity. 'There's a café on the Caledonian Road called Rudy's, four hundred metres south of the address you gave me. If you want the case, you meet me there in fifteen minutes, and this time don't even think about trying anything.' I hang up before he has a chance to say anything else, the show of power making me feel better.

Straight away, the phone rings again. This time I switch it off. I'm embarking on a high-risk strategy, but in my experience it's always better to stand tall in the face of intimidation rather than let yourself get pushed around. I take another sip of orange juice and settle down to wait.

The grilled chicken and mozzarella ciabatta tastes as good as it sounds. The meat is so thin and tender that it almost melts in my mouth; the lettuce is crisp and fresh; and the tomatoes actually taste like tomatoes rather than those flavourless pinkish things they grow in greenhouses in Holland. It's good to see someone taking pride in their ingredients, and when the owner comes over to collect my empty plate I tell him this. He beams from ear to ear, and thanks me. I also tell him that I have a friend coming in to meet me in a moment and request that he not disturb us for a few minutes. Politeness and flattery make an excellent combination, and he answers of course, that'll be no problem.

I finish my coffee and order another one. I'm beginning to feel better.

As the owner brings it over, I see a figure entering the café and heading purposefully towards my table. He's carrying a small Adidas holdall.

I tense. The case he's here to collect is by my chair, out of sight.

The owner moves out of the way and steps back behind the counter, giving me a better view of the new arrival. He's a big guy, six two or three, very muscular, with shoulders broad enough to carry dwarves on, and though he makes a conscious effort to move with at least a modicum of grace, he still lumbers a little. He's wearing a tailored navy-blue suit and open-necked shirt, and as he pulls back a chair and takes a seat opposite me, I'm almost overcome by the thick, cloying smell of eau de cologne. With his wavy, perfectly coiffed black hair and deeply suntanned skin stretched as tight as a drum where he's had more than his fair share of plastic surgery, he's not what I was expecting at all. Straight away I know I've never seen him before. Even with memory loss, his is a face you're not going to forget.

He glares at me through cold, tar-black eyes that are devoid of emotion. He's got a job to do, and that's all he cares about. There is no doubt he would put a bullet in my head without batting an eyelid – although I'm not entirely sure he possesses an eyelid.

'So you're the guy who's set me up?' I say, looking him up and down.

'Not me,' he answers. 'I'm just here to collect the case. Where is it?' His accent's foreign. Southern European, I'm guessing. Greek, possibly Albanian.

I sip the coffee, deliberately taking my time.

'Where's the case?' he persists.

'Down here.' I motion with my head towards my right foot, noticing at the same time another man, smaller and older, coming into the café. He says something to the owner and I recognize the language he's speaking from my days serving in Bosnia. It's Serbo-Croat, the language of the former Yugoslavia. I don't know what it is the guy's saying, and I don't much care. I'm far more interested in the fact that he's wearing a long black mac even though there's not a cloud in the sky and the temperature outside must be way over eighty by now.

The owner returns to the coffee machine while the new guy takes a seat two tables down with his back to the wall. He doesn't look at me, but he moves one hand inside the coat. The other hand holds a strong-smelling cigarette which he smokes while staring into space.

I don't like this situation, but I remain calm.

'And have you got what I want?' I ask the rubber-faced man in front of me.

'It's in here,' he answers, tapping the holdall without taking his eyes off me.

'Open it.'

He shakes his head. 'It doesn't work like that. You show me the case first.'

I lean over, pick it up and give him a glimpse, then put it back down again.

'Give it to me,' he demands.

'When I see that you've got what I want, you can have it.'

'You see the man behind me?' he asks, trying without much luck to stretch his face into a sneer. 'He's got a gun trained on you.'

As if to confirm this, the barrel of what looks suspiciously like a Mac-10 submachine pistol appears over the hem of the other guy's raincoat. He's resting it on his lap and still smoking his cigarette, but now he's looking my way, and the blank expression on his face tells me that he too isn't going to waste time worrying about pulling the trigger.

I shrug, keeping my cool. 'Fair enough. At least now we're equal.'

'What do you mean?'

'Well, if you'd care to look under the table, you'll see that there's a gun trained on you as well. And I've used it once today, so I know it works. Now, unless you want your balls to leave this place before you do, I suggest you open the bag.'

I rehearsed this last line before Rubberface and his friend turned up, and it sounds good when I say it. It also seems to do the trick. He reluctantly places the holdall on the table and unzips it, pulling the flaps aside.

I can't really see anything and I don't want to lean forward too much in case I make myself vulnerable, even though I can't see Mac 10 man opening up in here unless he absolutely has to. There are customers sitting at two tables outside on the pavement in front of the window, and the owner is tidying up behind the counter, oblivious to what's going on only ten feet away from him, or maybe he just doesn't want to look. Either way, if these men decide to take me out, they're going to have to walk past a lot of witnesses who could potentially ID them. Or kill everyone, which I'm pretty sure they're not going to want to do.

But still I'm careful. As casually as possible I put one hand into the holdall, keeping the other hidden from view, and move it around until I touch something wrapped in plastic. I slowly lift it until it appears in the gap, still concealed from view by the angle of the holdall. It's a large, thick-bladed knife heavily stained with dried blood, wrapped in clingfilm and sitting in a clear plastic evidence bag. Next to it in the bag is a silver DVD in its plastic sheath.

I swallow hard. It's the same knife from the film of Leah's murder, and the sight of it brings the memories of this morning right back to the forefront of my mind. For the first time in a while I come close to losing my calm. I let it drop back into the holdall, and Rubberface zips it up again.

'Now, let me see the case properly,' he demands.

I think of Leah alive and laughing with a glass of chilled white wine and experience a desperate urge to pull the trigger and watch this arrogant bastard scream. But I don't. Instead, I pick up the holdall and put it down beside me, then lift up the case and place it carefully on the table, with the handle facing him. He inspects it carefully for several long seconds, checking its authenticity, then stops.

We all stop.

I'm looking at the door, and Rubberface must have seen the flicker of alarm that crossed my face.

Two cops have walked in. They are unarmed, and look like community support officers. One is black and overweight, with a pudgy face and a belly that reaches the counter at least a second before he does. The other is white and small and middle-aged, and reminds me of my old maths teacher at school. If these two are the face of crime fighting in London, then law-abiding citizens everywhere are in trouble.

I try to gesture as naturally as possible for Rubberface not to look round, but subtlety's clearly not his strong point and his head's already turning. Mac 10 man's calmer, giving them only a cursory glance as they arrive at the counter, but I also see that his trigger arm has tensed.

I pick up my coffee and take a casual sip, a man without a care in the world.

Unfortunately, it's too late. In the periphery of my vision, I can see we've caught the cops' attention. The black officer orders bacon and sausage on white bread and leans a stubby elbow on the counter top, looking our way. He's got that sort of officious expression you often get on petty bureaucrats. He wants to show the world that he's got power, that he's not just some meaningless cog in the big wheel of life. That he's a man to be respected. And at the moment, this makes him very dangerous. The white guy, who's made an excellent culinary choice and gone for what I had on the menu, looks much more nervous, and I can't say I blame him. If we're innocent, then all we're doing is interrupting his lunch; if we're guilty, then it's going to be no easy collar. Rubberface could probably break him in half if he chose to, and I doubt he'd have too much trouble stomping his tubby colleague either.

Rubberface picks up the briefcase and gets to his feet, apparently satisfied that it's the right one.

'What's in the case?'

It's the black officer speaking, and my heart sinks. His tone's confident, almost playful.

'Business papers,' Rubberface says brusquely.

The officer nods slowly, his expression coolly sceptical. 'What kind of business papers?'

I ask myself why the hell he's doing this. Is it because he genuinely believes he's stumbled on some sort of clandestine deal, or is he just showing off to the owner? It's difficult to tell. On the other table, Mac 10 man is staring hard at both cops. The barrel of the weapon has moved ninety degrees too, and the black officer's ample belly is now directly in the firing line. A single signal from Rubberface and I know he'll pull the trigger without hesitation. I'm no hero, but I can't allow that to happen. The guy's an idiot, but he doesn't deserve to die in a hail of bullets.

'Just papers,' reiterates Rubberface, his accent becoming more obvious as he starts to walk towards the door.

The officer moves away from the counter, blocking his path, and I see that his hand has moved down towards the can of CS gas in his belt. Five feet separates the two men. Probably the same distance separates the officer from the end of the Mac 10. I wonder if he can smell the tension. But no, it seems he can't.

'Do you mind if I have a look?' he asks.

'Yeah, I do mind,' snaps Rubberface. 'I'm in a hurry.'

He goes to walk past, but the cop doesn't move.

'I'm afraid I'm going to have to make this official,' says the cop. 'I'm searching you under the terms of the Police and Criminal Evidence Act 1984 on suspicion of possession of drugs.'

'This is fucking ridiculous.'

'Don't swear, sir. Please put the briefcase down and put your hands in the air.'

Rubberface does neither of these two things. Instead, he and Mac 10 man exchange a brief glance. A silent message passes between them, and Mac 10's trigger arm becomes as taut as a drum.

Both cops turn in Mac 10's direction, as if seeing him for the first time. He stares back at them, his left hand out of sight under the table, the right still holding the foul-smelling cigarette. He puts the cigarette to his lips and takes a slow, contemptuous drag, before flicking ash directly onto the table top. The contours of his face are cold, dead stone. It's the gaze of a natural killer.

The whole room becomes still, as if the pause button's been pushed. No-one moves. Even the café's owner has stopped what he's doing. He looks petrified. The coffee percolator fizzes and froths in the background, and there is a certain inevitability about what's going to happen next.

The Mac 10 is a so-called 'spray and pray' weapon, designed for close-quarter combat rather than accuracy. With a rate of fire of twelve hundred bullets per minute, its thirty-two-round magazine will empty in under two seconds if the trigger is pulled while the weapon's set to automatic, the nine-millimetre bullets tearing apart anything in their path as they leave the barrel at more than six hundred miles per hour. In a confined space like this one, and with the pistol bucking in the shooter's hand, the effects will be devastating.

I need to move, and fast. Before the shooting starts.

The black cop turns back to Rubberface. For the first time, I see the tension in his features. He's unarmed and outnumbered, and he knows it.

But he won't back down. Even now, he won't back down.

'Please put the case down, sir,' he repeats, unclipping the strap on the CS gas holder, 'and place your hands in the air.'

The white cop's sweating, and I can see that his hands are shaking.

Mac 10 sits with Zen-like calm, as if he is above the petty fears of the others in the room. He is at peace with himself, if not with the rest of humanity, and I know that he's making the final preparations to commit an absolute minimum of two murders, and that I may well be number three.

'I'm going to ask you one last time,' says the black cop, his voice faltering, 'then I'm going to place you under arrest for obstruction.' Slowly, he removes the spray from its holder.

'This is stupid,' complains Rubberface.

He has his back to me, and I'm wondering if I can use him as cover.

Mac 10 is looking at his boss expectantly, waiting for the final nod. He's sitting back in his seat, giving himself support for when he opens fire.

Every second seems to crawl by. The air in here is like glue.

My legs tense and stiffen, and I begin, very slowly, to get up from my seat.

And then it happens.

The door crashes open.

A man has rushed into the café. 'Officers!' he shouts, clearly panic-stricken. 'There's been a stabbing in the shop round the corner. The assistant's been knifed. She's bleeding all over the place. You've got to come quick.'

The cops don't need asking twice. The white cop is already running for the door and tugging his radio free. 'Has someone called nine-nine-nine?' he shouts, the relief evident in his voice as he kicks up a real cloud of dust in his desire to get out of here. You have to give the black cop credit, though. As he follows his colleague out the door, he shouts at the three of us to stay where we are because he hasn't finished with us yet. He even manages to chuck an instruction to the café owner to keep his bacon and sausage sandwich warm.

And then they're gone.

For a moment, no-one seems to know quite what to do. Then, without looking back at me, Rubberface says something to Mac 10 in Serbo-Croat, and he gets up, his machine pistol hidden from view once again. They hurry out together in single file, taking the briefcase with them, while I slip the Glock back into the waistband of my jeans, pick up the holdall and get to my feet.

The café owner looks at me vaguely aghast. He knows something bad's gone on here but, like the coppers, he's not quite sure what. I take a ten-pound note from my pocket, walk over to the counter and put it in his hand. 'That was an excellent lunch,' I tell him with a smile, and before he has a chance to answer I'm walking out of there, knowing that Lucas won't be able to distract the cops with his story of an armed robbery gone wrong for very long.

13

Outside, the street's busy with passers-by, all of them oblivious to the drama that's just been played out right under their noses. It always amazes me how little people really see of what goes on around them. They're like sheep grazing contentedly at the edge of a wood full of wolves. I try to imagine what the scene would have been like had Mac 10 made one simple movement of his index finger and pulled the trigger. Two seconds of noise followed by blood, death and outright panic, and suddenly the writhing underbelly of society would have been thrust right into their midst.

I look down the road but I can't see the Yugoslavs any more. I'm guessing they arrived by car and left the same way. Now that I'm in possession of the evidence against me for Leah's murder, I'm not a hundred per cent sure what I'm going to do with it. I feel vulnerable carrying the holdall containing the weapon used to butcher her. I need to get rid of it.

My phone rings. Not the one supplied to me by Leah's killer, but the one belonging to Martin Lukersson Associates. The ringtone is 'Rhinestone Cowboy' by Glenn Campbell, and I remember that Snowy is a fan of country music and that all their phones announce incoming calls with famous country hits. Snowy's own phone plays 'Big Bad John' by Ron Jordan.

It's Lucas on the other end. 'Where are you?' he asks.

'Going north on the Caledonian Road. I've just passed Wharfdale Road. You sound tired.'

'Are you surprised? I've been running away from those cops. They got a bit pissed off when they found out that their stabbing victim only existed in my head. What the hell happened in there? Who were those guys?'

'I think they're Yugoslavs. They were speaking Serbo-Croat.'

'Since when have you had any run-ins with Yugoslavs?'

'I don't think I ever have. We never had any problems with the locals when we were serving in Bosnia, did we?'

'Not that I remember. I thought we were on pretty reasonable terms with everyone back then.'

'And it was more than ten years ago as well.'

'So it sounds like they're working for someone else?'

'It looks that way, but they're no off-the-street stooges. One of them was packing a Mac 10.'

Lucas whistles down the other end of the phone. As a former soldier, he can appreciate serious firepower. 'You've got yourself involved with some serious shit, Tyler.'

'Don't I know it. And it almost got even more serious. Those cops walked in right in the middle of the deal, and decided to get involved. It was a good thing you appeared. I think the guy with the Mac 10 was just about to start shooting.'

'It's all part of the service, sir. I trust you were suitably impressed with my acting skills.'

'Oscar-winning. So, where are they now?'

'Eastbound on the Pentonville Road. Snowy's on them.'

'I hope he's not drawing attention to himself.'

'We're professionals, Tyler. We do this every day. And anyway, he can hang back. The tracker on the briefcase emits a signal we can follow without being right behind it.'

I'd always known I was going to have to hand over the briefcase in exchange for the evidence linking me to Leah's murder, but that didn't mean I was going to give up the hunt for her killers. I'd got Lucas to plant a tiny GPS tracking device barely half a centimetre across in the narrow gap created in the material where the case opened and closed. It wasn't a perfect fit, but you'd have to look quite hard to find it, and Rubberface hadn't been looking that hard, especially after he was interrupted.

'Listen,' continues Lucas, 'I'm just getting it in my car now. I'm parked round the back of the station. I'll pick you up on the Caledonian Road in three minutes.'

True to his word, he pulls up beside me exactly three minutes later in the second-hand BMW X3 he bought from the showroom last year. I notice that it needs a clean as I jump inside.

He's talking on hands-free to Snowy, who's giving him a rundown of our quarry's location. Still talking, he pulls away and takes the first left turn. Snowy had been waiting in his car on double yellow lines fifty yards from the café and is now following the Yugoslavs who left the scene in a car driven by a third man. Snowy tells us that their vehicle's currently stuck in heavy traffic just east of the Angel, Islington, on the City Road, a distance from us of just over a mile. He's currently six cars back from the Yugoslavs, and one lane over. He talks us through what's happening, or more accurately what isn't happening, in a voice that's very similar to Lucas's – deep, confident, and in control. Lucas tells him that we're five minutes behind him. 'Call me with a status report in five minutes,' he says, 'or when you start moving again.' Then he ends the call. 'No point listening to him sitting in traffic,' he explains, pulling a battered pack of

Lucky Strike from the glove compartment and lighting one. 'He's not that interesting.'

Lucas looks dapper as usual in a short-sleeved white shirt with not a crease in it (ex-soldiers are always good at ironing), and a burgundy silk tie with matching Parachute Regiment tie pin, which he likes to wear in front of the punters, since he feels that it sums him up as a man of action, even though it's close to a decade since he wore the uniform. His charcoal-grey suit trousers are tailored and his black brogues smartly polished, although his cherished blond locks have grown just a little bit too wild and free. In my opinion, they need the services of a good barber to rein them in.

While Lucas smokes his cigarette and manoeuvres the BMW through the back streets of Islington, trying without much success to avoid the worst of the traffic, he asks me more about the details of the events I'm caught up in. So far, I haven't told him too much. There wasn't time when we were in his offices. Now, though, I figure that, having trusted him enough to ask for his help, I may as well trust him enough to say why, and I start talking. He interrupts repeatedly with questions which I do my best to answer. I tell him about Leah and the manner of her murder, and then the exchange of briefcases that ended in the deaths of four people.

He whistles through his teeth. 'And you shot two of them?'

I nod. 'It would have been three, but someone beat me to it.'

'You know, Tyler, if it ever comes to court, I'd avoid letting the jury hear that.'

'It was self-defence,' I explain. 'I had no choice. But, you know, after what happened to Leah, I'm not in the mood for showing a lot of mercy.'

'You really cared about her, eh?'

'Yeah,' I say simply, staring out of the window, 'I did.'

Seeing the expression on my face, Lucas decides to move on. 'And you've got no idea what's in the case?'

I shake my head. 'Just that whatever it is is being used to blackmail a businessman. I got the impression it was something . . .' I pause for a moment, trying to come up with the right words. 'Something very unpleasant.'

He raises his eyebrows. 'Really? Now I'm getting curious.'

'Also, the guy I was picking the case up from, he was someone from the regiment.'

Lucas looks surprised. 'From my time?'

'Yeah, I'm sure he was there when you were. He was a captain, first name Iain, I think. Medium height, thin face. About our age.'

'Ferrie,' he says decisively. 'His name's Iain Ferrie.'

'That's right,' I say, remembering now. 'I'm impressed. I never realized you had such a good memory.'

But Lucas is giving me a strange look. 'My memory isn't that good,' he answers. 'The only reason I know is because I've just done some work for him.'

14

'He came to see me twice,' explains Lucas. 'The first time he wanted a Land Registry search done on a property in Bedfordshire. That was back in May. I advertise sometimes in *Army News*, and he said he'd heard of me from there. I did all the relevant searches, and it turned out that the property belonged to an offshore company based in the Bahamas. He wanted to know the names of the directors. He was pretty adamant about that. Same way he was adamant that I kept things absolutely confidential. He didn't even want to involve Snowy. I got the directors' names – although as far as I could see they were just local Bahamian guys put there to make the paperwork all above board – and gave them to him. He paid me, and that was that.'

'And there was nothing untoward about the company?'

He shakes his head. 'No, didn't seem to be. Nothing that struck me anyway.'

'And the second time?'

'That was a bit weirder. It was about a month ago. He said he wanted me to look into the murder of Maxwell and Spann in Paris.'

'Ferrie mentioned them to me this morning. He reckoned they were murdered by the same person who'd been hired to come after him.'

'That's right. Someone he called the Vampire.' He emphasizes these last two words, pulling a face. 'He wanted me to find out all I could about their deaths. To be honest, I thought he'd been smoking something he shouldn't have. He was really agitated and kept insisting that I was totally discreet in my enquiries, like I was going to shout about it from the rooftops. I didn't really want to get involved, but he was offering money upfront, and I don't turn down ready cash.'

'And what did you find out?'

Lucas tells me pretty much exactly what Ferrie told me this morning. 'The guy Maxwell and Spann were guarding was a Russian mafia type,' he adds. 'He was supposedly something big in oil, but I spoke to the detective in Paris who led the investigation, and he reckoned that the Russian was also heavily involved in people trafficking – you know, bringing young women from the Eastern Bloc into western Europe, and setting them up as prostitutes. But he'd recently fallen out with his associates, and this is where it gets interesting.'

'Go on.'

'Apparently those associates were Yugoslavs. From Bosnia.'

'And did the detective identify them?'

Lucas shakes his head. 'No, and I didn't find out anything about this Vampire Ferrie was talking about either.'

'I still don't understand what all this has got to do with me,' I say, and it's true, I don't. I don't have the faintest idea.

'Neither do I.' Lucas stubs out his cigarette in the car's overflowing ashtray. 'Let's hope our quarry can provide a few answers.'

At that moment, his mobile rings again. It's Snowy. Our targets are on the move.

For the next ten minutes, Snowy gives us a running commentary of their progress as they continue down the City Road, then turn on to Vestry Street and the New North Road, heading away from the financial district towards the eastern edge of Islington. Snowy's hanging back a little now because he thinks they may be doubling back on themselves, which would suggest they're worried about a tail.

By this time, though, we're clogged in Friday-afternoon traffic near the Business Design Centre on Upper Street. There's been an accident up ahead between a four-wheel-drive and a Mazda full of Arabs, and the road's blocked.

I look at my watch. It's just turned five to three, and the sun's beating down out of a near cloudless sky.

Lucas curses and bangs the palm of his hand on the steering wheel. Cars have already backed up behind us, so there's no way back. We've just got to wait while the four-wheel-drive and the Mazda get out of the way, and at the moment there doesn't appear to be much chance of that happening. The 4×4 is like a tank; even if it mounts the pavement it will be difficult to get past it. The woman driver has her head out of the window and is shouting at the Arabs, who are clustered around the front of their own car, gesticulating wildly. A chorus of horns blasts away, and a guy in a white van jumps out and starts yelling for them all to move. It's a hot day in an overcrowded, smoky city, and tempers are frayed. I wish I was anywhere but here.

'Bravo One's turning right into Mintern Street one hundred metres ahead,' announces Snowy. 'I'm going to keep on going so I don't draw suspicion.'

'Good idea,' says Lucas. 'We're still in west Islington so currently ten minutes behind you.'

Although Lucas has already told me that the tracking device emits a signal that can be tracked remotely via the laptop in

Snowy's car, there is a slight problem. If the case goes inside a building, the satellite's view of it will be blocked and the signal lost, which is something I can't afford, because I've got a feeling that once inside, it won't be coming out again, and my best lead'll be lost for ever.

Snowy picks up the Yugoslavs again in a residential back street a few hundred metres further on. 'OK, Bravo One's fifty metres ahead turning right into Osman Road – now. Traffic's light so I'm running the risk of being compromised. What's your location?'

'We're still ten minutes away,' answers Lucas as the 4×4 finally pulls up onto the pavement and the Arabs cease their gesticulating and park up behind it, easing the bottleneck.

'Once I'm on Kingsland Road, I'm going to allow them to get ahead of me a little. OK?'

'No problem, Snow. We'll be with you as soon as we can. In the meantime, don't take any risks.'

'I won't.' He pauses for a moment before continuing. 'I'm turning into Osman Road, got visual. Car's pulling up outside a three-storey warehouse building halfway down. Big IC2 male, black hair, getting out.'

'That's him,' I say.

'He's got the case in his hand,' Snowy continues, 'and he's going to the door and speaking into an intercom. I'm going to have to stop talking while I pass.' There's a longer pause – ten, maybe twelve seconds – and by the time he comes back on the line again we've passed the 4×4 and are pulling onto Upper Street. 'I'm now coming up to the junction with Kingsland Road. IC2 male has entered building with the case. There's no number or name on it, but it's behind a fence and has blue-framed windows with mesh over them. Bravo One has now pulled away from the building and is driving behind me. What do you want me to do? Keep with him or wait with the case?'

Lucas doesn't hesitate. 'Keep with the case. We've got the registration on the car so we can always track it later. Pull up somewhere out of sight, preferably where you can get visual on the front of the building, then call me with the location, or if the case goes on the move again. See you in ten.'

15

As it happens, we're there in nearer fifteen.

Osman Road is a narrow, comparatively quiet street containing a varied mixture of warehouses, workshops and office buildings, most of which look like they were built in the sixties and seventies when aesthetically pleasing designs were a low priority. The building we want is a large, nondescript, three-storey warehouse with grimy concrete columns running up between the darkened windows, and cheap stone cladding filling the gaps.

There's very little traffic about, and only the occasional pedestrian, so it's easy to see why Snowy was concerned about getting spotted by his target. He's moved to a parallel street, so we turn right on Osman Road, then immediately left and drive until we get to the surprisingly leafy no-through road where his BMW – another from my showroom – is parked up. Lucas finds a space two or three cars down, backing on to a low brick wall beyond which is a tiny tree-lined park with a kids' climbing frame and swings. Through the closed windows of Lucas's car I can just about hear the faint shouts of kids playing. On the other side of the road is a five-storey block of neat, well-kept council flats, all of which have small balconies, and I'm surprised to see that none of them is occupied. Snowy's chosen this place well. It's secluded, and there's pedestrian access through to Osman Road at the end. Although you can't actually see the target building, by my reckoning it's barely fifty yards away, and if the case starts moving again he can be on to it quick and without drawing attention to himself.

We exit the BMW, and the sound of the kids playing gets louder. Over the top of the wall, I can see a young mother lifting her child onto the top of a slide, and laughing as she watches him disappear down it. There's pure love in her expression, and I turn away quickly, before I start thinking about Leah.

We walk over to Snowy's car, with me leading the way. I can see him sitting in the driver's seat.

But something's wrong.

He's not moving.

I stop a few feet away, and Lucas stops beside me.

'What is it?' he says, but even before the words are out, they're dying in his throat. 'Oh shit.'

Snowy is staring straight ahead, and for the first time I see the thick drops of blood on the inside of the windscreen.

Lucas sees them too. 'No,' he whispers, his voice laced with real pain.

He steps forward and tugs open the passenger door. Hot, fetid air wafts out as Snowy comes into view properly. Lucas moans. I gasp. Neither of us, I think, can believe what we're seeing.

A long, deep slice runs across Snowy's throat, pretty much from ear to ear, the pale flabby flesh hanging open like a burst seam. The wound's still leaking thick streams of arterial blood onto the shirt, so much so that I know it's a leaf-green colour only by looking at the material directly above the waistband of his trousers. There's more blood on the dashboard, as well as the drops on the lower end of the windscreen where it must have spurted. On his lap, perched on the protruding zipper of his fly, is the tracking device I saw Lucas insert into the lining of the briefcase. It's a tiny black thing, very close in colour to the leather of the case. Almost impossible to spot, I thought at the time, as I recall did Lucas, but it's clear we were both wrong because someone has not only spotted it, they've also spotted the tail as well, and decided to do something about it very quickly, very decisively and, of course, very brutally.

Even so, it's a clean killing. Someone's come up to the car unnoticed, leaned in the window, grabbed him by his mop of snow-white hair with a gloved hand, and used the other to inflict a single cut from a very sharp knife or razor without him having a chance to react or cry out. This place may be quiet, but it's hardly the dead of night, and it takes some serious balls to do what the killer did. And Snowy's no easy target either. He's an ex-para who's now a private detective, so he's the kind of guy who keeps his wits about him.

But he's still dead.

'Look,' says Lucas, 'they've searched his pockets as well.' He points to his former colleague's trousers, to where the threadbare material of the lining is hanging out.

'Jesus.'

I turn away, feeling sick, reminded of Leah's dead body and the way her blood soaked through the bedclothes. I'm also thinking about the Maxwell and Spann murders Lucas and I were talking about barely fifteen minutes ago. The Vampire. Is this his work?

The sound of the kids playing only yards away seems suddenly amplified, a grotesque contrast to the sight that has just confronted me. I move a few paces away from the car, unable to breathe in the smell of death any more.

'Get back in my car,' Lucas tells me, pulling on a pair of clear plastic evidence gloves. 'I need to check something.' He clambers into Snowy's BMW and shuts the door behind him.

I don't need asking twice and, keeping my head down, I walk back and get inside, taking deep breaths to fight down the nausea I'm feeling. I've fucked up, no question, and in the light of this latest grim development, I'm left wondering what the hell I'm going to do next.

But, of course, I know the answer to that one straight away.

The door opens and Lucas jumps back in the driver's seat.

'I'm sorry,' I tell him, not really sure what else to say.

He doesn't acknowledge the comment. Instead, he tells me that Snowy's pockets are all empty. 'They've taken everything,' he adds, the expression on his face uncharacteristically grim. 'His phone, his wallet. The whole lot.'

'Which means they'll know who he works for.'

He sighs. 'It looks that way. This is a warning. It's telling us to leave well alone.'

'I know, but I can't.'

'Somehow I thought you'd say that,' he says, starting the car and reversing out of the parking space. As he drives out of the road's only exit, with his free hand he plants a cigarette firmly between his lips and lights it.

'I'm going into the warehouse,' I tell him.

'Fuck it, Tyler, don't risk it,' he mumbles through the cigarette.

'Look, Leah's dead, Snowy's dead. That case is my only lead.'

'It probably isn't even in there now,' he points out as we drive aimlessly through the back streets, moving in a rough circle round Osman Road.

'It might not be, but there are going to be people inside who know something, and I'm still armed.'

'Listen, it'll be a lot easier and a lot safer for me to get the address and do a land registry search.'

'And you'll probably end up finding out that it belongs to some Bahamas-based offshore company, and that's not really going to tell me anything, is it?'

Lucas spits the cigarette out of the window. His hands are tight on the steering wheel, the knuckles red. There's perspiration forming in tiny droplets on the tanned, only faintly lined skin of his forehead, even though the BMW's air conditioning is blasting out on full.

I wish I hadn't involved him now, and I know he feels the same way. He wanted to help an old friend, but in one fell swoop his trusted colleague's dead and the business he's built up over years of hard work is suddenly in jeopardy, because Snowy's murder's going to get back to him. He may be sitting there dead with no ID on him and in a car I know is registered in his name rather than Martin Lukersson Associates, because I sold it to him; but even if the police are on a go-slow, they're eventually going to link Snowy with Lucas. And when that happens, when what they are working on comes out, my name's going to end up in the frame and the police are going to be looking for me. This is another reason why I feel I've got no choice but to go into the building and take my chances. Because already my time is running out.

Lucas tries hard to dissuade me as we drive round. He tells me that for a start I have no actual plan, and improvisation is hardly going to work, unless I'm prepared to kill again. And with two corpses to my name today already, do I honestly want to add any more? He also points out that the people inside may well be expecting me, knowing that there's a strong possibility I'll have discovered Snowy's body, and since I'm acting alone, and am therefore almost certain to be overpowered, that effectively means I'm a dead man. Lastly, it's going to be a lot safer to find out who we're up against using more conventional detection methods in which he is, if he says so himself, something of an expert.

He says all this in the space of about thirty seconds, and I've got to admit I'm impressed by the strength and breadth of his arguments. Unfortunately, they don't work. My mind's made up, and I don't want to hang around thinking about what might go wrong because that way something inevitably will. Soldiers should never think too much when they're going into battle, and generally they don't, which is why they still go rather than dwell on the reasonable statistical chance that death awaits them and high-tail it the other way. There's an old adage that when the bullets are flying, you never think you're going to be the one to get hit, and it's true. Which is why I tell Lucas to turn right and then right again, and soon we're driving back down Osman Road.

As we do so, I can see that a taxi has pulled up on the road directly outside our building, and two ordinary-looking business-men in suits emerge from it. They walk up to the black door, and one speaks into the intercom. By this time we're driving past and Lucas hisses at me not to stare. 'Look at me,' he demands. 'Casually. Like we're having a conversation.'

I do as he says.

'You never know who's watching,' he tells me, 'and we really don't want to stand out. Not after what's happened.' He takes a casual look in the rear-view mirror. 'You see, this is how we do it, using the mirrors. That way it looks natural. Right, the door's opened and those two guys have just gone in. Recognize them?'

'Never seen them before in my life.'

We're now coming to the end of Osman Road where it meets with Kingsland Road.

'OK, drop me off at the top here,' I tell Lucas. 'I'm going to go in the back way.'

'I hope you know what you're doing,' he says, fixing me with an intense expression that accentuates his high cheekbones and Nordic features. It's a look that suits him. He has very vivid blue eyes, the colour of tropical seas in winter holiday adverts, and at the moment they're filled with what looks a lot like genuine concern.

If I had the time, I'd almost feel touched. But I don't. The clock's ticking, and I need to come up with some answers, and soon. So all I reply is, 'Of course I know what I'm doing,' even though it must be obvious to all but the most deranged of observers that I don't. I lean over and put a hand on his arm. 'Thanks for everything, OK? I appreciate it. And I'm sorry for what happened to Snowy. But now you can go home.'

'Shit,' he snorts contemptuously as he stops at the junction, making no move to pull out, 'do you really think I'd leave you here alone?'

'I don't want you coming in with me. You've done enough.'

'I'm not going to come in with you, but I'm not going to desert you either. You've still got our phone, haven't you?'

'Course I have. I respect other people's property.'

'If I haven't heard from you in fifteen minutes, I'll raise the alarm somehow.'

'How?'

'I'll think of something.'

'I appreciate this,' I tell him, thankful that amid all the savagery of this day I've got someone I can rely on.

We watch each other for a long moment.

'Be careful, Tyler,' Lucas says eventually.

I tell him I will. We shake hands and I pull my hand away quickly, not wanting to drag things out, because if I do I know the fear will kick in and I'll lose the momentum that's been driving me forward all day.

I jump out of the car and he pulls away, turning left on to the main road. I start walking, watching the BMW as it disappears over the hump of a nearby bridge, and with each step I take I think about Leah and wonder why she, like Snowy, had to die for the mysterious contents of a briefcase.

It's time to find out.

16

When I get to the bridge, I see that it crosses a canal and that the buildings on Osman Road back on to the canal path, which gives me something of an advantage. I pick out the target building. It's bordered at the rear by a brick wall about eight feet high, with a set of double gates in the middle topped with two lines of rusty-looking barbed wire. It all looks fairly imposing, but looks can be deceptive, and I know I'll be able to get through security like that easily enough.

Taking a deep breath, I descend the steps that lead down from the bridge to the canal path and walk as casually as I can towards my destination. On the other side of the canal a couple of joggers run past, looking exhausted in the heat.

And then, finally, fate intervenes on my behalf. As I approach the gate, I hear someone talking behind the wall. Once again, the language is Serbo-Croat. I slow down and stop, and a second later I hear the gate being unlocked on the other side. There's nowhere to hide, so as it opens outwards, I step behind it and stand there, out of view.

A young guy in a cheap black suit emerges, letting the gate

swing back on its hinges behind him. He's talking into a mobile phone, and he's got his back to me as he walks slowly down the path. Taking my opportunity, I curl my fingers round the end of the gate and stop it shutting automatically, then slip inside, leaving it on the latch.

I'm in a car park about twenty yards square which leads to the back of the building. There are banks of windows lining each floor. Most have the blinds down and the others appear empty, which seems strange given that there are about a dozen vehicles of all shapes and sizes in the car park, including a Jag and a brand-new Merc CLK-Class Cabriolet.

As I step forward, I hear the gate reopening as the guy in the suit comes back in. He's off the phone now and has clicked the gate shut. I slip behind a metallic blue Land Rover Discovery and crouch down while he passes. He pauses to light a cigarette, then continues towards the back of the building. He's the only person I can see, and I walk behind him, my footsteps barely making a sound on the dusty concrete.

By the time he hears me, he's five yards from the back door and I've already retrieved the Glock from my waistband. He turns round, and I see that he's in his late twenties with bad teeth and ferret-like eyes which widen dramatically at just the moment when I smack him in the middle of the forehead with the gun's handle. He grunts in pain and goes down on one knee, so I smack him again, this time on the temple; the blow is easily enough to knock him unconscious. He'll be out for a good few minutes, which is the best I can hope for at the moment.

There's a wheelie bin a few yards away, next to a locked-up loading bay, with a pungent smell of old fish oozing out of it in the still heat. Shoving the Glock back in my jeans, I pull him roughly to his feet and drag him over to it. I remove the lid and the smell suddenly gets a lot stronger. I dread to think what the people here have been eating. You wouldn't want to dump your worst enemy in here – unless, of course, your worst enemies are like mine are turning out to be. I hoist him over my shoulder, toss him inside, replace the lid and take a deep breath of fresh air.

The back door's a fire exit and it's been propped open with a stop. I open it slowly and find myself in a darkened corridor with cement flooring. There's an empty kitchen area to my right, and another door directly ahead of me, which looks more promising. I try the handle. It's unlocked.

This time I find myself in a carpeted hallway with lighted chandeliers on the ceiling. The air conditioning's on in here, and I can hear the steady buzz of casual conversation coming through some open glass doors ahead of me. There's a peal of female laughter, and I wonder what kind of place I'm in. I pass a carpeted staircase on my left, and then I'm through the glass doors and into a narrow, windowless bar, lit up by the soft glow of half a dozen Chinese lamps. The decor's not what you'd describe as expensive, but it's definitely making the effort, and I'm surprised at how much better this place looks on the inside.

The tables lining one side of the room are teak in colour, and the low-slung armchairs around them are worn leather. Most of them are occupied by two types of people: thin young women who look barely out of their teens, wearing respectful, slightly vacant expressions, and skirts so short they're in danger of hanging themselves with them; and expensively, occasionally gaudily, dressed men with too little hair who, to put it politely, are a long way past their peak. None of them glances my way. The men are too preoccupied, and I'm guessing the girls wouldn't dare. This is, I realize suddenly, the public area of a brothel, and the people who run things will be somewhere else.

The barman – who's wearing a burgundy waistcoat the colour

of the wallpaper and a minute bow-tie, and is the only man in here younger than me – looks my way with interest. I smile at him and turn away, heading back out and over to the staircase.

As I take the first of the steps, a door opens to my right and through it comes a short, squat guy with a razor-sharp widow's peak and a more than passing resemblance to Bela Lugosi in his glory days as Count Dracula. We're only three feet apart. He scowls and opens his mouth to say something, but the gun's out of my waistband in one movement. I shove it hard against his belly before he can react, and move in close to him, putting a hand behind his neck so that we're almost in an embrace. He smells of stale and very cheap cigarette smoke. He looks extremely angry too, his features wrinkling into an expression of almost unhinged aggression. But he's not stupid. He can feel the Glock's barrel and doesn't resist as I give him a cursory pat-down, retrieving a four-inch flick knife from his trouser pocket.

I press my thumb into the pressure point just below his ear. 'I've killed two men today,' I tell him calmly. 'Unless you tell me what I want to know, you're going to be number three.'

He grunts something unintelligible and meets my eye to show he's not intimidated.

I know I haven't got much time. Any minute now, someone's going to come past, see what's happening, and raise the alarm.

'I'm looking for a big man with dark hair and very brown skin.'

He looks blank.

'He's had a lot of plastic surgery,' I add, hoping this'll help identify him.

He looks totally confused. 'What you say?'

I suddenly see what Lucas meant about not having a plan. It's time for decisive measures. Returning my hand to his neck, I slam my thumb into the pressure point and he gasps in pain, his legs wobbling. I could easily knock him out, but again, I doubt if he'd be under for more than a few minutes, and I really don't want to go through this whole building temporarily incapacitating every thug I come across, because, one way or another, I've got to get back out of here again.

'Right, up the stairs,' I snap, swinging him round and shoving the gun into the small of his back. 'You're going to take me to the guy who runs this place, and if you try anything, you'll be in a wheelchair for the rest of your life.'

I push the Glock's barrel right into his back, just so he's in no doubt that I mean business, and he starts up the stairs. I follow very close behind, my breath on his neck. I hear more laughter coming from behind me, this time male, and the sound of chairs scraping across the carpet. I'm guessing that some of the men in the bar are getting ready for their main course, and they'll soon be heading up the stairs as well. I give Dracula a shove to speed him up.

'You know who I'm talking about, don't you?' I whisper, and this time I flick open the blade on the knife and jab it hard against his cheek, almost but not quite breaking the skin.

He grunts again, a defiant sound, and I know this guy's not the sort who intimidates easily. I may have to make him bleed to get where I need to go, but I'm hoping he'll see sense. I was a soldier, not a torturer, and the idea of carving a blade across a helpless man's face is not a prospect I relish.

When we reach the top of the stairs, he turns left and we start to walk down a long hallway, the kind you get in a hotel, running the length of the whole floor with doors on both sides. All the doors are shut, but from behind several of them I can hear the sound of women faking sexual pleasure, as well as the occasional animal growl of exertion. The hallway itself is empty, everyone being far too busy to be hanging around in corridors, but already I can hear the new arrivals from the bar starting up the stairs.

I give Dracula another jab with the knife. He continues to walk, then stops at a heavy fire door close to the end of the hallway, and tries its handle.

'It's locked,' he grunts.

'Unlock it, then. I know you've got keys. I felt them when I searched you earlier. And hurry up.'

I jab him again, and this time the skin breaks and a tiny drop of blood comes out. Dracula flinches slightly, and pulls a bunch of keys from his pocket. I watch as the droplet trickles very slowly down his cheek, and for a moment the sight of it makes me nauseous.

He opens the door just as the punters and the girls come into view. Before any of them turn our way, I push him through and follow behind, hoping they haven't spotted us.

We're in a small alcove with stairs leading up to the next floor. We stop at the bottom. I can't hear anything coming from up above, not a sound, which concerns me. This building's only three storeys, and if there's no-one up here, I really don't know where else to look.

'Where's the man I want?' I demand.

He motions with his head towards the top of the stairs, and I wonder whether I'm being led into a trap. I watch him carefully. A line of blood runs all the way to his jaw where I've cut him. He's beginning to look nervous.

I click the knife's blade shut and put it in the back pocket of my jeans, then place an arm round Dracula's neck and pull him close, using him as a human shield as we lumber up the stairs together like some sort of pantomime horse.

'Next time there'll be no jab with the knife,' I hiss in his ear, ignoring the smell of wax and stale smoke that comes from there. 'I'll just settle for blowing your spine out.'

On the third or fourth step from the top, the third floor comes into view. The layout is the same, but the lighting is much harsher and the walls are painted a stark white which has stained with age.

Suddenly a door to the left opens, and lo and behold Rubberface appears. He's turning round and talking in Serbo-Croat to someone I can't see.

Moving fast, I shove Dracula up the last couple of stairs and swing him round so he's facing Rubberface.

Hearing the commotion, Rubberface turns our way and immediately curses. He's been caught off guard, and he freezes for a moment.

I know it's not going to take him long to gather his senses, and as soon as he does he's going to try to get back inside the door. I pull the gun away from its position against Dracula's spine, and point it straight at his torso.

'Move, and you get a bullet in the gut,' I state in tones that tell him I'm the one in control of this situation.

Unfortunately, I'm not. No longer under direct threat from the Glock, Dracula seizes his chance and grabs at my wrist, bucking and kicking as he tries to break my grip on his neck. I stumble back, and Dracula uses his free arm to try to elbow me in the belly; but I twist away from the blow and put every ounce of my strength into squeezing the air out of his throat. He chokes and gasps but keeps struggling, and I'm sent crashing backwards into the wall, my gun arm thrust high in the air as Dracula yanks at it. Rubberface is yelling something else in Serbo-Croat, and now I know that I've got seconds to retrieve matters, otherwise I'm finished.

Bouncing back off the wall, I slam my knee into Dracula's coccyx. I'm sure he would have cried out in pain had he been able to breathe, but the pressure he's under finally takes its toll. His grip on my wrist loosens, and I pull my arm free. I'm swinging it back to smack him in the head with the barrel in a final effort to take him out of the equation when he grabs my wrist again, stopping the gun's trajectory at just the point when the barrel's facing his temple.

It's a mistake. My finger's already tight on the trigger, and the sudden force he applies causes a further involuntary tightening.

The noise of the Glock firing explodes in my ears, and I feel a warm splash on my arm as a gout of blood from what's left of the side of Dracula's head lands there. More blood splatters heavily on the carpet, and he goes limp in my arms. It may have been an accident, but it was also a perfect shot, straight into his temple, killing him near enough instantly.

Military training emphasizes the need in battle to compartmentalize your feelings. You need to kill without compunction or emotion, and then to move straight on to the next target, so I drop him to the floor and step straight over his corpse, the Glock held tight in both hands as I approach the door Rubberface has just disappeared through. No more than five seconds have passed since he made good his escape, but I've lost my most effective weapon, surprise, and now the whole dynamic has changed because they know I'm coming. As soon as I step through that door, I'm likely to take a bullet. If I go in commando-style, rolling, I'll have no idea where my targets are and I'm still going to end up shot, particularly if that rat-faced bastard with the Mac 10's in there. I need to think of something else, and fast.

Then a girl screams.

It comes out of nowhere; or, more accurately, it comes from somewhere behind the door. It's full of panic, and it stops me dead in my tracks. I hear it again, louder now. There's pain there, too, I'm sure of it, and my adrenalin goes into overdrive all over again.

The door begins to open.

'Help me,' I hear her beg. 'You've got to help me.'

The door's open about six inches now, and I can see a head appearing in the gap. I stand frozen to the spot, the gun outstretched in my hands, the end of the barrel barely a couple of feet from her. I have no idea what is going on.

'Come out here slowly.'

'They've hurt me,' she sobs.

I repeat the instruction. I'm not going in there.

The door opens further, and a terrified-looking young woman with a mane of blonde hair, dressed casually in jeans and a T-shirt, rushes towards me, oblivious to the gun, an expression of huge relief on her face.

I'm already lowering the gun as she runs into my arms, burying her head in my shoulder. I breathe in her clean, musky smell, and then she pulls back and her eyes meet mine. I'm transfixed. It's like gazing into dark pools.

Which is unfortunate, really, because by the time I realize she's holding something by her side, it's far too late.

One hand whips out and, with surprising strength, knocks the Glock out of my grasp, while the other slams the stun baton into my side, and for the second time that day I judder wildly as God knows how many volts go shooting through my body.

I just have time to curse myself for being so damn stupid before my legs go from under me and I crash heavily to the floor.

17

I'm not out for long, probably no more than three or four seconds. When I come round I can feel my shirt being pulled off, along with my bulletproof vest. I'm dragged to my feet by more than one pair of hands and led stumbling down the hallway, then up some more stairs, even though I didn't think there was another floor. No-one speaks.

A door appears, and I'm pushed through it. It's dark in here, and cooler than outside. I'm shoved into a chair, and I finally see who my captors are. One is the girl. The other is Rubberface, who slaps me hard across the face. There's real force in the blow, and it knocks me sideways. I kick out, catching him in the shin, and try to stand up, but he slaps me again, knocking me back down. My right cheek feels like it's on fire.

'Move again, and you get another dose of the baton,' he snarls, coming in close and showing perfect white teeth.

There's a leather restraint on the chair, which gives me a good idea what they use this room for, and which is why I'm not keen to remain in it. Rubberface pulls it round my midriff and buckles it at the back, pulling it tight. While he does this, the girl holds the stun baton against my leg. I glare at her, and she turns away. I can tell she's not really enjoying this.

'What are we going to do with him, Marco?' she asks, sounding worried.

'Forget him,' he snaps. 'And don't use my name, even in front of a dead man. OK?'

He grabs her arm roughly when he says this, and she gives him a frightened look of compliance. It's obvious she knows her place. Even after what she's done to me, and the fact that she's responsible for whatever's coming next (and Marco's kind of given the game away now), I still feel sorry for her.

He turns and gives me a contemptuous glare, then snatches the baton and thrusts it right into my groin. The pain is like nothing I've ever felt before. It literally takes my breath away. I shiver and twitch under my restraints while simultaneously gasping for air. He holds it there. The bastard holds it there, the drum-tight skin of his face forming a pathetic version of a smile.

'That's for trying to fuck me about,' he says.

I feel myself blacking out as he pulls the baton away. I fight unconsciousness, but it creeps up on me, and the world of violence that is all I've experienced today fades away like a headland in a sea mist. I hear the door shutting, then nausea rises up in me and I heave twice before throwing up all down my front. It's a horrible feeling, but it stops me from going under and brings me back to the real world with a bang, although it's debatable whether or not I actually want to be here.

I spit out the last of the vomit, sit back in my seat and take a couple of deep breaths, ignoring the foul taste in my mouth. I look around the room. It's small, with a low ceiling and bare concrete walls, and it smells of damp. The only light comes from a tiny window to my right which illuminates the thousands of dust particles floating in the stale air. The window has a long crack in it that runs left to right at a crooked angle, and the threadbare carpet is dirty and stained dark in patches. There's not much in the way of furnishings: a couple of cheap wooden chairs, and beyond them an ancient piece of machinery that I think must once have been a workman's lathe. Also, next to my chair is a rusty electric cooker. I try not to think about whether it works, and if so, what it gets used for.

The door opens again and a man in a boiler suit walks in. He's small and middle-aged, with big glasses. He shuts the door behind him, walks over to the chair opposite me and sits down. He's holding a jumbo packet of pistachio nuts, and he takes one out, flicks off the shell with an expert touch, and chucks it into his mouth. As he chews, he watches me with interest. Underneath the thick lenses of his outsize spectacles his eyes are bright with malignance, and utterly without mercy.

'What do you come back for, man?' he asks, his voice soft and lilting, his accent, like the others, Eastern European. As he speaks, he snaps the shells off another couple of nuts and tosses them onto the carpet.

Sitting here, trapped, I'm asking myself exactly the same thing. I'm also wondering how many more minutes there are left before Lucas raises the alarm.

'You told my boss that you knew the real name of the man you picked up the briefcase from. Yeah? Tell me. What is it?'

Not for the first time, I curse myself for letting this slip. 'I don't know.'

He grins. 'You think we won't get it out of you? Sure we will.' He pops another nut. 'The man you just shot is called Pero. That was real stupid, scaring our customers like that.' He shakes his head. 'Now, I got to be honest with you, man. You're going to have to die. We can't have someone forcing his way in here and killing one of our people. It's disrespectful, you know? But there are different ways of dying. Some can be pretty painless, like the bullet in the back of the head.' He makes the shape of a gun with his thumb and forefinger, puts it against his temple, and imitates pulling the trigger. 'One shot, and bang, it's all over. No more problems, no more hassles. Just a nice long sleep. But there are other ways too, man. Ways that aren't so nice.' He pauses again, but this time it's for effect rather than sustenance. 'Pero, the man you killed ... His cousin's here, and man, he loves to hurt people. And now, after what you've done to his cousin, he really wants to work on you, too.' He gives a mock shudder. 'But I can stop him. All you have to do is tell me the real name of the man who gave you the briefcase, and anything else you know about him, and I'll make it quick. OK? Is that a deal?'

He tries to smile, and I feel a pang of real fear.

Using the end of the nail on my middle finger, I have gained some leverage on the flick-knife handle, and millimetre by millimetre I am lifting it up in the pocket. It requires immense concentration, but I can't afford to look anything other than interested in the offer that's being put to me.

'How do I know you won't let him torture me anyway?' I ask.

'You don't,' he answers with an honesty I wasn't expecting. 'But that's a risk you're going to have to take.'

I look like I'm thinking about it. The handle's exposed about a quarter of an inch now. I try to grab it with my thumb and middle finger, but can't quite get a grip.

'Don't fuck me about, man,' he snaps. 'What's his name?'

It's clear they still think Ferrie's holding something back from them, and I briefly wonder what it can be. 'OK, OK,' I say, making it sound like I've come to a decision. The end of the nail's hooked under the handle again, and I continue to try to get it out of my pocket. 'His name's Terry Douglas.' It's the first name that comes to my head. The father of my first girlfriend.

An ex boxer turned property developer who never thought I was good enough for his daughter. 'I, er . . .' I pause, buying time, because as soon as I give him the rest of the information I'm dead.

I try once again to get a proper grip on the handle, and this time it comes free. I feel for the button that releases the blade, and find it. I am ten seconds away from death. My torturer is looking at me expectantly, and I'm trying to work out whether or not he's armed and whether it'll be him who delivers the fatal shot. I am absolutely terrified, and it takes all my willpower to keep my hands from shaking.

'We served together in the police,' I say, more loudly than I need to so that I muffle the click of the blade opening.

'The police?' He shakes his head angrily. 'You're fucking me about, man. We know all about you. You weren't in the police.'

I've made a mistake. I should have thought of that. But I've also bought myself a few seconds of time. I use my thumb to feel for the sharp edge of the blade and touch it against the leather restraint. Slowly I start sawing, hoping that he's not going to notice that my right hand is moving ever so slightly backwards and forwards.

'No, I didn't mean the police.'

'The army? Did you serve in the army with him?'

These guys may well know a lot about me, but they don't seem to know much about the man blackmailing them, and it strikes me that I shouldn't be helping them fill in the gaps. Ferrie might be dead, but it's possible he can still provide clues. I think back to Lucas's advice, that we should concentrate on conventional detective work rather than run into the hornets' nest, all guns blazing, and I realize that he was right. If I get out of here, we're definitely going to do things his way.

'Yeah,' I answer, 'that's where I know him from.' But I say it in a relieved way so that once again he'll think I'm bullshitting.

Playing for time. I am playing for time.

He gets to his feet and turns towards the door, shouting something in Serbo-Croat. I saw frantically for three or four seconds, until he turns back.

'I've had enough of your lies, man,' he says dismissively. 'I gave you the chance. You fucked me around. Now you're really going to pay.'

He returns to his seat as the door opens, and as I catch sight of the man who comes in, my eyes widen.

18

He's naked from the waist up, his body muscular and only just showing signs of running to fat around the midriff. I recognize him instantly, even though his face is concealed behind the tight black fetish mask, criss-crossed with metal zips, that covers his entire head. The one he was wearing last night when he plunged the knife into Leah.

The fear evaporates in an instant, replaced by an intense rage that shoots right through me. I struggle violently in my seat, trying to break the restraint. I want nothing more in the world right now than to kill this man, and know with an absolute certainty that I cannot die before I do.

As he turns to draw a bolt on the door, I see that there are no signs of the scars on his back from last night. He turns back to face me again, and for a moment he stands there studying me through the eyeholes in the mask. His eyes flash with an undisguised hatred that I know is reflected in mine.

In one hand, he's got a two-litre bottle of vegetable oil; in the other, a metal saucepan and a ladle.

I stop struggling as he walks towards me and stops by the side of the ancient cooker. He turns on one of the hotplates, puts down the saucepan and fills it almost to the top with the oil. He's beside me now, almost within touching distance. If he looks in the right place, he'll see the knife in my right hand.

But he doesn't. He's staring me out. I stare back, not daring to resume the sawing.

The guy opposite smiles malevolently. 'You know what my man here likes the most? Burning. It's his passion, man. He gets the oil nice and hot, and when he ladles it on, the flesh just drips off like water. And the screams, man. You should hear the screams.' He leans forward in the chair. 'Now, tell us the truth. Who gave you the briefcase?'

I don't speak. My interrogator gestures to the guy in the mask who produces a cut-throat razor from the pocket of his trousers. He flicks it open. I wonder then if he's the one who's just killed Snowy, the contract killer Ferrie called the Vampire. The blade on his razor shines brightly, but there's no blood on it.

'I want you to have a little taste of what's to come,' says my interrogator. 'Radovan, while we wait for the oil to heat up, cut one of his eyes out.'

Radovan leans forward, and I struggle wildly again, but the strap holds. I desperately crane my neck away from him, trying to tip over the chair, but he grabs my chin and wrenches me round, holding it steady. The curved tip of the blade takes up my whole field of vision, approaching inch by inch.

I break. 'I'll tell you, I'll tell you. I swear it. I'll tell everything.' I mean it, too.

The blade stops moving. It's an inch from my right eye. I can feel Radovan's breath on my face. It smells savoury, like meat on the turn. I can smell something else, too, something coming from outside the room. Smoke. And although I can no longer see him,

I can hear my interrogator moving about in his chair. Can he smell it too?

Then, just as I'm about to speak again, a fire alarm goes off, its shrill ringing reverberating through the building. I can hear faint panicked shouts which sound like they're coming from downstairs.

There's a loud knock on the door.

Radovan steps back, the blade retreating with him. His comrade is out of his seat, looking concerned.

'Who the hell is it?' he shouts.

'It's me, Alannah,' answers a female voice. 'We've got to get out. The place is on fire.'

She bangs frantically on the door, and my interrogator pulls across the bolt and opens it a few inches. Smoke drifts in, and the smell gets a lot stronger. I catch a glimpse of blonde hair – it's the girl who caught me with the stun baton. But I'm not concentrating on her. Instead, I'm sawing once again, this time as fast as I can. Because if they don't kill me, the fire will, and I wonder why the hell Lucas set it because surely he must have known that if I was trapped in here, then burning the place down isn't likely to help.

I feel the material beginning to give way, and luckily Radovan is looking towards the door, the razor still held tight in his hand.

'All right, we're coming,' says the interrogator. 'We're coming.'

'Is he still in here?' the girl asks, trying to push her way inside.

'What do you want to know for, bitch?' he demands, trying to push her back out again. 'This is none of your fucking business!' He turns to Radovan, and beneath the spectacles his eyes are wide with tension. 'OK, no time for fun,' he shouts. 'Cut his throat.'

Radovan is still only a couple of feet away from me, and in one movement he swings the razor round in a neck-high arc. But

I'm prepared for him and I lash out with my right leg, knocking him off balance. The blade misses the flesh of my throat by inches, but I've only bought myself a split second. I stop sawing and strain against the leather, knowing that this is my last chance. Out of the corner of my eye, I can see the interrogator pulling a revolver from one of the pockets of his boiler suit; but in this single moment he's utterly irrelevant because my whole existence stands or falls on whether or not I have the strength to break free from my restraint.

Radovan has danced off to one side, out of range of my legs, and the razor's coming back again.

And this time it's not going to miss.

There's a splitting sound. The material has finally come apart, and I'm flung forward onto my knees. I feel a hot, very intense pain as the razor catches me on the scalp, slicing open the skin, but it's not a deep enough cut to slow me down. Almost as soon as I've landed, Radovan grabs me by the hair, lifting me to my feet as he moves in for the killing slice. I catch the briefest glimpse of his colleague through a thin pall of smoke. He's raising the revolver and pointing it calmly at my chest, preparing to fire. I am caught between a rock and a hard place, but I can do no more than deal with one thing at a time, and as I'm dragged back into Radovan's choking grip, I reverse the flick knife in my hand and drive it up to the hilt in the murdering bastard's thigh. He lets out a deep gasp – the first sound I've heard him make – and I dive clear as he staggers backwards, knowing that I've got to avoid a bullet. I can see the revolver's barrel tracking me as I slide across the carpet, and without my vest I know I'm a sitting duck. A shot rings out but it misses, and I hear the gunman curse. 'You bitch!' he cries, and to my surprise and relief I see that the blonde girl's struggling with him. The revolver's raised towards the ceiling, both their hands on it. It goes off a second, then a third time.

The smoke's really billowing into the room now; I can even hear the faint roar of the fire. Already I'm beginning to choke on the fumes and I sneak a look over at Radovan. Rather than wasting time with the knife in his thigh, he's limped over to the cooker where he's now picking up the saucepan of sizzling oil.

The gun goes off again, the bullet a lot closer to me this time and I see that the struggle between my interrogator and the beautiful blonde continues unabated.

Radovan's turning round now, holding the saucepan with both hands. The blood from the stab wound is pumping out fast and running down his trouser leg, but he ignores it. He may be a ruthless, cold-hearted torturer, but the fact remains that I've killed his cousin, and whether it's about honour or emotion – and I'm guessing by the look of him that it's going to have to be about honour – I've still got to pay. But his hands are unsteady, and he's having difficulty walking. Oil drips over the top, splashing onto his shoes, where it sizzles away angrily.

This is the bastard who butchered Leah on camera while she lay helpless and terrified, who probably cut Snowy's throat as well, and now's my opportunity to make him pay. I launch myself from the floor with a speed that I'm certain he wasn't expecting, and before he can react I lash out with an ungraceful but accurate karate kick that catches the bottom of the saucepan and sends a much bigger splash of oil over his torso. This time he howls in pain, and it's a sound that pleases me. He drops the saucepan and smacks wildly at the fat as it eats away at his flesh. As he does so, I charge him low, smashing my head into his groin and sending him crashing backwards into the cooker. I can smell burning meat, and my scalp feels like it's on fire as I make contact with the oil that runs down him. He gasps, winded, in no position to fight back, and I slam the palm of one hand onto his masked head and drive it down onto the hotplate. At the last moment, he puts up some resistance, but it's too late, and his head hits the hob side on with a sound like bacon sizzling in a pan. He screams and tries to struggle free, but the leather of the mask is already melting and he's stuck fast. I push down harder, this time with both hands, ignoring the waves of heat emanating from the metal and remembering the DVD I was forced to watch of Leah being torn apart. His hands slap uselessly at me and his legs kick out, but he's finished, there's no doubt about that.

The room's filling with smoke now, and I'm having difficulty breathing. I can see no sign of the other guy or the blonde girl, and I can't hear them either. But I can hear the roar of a spreading fire.

It's time to go.

19

As I feel my way out I'm assailed by more thick waves of choking black smoke as it pours up the stairs. There's surely no means of exit down there, which doesn't leave me much in the way of alternatives. I can feel panic rising in me, but I force it down and stagger blindly away from the stairs along a short corridor. I bang into something and stumble, only just managing to regain my footing. Through the haze, I see it's the prone figure of my interrogator, and he's unconscious. I won't be getting any answers out of him now, and there's no way I'm going to make it out of here carrying him, so I step over him and keep going.

There's a door at the end of the corridor and I open it, grope my way through, then slam it shut behind me. I'm in what appears to be a storage room. There are various bits and pieces – mainly boxes, and the occasional solitary item of furniture – piled high against all the available wall space, but my attention is immediately drawn to a large aluminium beer barrel standing in the centre of the room. I feel a rush of relief. It stands directly beneath an open skylight. Someone, it seems, has already made good his or her escape from the building this way. It's got to be the girl. I hope so.

I am exhausted, panting, breathing in acrid smoke, running on empty, but a desperate desire for fresh air drives me on and I clamber onto the barrel, reach up on tiptoes and just about manage to get a decent grip on the edge of the frame. I heave myself up, push my head through the gap in the window, and gulp down the fresh, warm summer air.

An explosion comes from somewhere below me, and the whole building shakes. Christ, what are they storing in this place? Dynamite? I'm not out of either the frying pan or the fire just yet. Using my arms as leverage, I drag the rest of my body through the gap until I'm lying on the tiles of the warehouse's sloping roof, facing out towards the canal and the buildings on the other side. Joggers and shifty-looking kids in school uniform are lining the towpath on the opposite bank, staring towards the inferno in front of them, and I can see Lucas's car parked up on the pavement on the bridge over the Kingsland Road, with the hazards on. He's stood beside it, and when he spots me he waves enthusiastically like I'm the long-lost cousin he's been waiting for in Airport Arrivals. He's at least forty yards and a very long drop away. At the very least, I think he ought to be looking for a ladder.

I roll down the slope of the roof until I reach the guttering on the edge, and look down. I'm right about the drop – it's far too high for me to jump, even with my training. Below me I can see smoke billowing out of windows and flames licking the walls on the ground floor. The wheelie bin in which I deposited the guard is completely engulfed by fire, and I wonder whether he escaped or whether, more likely, he's another person who's been killed today.

I can hear fire engines approaching from several different

directions, but I'm in no position to wait for them. An old building like this one is going to come down fast. Already I can feel the tiles beginning to grow hot.

I turn my back on Lucas and make my way along the tiles until I reach the western edge of the building. The roof of the adjoining property is about fifteen feet away. That's a long way when you're jumping at height, but if I make it I know I'm home free because I can see it's got a two-storey extension sticking out the back, meaning that I can get back down to ground level without too much difficulty.

There are men in grubby overalls staring up at me from the yard down below. 'You're going to be all right, mate!' yells one, which is easy for him to say, I think.

Thin trails of smoke are now coming through the gaps in the tiles. Not long now until the roof collapses. From somewhere down below I hear another explosion, and once again the building shudders, as do I, almost losing my balance and heading for the ground quicker than I'd anticipated. Through the gap between the two buildings I see a police car pull up and an officer jump out, holding a radio to his mouth.

I take a few steps backwards, moving off the guttering so that I'm standing at an angle on the sloping, smoking roof, and then I make a run for it. Two seconds later, I'm sailing through the air, legs flailing as I try to maintain my momentum. My feet land on the edge of the other roof. One slips and kicks out into space, but my hands scrape at the tiles, and before I know it I'm rolling down the roof in the direction of the two-storey extension. I roll straight off, one hand grabbing a piece of guttering to ease my fall, and somehow manage to land on my feet on the extension's flat roof. I run across it, feeling more confident now, and do a single hanging jump that lands me in the burly arms of two of the overalled workmen. 'It's OK, mate, you're safe now,' says the one who offered me the encouragement earlier, but he doesn't know the half of it. I'm not safe until I'm well away from this place.

I cough violently, and someone thrusts a bottle of water at me. I take a long drink.

'You need to sit down, mate,' says the one who gave me the water, putting an arm round my shoulder.

'Is it a brothel in there?' asks someone else.

'I've got to run.' I wipe my mouth. 'Is there a back way out of here?'

Someone points past a workshop towards a gate set into a whitewashed wall. 'It's open,' he says.

'Don't want to get in trouble with the wife then, eh?' shouts someone else, obviously the comedian of the bunch.

I break free of the group and run for the gate. The sirens are coming from all over the place now and great sheets of flame burst forth from the burning building like dragons' breaths. My lungs are bursting as I fling open the gate and stumble through onto the canal path. Lucas is still there on the bridge. I run towards it, ignoring the pain, and force myself up the steps.

By the time I reach the top I have virtually no strength left, but it doesn't matter because Lucas grabs me and hauls me over to the car. The passenger door's open and I clamber inside, keeping low while he slams it behind me. Then he's in the driver's seat and pulling away into traffic, heading north up the Kingsland Road.

'You stink,' he comments as we pass through the first set of lights, swerving to avoid a fire engine screaming down the other way with all horns blaring.

'Well, that isn't really any surprise, is it?' I answer eventually, when my breathing's evened out a little and I've finished coughing. 'I don't want to sound ungrateful or anything, but what the hell were you doing setting a fire like that?'

He turns to me with a look of mild incredulity on his face. 'What the hell are you talking about?' he says. 'I didn't set any fire. I thought that was you.'

20

If Lucas didn't set the fire, who the hell did? And why?

Neither question is one I'm in any position to answer as I sit back in the seat and watch the shabby, cheap shopfronts of the Kingsland Road scudding past, relieved simply to be alive. I feel a small twinge of satisfaction at having dealt with the man who murdered Leah, and maybe Snowy too. Was he the man Ferrie thought had been hired to kill him, the one he called the Vampire? If he was, then he's paid for his sins now. I think back to his grunts of pain as his mask crackled and burned, and hope that he suffered in the same way Leah must have. But the reason I'm not more satisfied is I still don't have the slightest idea why someone's gone to so much trouble to set me up, or who that person might be. And it's something that, now more than ever, I've got to find out.

'Where's the holdall?' I ask, looking down at the empty space by my feet.

'It's in the back,' Lucas replies, adding quickly when he sees me turn round to grab it, 'but it's empty.'

'Empty? What do you mean?'

'I took the liberty of getting rid of the knife in the canal while you were inside. I thought it seemed as good a place as any.'

I'm a bit concerned by this. It doesn't feel like as good a place as any to me. With at least two people dead inside the brothel, possibly more, the area's going to turn into a major crime scene, which means they may end up dredging the canal for clues as to what might have happened.

Lucas reads my thoughts. 'Don't worry, I wiped it clean. There's no way it'll ever get back to you.'

'And the DVD?'

'I've still got it.' He taps the waist pocket of his suit jacket. 'We'll destroy it when I've had a chance to watch the footage.'

I nod slowly. 'OK.'

I'm too exhausted to think straight, but even so, I can't help feeling an odd twinge of suspicion. Why the hell did he do that without talking to me first? I tell myself to stop feeling paranoid, and settle back in my seat. Lucas has just lost a good friend; he can't be in on this.

We take a roundabout route back to his offices in Commercial Street and it's just turned four o'clock when he parks up in an alley round the back. He wants me to stay in the car. 'I'm only going in to collect the file on Ferrie. It's not safe to hang about round here at the moment. Whoever killed Snowy will have got the company's address from his business cards.'

'And it's possible they could be waiting for you. It's better if I come in.'

'You look like shit,' he answers. 'You're going to stand out a mile walking round like that. Even in an area like this.'

I check myself out in the rear-view mirror and have to conclude that he's right. My head looks like it's been shoved up the exhaust pipe of a speeding lorry. Every square inch of exposed skin is smoke-blackened, and my hair, usually neat and

fashionably cut, is sticking up all over the place in bizarre for-
mations where the blood from my scalp wound's matted. There's
more dried blood on my neck, and to top it off, a rust-covered
puke stain covers my shirt. 'I'll be fine,' I say, removing the shirt
and wiping my face with the cleanest part of it. I try to force my
hair back into shape, and when that doesn't work, Lucas produces an old beanie hat from under his seat, and I put that on.

'Come on,' he says with a sigh, 'let's get going.'

We go in the back door, and although Lucas is feigning confidence, I know he's nervous. He moves carefully through the
gloomy foyer and up the winding staircase to his office. I've
never quite understood why he doesn't run his operation from
home. He's got a nice apartment in a modern block in Islington
which would impress the punters a damn sight more than a
couple of rooms above a shop on a rundown street like this one.
He told me once he liked to have a base near to the City because
that's where all the big money is, and to be fair his office is only
a few hundred yards away from the gleaming spires of Aldgate;
but this is London, where a few hundred yards can sometimes
feel like a thousand miles. Whatever Lucas likes to think, he's
based in Whitechapel. This is Jack the Ripper country, the real
East End, and most definitely not the financial district. As he's
probably found out, people from the latter don't tend to venture
into the former.

It's an ideal spot for an ambush as well, I think, as we reach
the top of the stairs and he opens the door. It's an old building
with plenty of alcoves, and, unfortunately, at the moment I'm
unarmed, my gun having been taken from me back at the
brothel. And without the security of the vest, which has probably
been burned to a crisp by now, I feel both naked and vulnerable.

We step inside, and Lucas shuts the door behind us. As he
surveys the room, he shakes his head slowly. There are two large

desks with monitors and phones on them, arranged so that they are both facing the door at an angle. The right, and slightly larger of the two, belongs to Lucas. It's tidier than I was expecting, with everything arranged perfectly symmetrically. Snowy's desk is messy, with pens and bits of paper everywhere, as well as two empty mugs, one of which says World's Best Uncle.

'I can't believe he's dead,' Lucas says, walking up to his former employee's desk.

'Has he got family?' I ask, realizing that even though Snowy and I served together I never really knew that much about him.

Lucas lights a cigarette before answering. 'A brother, that's all. His mum and dad are dead. I think he's quite close – was quite close – to the brother. Poor sod didn't really have anyone else.' He picks up a photo on the desk and views it wistfully. 'He loved that cat,' he explains, showing me a picture of a very fat tabby cat with one eye shut sprawled next to an electric fire. Just looking at it makes me want to go to sleep.

'Cats are independent,' I say. 'He'll be all right.' Although I'm not sure this one will be. He looks like he enjoys the high life, and with his master gone who's going to provide that for him?

Lucas puts the picture down and goes round to his own desk. There's a red light flashing on his phone.

'Messages,' he says, pressing a button.

There are two of them. The first is from a guy called Kevin who wants to know how far Lucas has got in proving his wife's infidelities.

'Too far,' Lucas says to me as we listen. 'She's slept with three men in the past week.'

The other message is from someone calling himself Phil. He says that the Lexus LS 600 Lucas was interested in, registration number Whisky Three Two Three Bravo Charlie Sierra, is registered to a Mr Trevor Blake of 14 Tennyson Way in Bermondsey, a forty-four-year-old married insurance salesman with a nine-year-old son and no criminal record. Lucas writes this down on his notepad and tears off the page.

'That was the car Snowy was following,' he explains. 'The one carrying your Yugoslavs. It looks like they were false plates. Let me get the details on Iain Ferrie, then we'd better leave.'

He goes into a storage room and returns a few seconds later with a thin file under his arm.

'Listen, Lucas,' I tell him, 'you've done enough for me. Just give me the information you've got and I'll take over from here.'

He shakes his head firmly, his jaw set hard. 'No, it's personal for me now. They've killed my friend. All he was doing was his job. They're also trying to kill another of my friends. The thing is, Tyler, I've got a lot of acquaintances, women and men, but I haven't really got many people in this world I genuinely care about. He was one of them. You're another.'

I'm touched, especially after all I've been through today.

'But I don't want you to get in any trouble,' I say. 'At the moment, you haven't done anything wrong. We go too much further down the line and you might end up doing something you regret.'

He drags hard on the cigarette. 'Let me worry about that.'

'It's not going to take the police long to ID Snowy. I sold him the car so I know it's registered in his name. Pretty soon they're going to come knocking on your door.'

'And when they do, I'll answer their questions.'

'They'll know you made calls to him very close to the time he was killed. You're going to have to tell them the truth and give me up. If you come up with a false story they'll be on to you, and I don't want you falling under suspicion on my behalf.'

'And I don't want to be putting you in the firing line either.'

'You're going to have to,' I tell him. 'You've got no choice.'

'That means that you haven't got much time to find out who's behind all of this. You need all the help you can get, so until the cops do turn up, I'm it.'

'Thanks, mate,' I say, feeling genuinely emotional. I take a deep breath and tell myself it's shock, a delayed reaction to all I've been through today. I've never been the most tactile of people. I'm an old-fashioned Englishman who believes that physical contact between men should be limited to a firm handshake. But as Lucas comes past me now I put a hand on his shoulder and pull him into an embrace. It feels weird so I pull back quickly. Lucas looks as shocked as me by this totally unexpected show of affection.

'This is turning into a very strange day,' he says, walking towards the door.

I follow him out, inclined to agree. The clock on the wall says 4.07 and I wonder, with what I think is justifiable apprehension, what the hell this strange day is going to bring next.

21

The first thing that happens is that we drive to Lucas's Islington apartment, or duplex as he prefers to call it, since the living accommodation is actually set over two floors. It's part of a swish glass building that stands out on a street of low-rise, low-cost 1960s houses in the slowly gentrifying area west of the bottom end of the Holloway Road. We deposit his car in the secure underground car park and go inside, pleased to find that there's no ambush or police here either.

'Let's start at the beginning,' Lucas says when we're in his study and he's got his laptop booted up.

We're both drinking coffee, sitting in matching and very comfortable black leather chairs at opposite ends of his enormous glass desk. It's now twenty to five, and I feel a lot better. I've showered and am dressed in a pair of Lucas's Armani jeans and a short-sleeved cotton Hugo Boss shirt. I wanted a pair of his shoes as well but he said his friendship only went so far, so I'm still in my tatty smoke-stained Timberlands.

'Do you still not remember anything at all about last night?' he asks.

'I can't really remember anything about yesterday. I vaguely recall driving to the showroom yesterday morning, but even that I'm not a hundred per cent sure about. I have no recollection of calling you.'

'It's a pity we can't do something to unlock your memory. Obviously, the people who set you up have gone to great trouble to conceal the location where you spent last night. Which means they think your memory might come back, or . . .'

'Or what?'

'Or it's a place that's familiar to you.'

I shake my head. 'I've never been in that bedroom before.'

'No, but you might have been to the house.'

'I don't think so,' I say. 'The place where I woke up this morning is somewhere north of London. Hertfordshire, maybe the edge of Essex. I don't know anyone who lives there.'

'OK,' he concedes. 'Now I need to take a look at this DVD. See what it shows up.'

He takes the case from his pocket and removes the disc.

'It's really not pleasant,' I warn him.

He lights a cigarette and views me through the smoke. 'I know, and you don't have to stay in here. In fact, it might be better if you didn't. There's no point putting yourself through it all again.'

Lucas is right, and as he inserts the DVD into his laptop I get up and leave the room. I want to remember Leah as she was when we first met: a mischievous, smiling young woman with beautiful doe eyes and a cute upturned nose, not the cold, lifeless corpse she became, nor the bleak, bloody way she met her end.

I take a seat in Lucas's lounge and stare at the blank screen of the giant plasma TV that hangs on an even blanker-looking wall. Lucas's place is a typical bachelor's pad, minimally furnished with most of the money going on the electrical goods. There are no pictures on any of the walls, and the sofa and matching chairs are carefully and immaculately arranged, giving it a showroom feel. It's all undeniably flashy – which makes me conclude that the PI trade pays a lot better than I ever thought – but bland and utterly devoid of character.

While I wait, I force the thoughts of Leah out of my mind and instead go back through the events of the day, trying to come up with some answers. I've been targeted by a gang of violent criminals with whom I have no previous connection. A former soldier, Iain Ferrie, whom I served alongside but hardly knew, had something in a briefcase that these people wanted desperately, but instead of sending one of their own associates to collect it, they decided to use me, going to elaborate lengths, including setting me up for murder, to make sure that I followed their instructions. Ferrie refused to tell me what was in the case but suggested that it was something 'very bad', and his demeanour – extremely tense and agitated – makes me think that he was telling the truth.

What's also true is that the men to whom I delivered the brief-case are determined to hang on to it, and will not hesitate to kill anyone who, like Snowy, gets in their way. They've taken some losses at the brothel, but I suspect there are more of them, and they still have the case. They also believe, it seems, that Ferrie was holding something back from them.

Iain Ferrie. Whichever way I look at it, he is the key to all this, the starting point.

I get up from the sofa just as Lucas opens the door of his study and steps into the lounge. I'm about to tell him that we need to learn more about Ferrie when I stop. The expression on Lucas's face is one of shock and confusion.

'It's bad, isn't it?' I say.

'It's horrible,' he answers, shaking his head slowly. 'Awful.'

'I know,' I say. But of course I don't. I couldn't bring myself to watch it all earlier, so I can only imagine the savagery and terror on that DVD.

'But there's something else,' he continues, with a sigh. 'Something I've got to show you.'

'I don't want to see any part of that film ever again,' I tell him.

'It's not something on the film.'

Puzzled, I follow him into the study and stand next to him in front of the laptop, which is displaying the 'My Computer' screen where the documents and various internal and external drives are listed. As I watch, Lucas leans down and right-clicks on the DVD drive icon. A menu of options appears, and he double-clicks on the 'Properties' icon. A table with a pie chart in the middle appears, stating that the disk has 83 per cent available space. Beneath the pie chart there's a single untitled file listed.

'Look at the date on the file,' Lucas says, touching the screen lightly with a forefinger.

The text to the right of the title 'Unknown File' reads 'date last modified', and that's the moment when it finally clicks. I turn and stare at him, and I'm guessing my expression is as confused as his was when he first came out of the study.

'This is the DVD they gave me, right? The one with the murder on?'

He nods. 'That's right. The one that was supposedly filmed last night featuring you and Leah. But you can see, can't you? It wasn't. This file, the film of the murder, was made at 11.47 p.m. on Wednesday.' He taps the time and date on the screen. 'In other words, two days ago. Someone's really fucking you about, Tyler.'

I step back from the machine, suddenly feeling flushed. 'What the hell does this mean? That it was all an act? But Leah was dead, Lucas. I saw her. And she sure as hell hadn't been dead for that long.'

He sighs. 'The film looks real enough. If it's a fake, it's a damn good one.'

I slam my hand down on the desk so hard the coffee cups rattle and Lucas flinches. Frustration hits me like an icy slap, and I'm reminded once again how impotent my memory loss is making me.

'What the hell does this all mean?' I repeat, my voice rising.

'It means', says Lucas calmly, 'that Leah may well be dead, but it wasn't her you woke up next to this morning.'

22

'How well did you really know her, Tyler?' asks Lucas quietly.

I can hear something vaguely accusatory in his tone, and I don't like it.

'Well enough,' I tell him. 'She's not involved in this, Lucas. She's . . .' I pause. 'She *was* a really good person.'

'I know, I know, but—'

'But what? Leah's dead, for Christ's sake. She was murdered. How can she have been involved?'

He sighs. 'Listen, Tyler. How long have I known you?'

'A long time,' I admit reluctantly.

'Exactly. You're my friend. I respect your judgement. I know you really cared for Leah, but I've got to be honest with you . . .' He stops and fixes me with an intense stare. 'There's something wrong.'

I open my mouth to argue, but something stops me. Instead, I sit back in the seat and listen. I think back to the night we met, how much I felt for her even then, and I feel a knot forming in my stomach.

'You came to me yesterday asking for information about

Leah,' Lucas continues, 'which means you weren't entirely sure about her yourself. Also, the DVD shows quite categorically that she wasn't murdered last night or early this morning. She was killed late on Wednesday.'

I wipe a hand across my brow, not sure what to think. The three weeks we spent together were some of the happiest of my life. For once, everything felt absolutely right. I can't bring myself, even now, to believe that it was all an act on her part.

'So, what is it you're saying, Lucas?'

'That it's possible she was working for whoever's set you up. That maybe she was used to lure you in, but was more expendable than she thought. She was used, then killed, to seal your co-operation.'

'But if I didn't see her yesterday, who was it who lured me to that house? And who did I wake up next to this morning?'

'I have no idea,' he admits, with a weary shrug. 'Neither, unfortunately, do you. Remember the anagram. Leah Torness. She's not real.'

I still think there must be some mistake on the timing shown on the DVD, because I know who I saw this morning, and I'm absolutely positive it was Leah. The body shape, the jewellery, the tattoo. They were all hers. But I don't press the argument. There's no point.

Lucas sighs. 'All right,' he says, 'we're going to have to look at things from another angle.'

'How about starting with Ferrie?' I suggest, forcing myself to start thinking properly again.

'Good idea.'

He pauses for a moment, mulling things over. I let him get on with it. He's the detective, after all. As he thinks, he doodles on a giant desktop notepad. Finally, he lights a cigarette, blows a line of smoke towards the ceiling, and looks my way.

'When you went to exchange the briefcases this morning, you told me that you were sent to one address but were immediately taken to another one?'

'That's right. A house just up the road.'

'How far up the road?'

'I don't know. Fifty yards?'

'Not far, then. Ferrie would probably have had to give them the location to send you to a while before you turned up.'

'He did. The guy blackmailing me told me where to go an hour and a half before I got there.'

Lucas jots something down on the notepad, the cigarette dangling from his mouth.

'Did the place where you finally met Ferrie look lived-in to you?' he asks.

I shake my head, recalling its sparseness. 'No, it didn't.'

He nods slowly. 'That's what I thought. I can't see a guy as nervous as you say Ferrie was swapping the cases at his home, or anywhere near it, so I reckon it's safe to assume he lived somewhere else. We need to find out where.'

'He was acting really paranoid this morning. It's not going to be easy.'

'Let me worry about that,' he says sharply. 'Now, when you were given the address, you weren't told the name of the person you were going to see. Is that right?'

I nod. 'They don't know his real name. It's one of the things they wanted me to tell them.'

'Which gives us an advantage, because we do know it. Even if he's covered his tracks, we'll find him.' He sends another pall of smoke skywards. 'Trust me, I'm a detective.'

So I sit there drinking my coffee and trying without much success to relax for the first time today, while he continues to detect. And it soon becomes clear that Ferrie had indeed covered his tracks. When he hired Lucas, he paid for his services upfront and in cash, declining to give an address where he could be reached. But we're lucky with the name. It's comparatively unusual, and there are only four Iain Ferries on the electoral roll in Greater London. A combination of surfing the net and telephoning strategically placed contacts confirms to us that none of them has ever served in the military. A dead end? Lucas is undeterred.

'You can find anybody if you want to,' he tells me between phone calls. 'As long as you know where to look. There's all this shit with the Data Protection Act and how you've got to protect a person's personal details, but the thing is, they're held on so many different databases it's impossible. And the security on those databases is worthless half the time. If you know a decent hacker, he'll get inside and they'll never have a clue he's been there.'

And Lucas does know a decent hacker. He's got the business card of someone with the bizarre name of Dorriel Graham who advertises himself as an IT security consultant. 'This guy's the best,' he tells me, calling the number on the card.

While he's not looking, I write down the number myself. You never know when skills like that may come in useful.

And come in useful they quickly do. Lucas gets him to hack into the Ministry of Defence computer systems. Now, given that the MOD are supposedly in charge of defending the realm, I would have thought this would be near enough impossible, but it seems some of their systems are more secure than others, and the database that contains the details of serving and recently demobbed soldiers is eminently hackable. Ferrie may have left the army some time ago, but the MOD still have a record of him, and within fifteen minutes of Lucas's call a two-page document with photograph is coming through on his printer.

'This'll help us,' he says, reading through it. 'Ferrie might not be on the electoral roll or the Land Registry, but people close to him will be. See, it says here he was married in 1999 and that his spouse is a Charlotte Melanie Priem. There'll be a record of her somewhere.'

His next port of call is the Register of Births, Marriages and Deaths, a database that any member of the public is allowed to access. Armed with the date of the marriage and the names of the couple, he quickly finds that it ended in divorce in December 2003, on the grounds of Mr Ferrie's unreasonable behaviour. No further details of what he did are given, but we don't care about that. What we care about is the fact that the petitioner, Miss Priem, gives a flat in Enfield as her permanent residence. A check on the Land Registry shows that she still owns the flat, and a quick call to his contact at BT gets Lucas its landline number. It's all very easy if, as he says, you know where you're looking.

'Let's hope she's in,' I say.

He shrugs. 'It doesn't matter if she's not. Chances are she'll have a mobile registered to that address – I'll just get hold of that. More importantly, does she know where he is?'

He lights another cigarette and calls the number.

Ten seconds later, Lucas embarks on some time-honoured patter. 'Hello, Mrs Ferrie? Oh, I'm sorry, Miss Priem. I apologize for bothering you but I've been trying to locate your ex-husband.' He tells her he's a former soldier who served with Iain, and wants to invite him to a regiment reunion. Something about his manner – all chirpy, cheeky charm – clearly works for the ladies because within seconds they're chatting like old friends. From the way he's speaking, it sounds like she's firing off a lot of not very flattering comments about her husband, which comes as no surprise. 'Oh, that'd be great if you could do that, Charlotte. You're very kind.' He winks at me as he speaks and gives the thumbs up. 'Thanks, that's really helpful . . . No, to be honest, I didn't get on with him that well, but I'd feel bad if he didn't get an invite, and there are a couple of people who do really want to see him.'

There's a short pause, then Lucas scribbles something down on the notepad. It looks promising.

'I agree,' he says into the phone, 'if he was like that, then it's inexcusable . . . No, you should never do that . . . That's right, you couldn't have known . . .' He rolls his eyes at me. 'Don't I know it? We always find these things out too late . . . What do I do now? I'm a forest ranger . . . Yes, I've always loved the out-door life. Now, if you'll excuse me, I really have to go . . . Yes, thanks . . . thanks . . . Definitely, if I get the time . . . OK . . . Bye.' He slams the phone into the cradle. 'Jesus, *I'd* be behaving pretty fucking unreasonably if I had to live with her. She wouldn't shut up.'

'But we've got what we wanted?'

He nods, ripping the paper containing the address from the notepad and stubbing his cigarette out in the ashtray. 'Yeah, she saw him three months ago. He was living in a flat in Southgate. She thinks he's still there. A place called Frobisher House.'

I could do with a longer sit down, but it's already gone five, about two hours since Snowy was murdered in broad daylight, and pretty soon the police are going to be phoning Lucas about it.

I think he's thinking the same thing because we get to our feet simultaneously and three minutes later we're in his BMW and heading north on the Holloway Road.

23

Frobisher House is the second of a row of five low-rise blocks of cheaply designed 1970s flats that share an award-winning blandness, and which take up one side of the street, looking like unwelcome invaders when compared to the pretty terrace of Edwardian cottages opposite. A group of kids are playing football in the car park that runs along the front of the flats as Lucas and I pull up half an hour after setting out. If anything, the day is getting hotter as it moves inexorably towards evening.

We get out of the car and walk up to the front entrance of Frobisher House.

'I'll tell you something,' says Lucas as we open the scratched and ancient Perspex doors, 'if I lived in a dump like this, I reckon *I'd* resort to blackmail.'

I know what he means. There's fresh, illegible graffiti on the adjoining wall, and as we step inside we're assailed by a stale smell of feet and sweat which reminds me of a schoolboys' changing room.

'I heard he was a gambler,' I say. 'I guess he just wasn't a very good one.'

Ferrie's place is on the second floor, at the end of a corridor that smells vaguely of bleach, which is a far more tolerable odour than the one lingering at ground level. I can hear a woman shouting at her kids in one of the flats and a baby is crying irritably in another, but the corridor itself is empty. The front door to his flat is made of plywood, in keeping with the general cheapness of the rest of the building, and there are two locks on it, a Yale and a Chubb, the latter having been added recently.

'You know,' says Lucas, pulling a set of skeleton keys from his pocket, 'if I had something valuable, worth all that money to someone else, there's no way I'd hide it in here. It's not exactly secure.' Wanting to prove his point, he gets to work on the locks, telling me to act natural. 'If anyone asks what we're doing, we're cops, OK? I've got some ID I can show them if they get too nosy.'

Lucas, it seems, has some fairly eye-opening working practices, and if ever the private detective work dries up, he's definitely got a career alternative as a burglar. It takes him about a minute to pick the Chubb and half that time to do the Yale. I have to admit I'm impressed as the door opens and I follow him inside.

It leads directly into a poky little box-like living room that's most definitely been lived in. It's at the opposite end of the bachelor pad spectrum from Lucas's. A threadbare sofa and a couple of armchairs that don't match it are arranged in a very tight semicircle around a portable TV, which sits on a cornflakes box. There's an overflowing pub ashtray on the sofa's arm and another one on the floor, as well as various bits of used crockery that haven't quite made it back to the kitchen. Bookshelves, groaning under the weight of piles of paperbacks, line two of the walls, and a framed poster showing an exotic beach scene, complete with turquoise sea and hanging coconut palms, takes up most of one of the others. It's entitled 'Paradise', which I'm guessing is where Iain Ferrie was planning on heading if he hadn't been so rudely interrupted. As if to prove the point, there's a battered Samsonite suitcase next to the front door with a passport and an airline ticket balanced on top.

So Ferrie had been telling me the truth about getting out of the country fast, and given the trouble he was getting himself in, who could blame him?

Lucas puts on some plastic evidence gloves and hands a pair to me. He picks up the passport and opens it at the photo. 'It's him, all right,' he says. 'So at least we're in the right place. Let's see where he was going.' He inspects the airline ticket. 'Caracas, one way. Very nice. The sort of place I'd head to if I was a fugitive.'

He puts the ticket and passport in the inside pocket of his suit and walks across the living room and into a tiny hallway, which has three doors leading off it– presumably the bedroom, bath-room and kitchen. They're all closed and Lucas has a quick check behind each of them before coming back into the living room.

'There's no laptop or computer in here,' he says.

'What about in his suitcase?'

He steps over, presses the handles, and it falls open, revealing a load of clothes, some shoes and a few more books, but no lap-top. He shuts it again and stands back up, taking the time to look round the room with an expression of distaste etched firmly on his features, like he's just stepped in dog mess.

'OK,' he says at last, 'the sooner we start, the sooner we finish. Rules are these: we try to be as quiet as possible but we turn over everything. And I mean everything, including the carpets. He was a blackmailer, so he wouldn't just leave stuff lying around. If you find anything with his handwriting on, however innocuous it looks, put it to one side so we can check it later, because he might be writing stuff down in code. And keep a real eye out for electrical devices. Blank CDs, flash drives, anything he might have stored information on. And definitely mobile phones. I'll start in here. You take the bedroom. Let's go.'

Ferrie's bedroom is less cluttered than his living room. There's a double bed with matching bedside tables on either side, another bookshelf full of books, and a built-in wardrobe. The doors to the wardrobe are open and I can see that most of the clothes have been removed, although there are still a couple of winter coats hanging up among the empty coat hangers.

There's a six-by-four photograph in a garish silver frame of Ferrie and his bride on their wedding day on top of one of the bedside tables, and before I start I pick it up. In the picture, a younger-looking Ferrie wears a morning suit dotted with confetti, and a purple cravat. Standing next to him, her head almost touching his, is a pretty, wholesome-looking blonde woman of about the same age in a wedding dress. They're both smiling at the camera, although her smile is wider and looks more genuine than his.

Looking at the photo now, I find myself feeling sorry for him. I know he brought his demise entirely upon himself, but it's still hard to see a picture of someone smiling on what I'm assuming was one of the happier days of his life, knowing that his life was snuffed out violently only hours earlier. It's an unwelcome reminder of my own mortality. The same bullets that killed him were also meant for me, and it's only through a combination of luck and training that I'm still standing. Nor is it over yet. There might come a time, and it could potentially be only hours away, when a world-weary detective stands in a bedroom not so different from this one, gazing at the old wedding photos I still keep in one of my drawers, wondering whether the man whose death he's investigating deserved his fate.

It's an unpleasant thought, and I swiftly shut my mind to it as I put down the photo and get to work, moving methodically through the room from right to left, occasionally stopping to wipe sweat from my brow. It's hot in here, and with the window closed the air's stagnant. I hear a lot of shouting coming from next door, and although there's a dividing wall separating us, I can hear every word. A teenage boy is having an argument with his mother. He swears a lot and is so disrespectful to her that if I wasn't stuck in here with my own problems I'd go round and clip the little bastard round the ear. His yelling reaches a spoilt, inarticulate peak, then a door slams and I'm left once again in heavy, humid silence.

I take the books from the shelves one by one and give them a quick flick through to check if there are any loose slips of paper inside, before discarding them on the floor. I find myself interested in Ferrie's reading habits. He likes crime fiction, and he's got quite a few old classics – Raymond Chandler and Mickey Spillane from the States, as well as a whole heap of Agatha Christies. He's got some contemporary stuff as well by a bunch of writers I've never heard of, but then I don't read so much myself these days, and when I do, it's usually biographies.

It's no fun searching the home of a dead man, but at least you don't have to worry too much about being tidy. Having found nothing of use among the books, I tear up the carpet (nothing under there either) before stripping the bed of its sheets and turning it on its side. But, as that too turns up a blank, I'm beginning to doubt we're going to find anything of use. Ferrie was planning on leaving the country as soon as he got his money, so there was no reason to leave any kind of clue behind. 'Something you don't ever want to see' were his words to describe the briefcase's contents. If it was truly something that bad, surely he would want no evidence of what he was involved in to remain in circulation.

But the guy with the pistachios back at the brothel hadn't been convinced. He'd wanted Ferrie's real name, even when he knew he was already dead, and the only possible reason for that is that the people he was blackmailing believed he might be holding something back. So I keep beavering away, conscious that with each passing minute the trail is going that little bit colder, and bringing us closer to the time when Lucas will be questioned by the police about Snowy's murder. And then they will be after me too.

To be honest, this particular thought's really beginning to play on my mind, so it hardly registers when my fingers find something in the pocket of one of Ferrie's winter jackets. But when I pull out a little black book with a single word embossed in gold on the front, it makes me want to praise the Lord aloud. It says, simply, 'Addresses'.

I leaf through it quickly. There are scores of names in here. I don't recognize any of them, but why should I? I never really knew the guy, and he never really knew me. Just to confirm this, I check whether my own address is there. It isn't, but Lucas's is. His office one, anyway.

Then I have an idea. I check under M, but the name I'm looking for isn't there, so I start again from the beginning of the book, reading the names of the contacts one by one. An old army name pops up in the 'E' section, Neil Ellison. I remember him vaguely. He left years back and I haven't seen him since. 'F' comes and goes with a few family members; 'G' and 'H' have only one name apiece, which makes me think Ferrie wasn't one of the world's more popular guys; and then in 'I' I finally find what I'm looking for. In the brothel, the blonde woman who incapacitated me with the stun baton before intervening when I was about to get shot, referred to the big guy, Rubberface, as Marco. Staring up at me from the page is the name Marco Itinic, and beneath it a London address in the postal district of W2. I think about carrying on through the rest of the address book, but I know that someone like Ferrie is not going to know two men called Marco.

I can't hear much in the way of activity next door in the living room so, thinking that perhaps I should be retraining as a PI since I've obviously got the knack for it, I stride through to show Lucas what I've found.

But as soon as I get inside the living room I stop. It looks like Lucas has found something too. It's in his hand, and he's inspecting it carefully with a shocked expression on his face.

For a moment, he doesn't acknowledge my presence, so lost in thought is he; then, slowly, he looks my way, and as he does so he lifts the object up between his thumb and forefinger so that I can see it clearly.

At first I can't work out what it is, but when I step forward to take a better look, I recognize it instantly. I've seen such things before, spilling out of the muddy earth in the genocidal killing grounds of Kosovo and Sierra Leone like grisly offerings. Yet still I hear myself taking a sharp intake of breath.

Because what Lucas is holding, stained and dark with decay underneath the thick seal of clingfilm wrapping, and with the first, jaundiced glint of bone showing through, is a human finger.

24

'Where did you find it?' I ask him, trying to keep down the sense of dread that's rising within me.

'Down the side of the sofa,' he answers, his voice quiet. 'Can you believe it?'

'Jesus, what the hell was Ferrie involved in?'

He shakes his head. 'Christ knows, but whatever it is, it's bad. This is real, no question.'

I stare down at the finger. The skin is pitted and badly discoloured where it's been wasting away, but it's still possible to tell from its size, combined with the manicured curve of the fingernail, that it belonged to a woman. The extent of the decay means there's no way of telling how old she was – or is, I suppose, since if you want to be pedantic about it, we don't know for sure that she's actually dead.

'How long since this was removed from the rest of her, do you think?' I ask Lucas, finally turning away from his gruesome discovery.

'I've got no idea,' he answers. 'I suppose it depends on what conditions it's been kept in. If it was out in the sun for any time in this heat, it wouldn't take very long to decompose.'

He stares at me for a moment, and I can see that his pale blue eyes are filled with concern. Lucas, I have to remind myself, has been a civilian for years. He may not have forgotten his other life entirely, but the danger that was such a part of it is all a long time ago. He's a carefree bachelor now, running a thriving business. At least he was until a few hours ago. Now, like me, he's in it up to his neck.

He sighs, furrowing his brow. 'I never liked Ferrie that much, but I never had him down for a killer.'

'Maybe he isn't,' I say.

'Maybe not. But how else would a finger have got here? It wasn't planted by someone. It was too well hidden for that.'

'If he was a killer, why keep a souvenir of what he's done round here?'

'I don't think he meant to. He obviously wasn't coming back, so he must have left it by accident.'

I think about this for a moment, but I'm unconvinced. I don't know why, but like Lucas, I just don't have Ferrie down for a murderer. Certainly not one who cuts off fingers and leaves them down the side of his sofa.

'You think it's got something to do with whoever it is he's blackmailing?' Lucas asks. 'How does that work? Blackmailing them with . . .' He searches for a suitable description. 'Human remains?'

'I don't know. But why else would he have it?'

It's a good question, one Lucas makes no attempt to answer. Instead, he stands in silence, surveying the finger for several seconds. Finally, he drags his gaze away.

'It still doesn't move us on though, does it?' he says.

'No, but this might.'

I show him the address book and open it at the 'I' section, explaining its significance.

'W2,' he says. 'That's the Paddington area.'

'I'm going to go there. But you don't need to come.'

'No,' he answers. 'We're in this together, we'll go there together.'

'I lost my gun back at the brothel, so we're unarmed. It could be dangerous.'

'I think I might have a way round that.'

'No, Lucas. You don't need to do anything else. I'm not dragging you in any deeper. At the moment, I've got nothing to lose. But you have.'

'Listen,' he says, as if he hasn't heard me, 'I brought back some souvenirs from the first Gulf War. A couple of pistols and an AK-47 that supposedly once belonged to Saddam Hussein's son-in-law.'

Believe it or not, it isn't unheard of for soldiers serving in overseas war zones to smuggle weapons back with them into the UK when they return with their units. Since they come through military airports rather than civilian customs, they're rarely subject to searches and there's ample opportunity to hide their illicit ordnance among all the other equipment and weaponry. Although most of them are brought back, like Lucas says, as souvenirs, a fair number end up sold to criminals, and I've often wondered why the government hasn't done more to combat the problem.

'The AK-47 doesn't work any more,' continues Lucas, 'but I'm pretty sure the pistols do.'

'Where are they?'

'In my loft at home.'

I sigh. 'Let me think about it.'

He nods. 'Fair enough, but let's go. It's not safe to hang round here.'

'What are you going to do with that?' I ask, indicating the decaying finger.

He reaches into a pocket and produces a crumpled, clear plastic bag, which he shakes open. 'It's evidence,' he answers, putting the finger inside and returning the bag to his pocket. 'Evidence of what I'm not sure, but it's got to be worth hanging on to.'

I don't question his rationale, and I need no second invitation to leave Ferrie's squalid little residence, with its stale, lingering air of death. We're out of there quickly, neither of us looking back as we walk, relieved, into the brightness of the early evening heat.

Almost immediately, Lucas's mobile rings.

'Anonymous call,' he says, stopping to check the screen.

But it's soon clear that it is in fact the police. Two and a half hours after we first discovered Snowy's body, they've finally traced him back to Lucas. I stand listening as Lucas first feigns shock at hearing of his colleague's death – something he does extremely well – then agrees to meet with the officers as soon as possible to make a statement. 'I can't believe it,' he keeps saying, sounding utterly deflated. He is, I have to say, a very able actor and he almost convinces me that this is the first he's heard of what's happened. He finishes the call by saying that he'll be with them in twenty minutes.

'They're going to come to the apartment to question me,' he says as we get into the car. 'There was no way I could get out of it.'

'Don't worry,' I tell him, 'I know that.'

'I don't know what I'll be able to do about the guns, either.'

'Forget it,' I tell him. 'It's OK.' But underneath I'm concerned. Once again I'm on my own, and without any obvious means of protection.

Still, I tell myself in an effort to raise my spirits, I have a lead. I know one of the people involved in Leah's murder, and this time I'm not going to let that bastard Marco slip from my grasp.

25

When Lucas drops me off at Holloway Road tube station, he reaches under his seat and pulls out a cylindrical device about a foot long with a handle running its entire length. I recognize it instantly from my days serving in Northern Ireland. It's an Enforcer, a heavy bludgeoning device used by the police to break the locks on doors. Something of an anachronism in these days of hi-tech gadgetry, but still one of the most highly effective means of gaining entry to a locked house.

'A present,' he says as he rummages around in the back of the car. 'It might come in useful.' He finds the holdall I was given earlier and drops the Enforcer inside before handing it to me.

'Thanks, mate,' I tell him. 'It's appreciated.'

We shake hands, and he says he'll call me later. I remind him once again that he's got to tell the truth to the cops, whatever it means for me. He tells me that he will, and then he's gone. It's just turned quarter past six.

At this time in the evening there's no point grabbing a taxi. The traffic's too heavy, and I've got to cross the centre of town. So I take the Piccadilly Line down to King's Cross and then the

Circle Line to Paddington. The journey takes me just under half an hour, and because I don't know the area that well I buy a pocket *A to Z* from one of the news stands in Paddington station. The address I want is in the Little Venice area, over the other side of the Westway flyover.

Once again, my plan is simple: get in, get answers. Use the element of surprise to catch my quarry off guard, then force him to talk. And if he isn't there, I wait. You could say that this kind of direct approach hasn't worked for me before, and you'd have a point, but unarmed and still completely ignorant of the reason I've been targeted, I figure I have no choice. Marco is a trusted member of the gang, otherwise he wouldn't have been sent to pick up the case, which means he'll know what's going on and who's behind it. After the discovery of the finger at Ferrie's place, I'm also very curious to know what it is the case actually contains.

As I walk through the fading sunshine, my thoughts drift back to Leah. I've tried to keep her out of my mind these past few hours, but now that I've got time to myself, it's proving impossible. I go back through our three weeks together, from start to finish. Our first meeting in the supermarket, the lovemaking that night. The picnic on Hampstead Heath the next day. Each and every date we shared. And in what I still can't help feeling is an act of betrayal, I look for signs: anything unnatural in her behaviour during that time; a mistake in her back story; a moment of evasiveness. But there's nothing. It was two people falling in love. Whichever way I look at it, that's how it was. It was also Leah there this morning next to me. I am sure of that. Poor, innocent Leah.

After ten minutes, I come to a quiet, tree-lined road of expensive white-washed Georgian townhouses. I soon find the house I want, a grand place with hanging baskets filled with flowers on either side of an imposing front door. Not the sort of place where you'd expect to run into a low-life gangster, but then, you have to remember, there's a lot of money in crime these days. Marco's address is the basement flat, which is reached via a short flight of stone steps protected by a locked, wrought-iron gate with an intercom security system. The top of the gate barely reaches my chest. I clamber over it without incident, conscious that with my holdall I must look like a burglar, and make my way down the steps and through a pretty walled garden, heavily planted with thick foliage.

When I reach the front door, I notice that there are bars on the adjoining windows. This is London after all, and if you have money, you don't want to make it easy for the area's burglars, even if the result does make your home look like a plush version of a prison cell.

I put my nose against the cool metal of the bars and find myself looking into a spacious kitchen. The worktops are empty, and the pots and pans hanging from the racks that run along the shelving units all look untouched. I move over to the front door and try the handle. It's locked. I put down the holdall, open the letterbox, and peek inside.

The entrance hall's empty, but I pick up the sounds immediately. Clear and unmistakeable as they drift through the open door of one of the rooms.

Someone's gasping for breath.

The attempts are utterly desperate, like those of an asthmatic having an attack. And they're accompanied by the sound of someone else, a man, grunting with exertion. Either it's a couple having a particularly wild bout of passionate sex, or he's trying to kill her, and straight away I know it's the latter, and that the way things are going it's not going to take him too much longer.

I unzip the holdall as fast as I can and pull out the Enforcer.

I've been on enough arrest operations in Northern Ireland to know how these things work. Standing with my right side to the door, I lift it back in a low arc and then smack one end hard against the lock. Wood splinters, and the door flies open on its hinges.

The adrenalin's surging through me as I charge inside, dropping the Enforcer on the floor (it's too unwieldy to use as a weapon) and running towards the source of the noise. I've still just about got the element of surprise, and I hope this'll help as I barge my way into a bedroom where a life-size poster of Pamela Anderson in her *Baywatch* swimsuit smiles back at me.

A powerfully built man with dyed black hair sits with his back to me astride a young woman on a kingsize double bed, his gloved hands round her neck in a tight, savage embrace as he throttles the life out of her. The woman's legs kick wildly as she struggles beneath him, and I notice that one of her shoes, a golden open-toed sandal with a stacked heel, is missing.

Marco's already turning his head so I launch myself at him, knowing I've got to move fast. My momentum knocks him off balance and I grab him round the neck and twist hard, prepared to break the damn thing if I have to. But I've made a mistake. I should have disabled him with a throat punch, not tried to use my weight against him, because I'm always going to be at a disadvantage in this kind of struggle. Marco doesn't panic either, which is always a bad sign, and for a big man he's quick. As I force his head into the crook of my arm, pulling him backwards, he reaches round and manages to clamp a meaty hand firmly over the most sensitive and important part of my body, and squeezes savagely.

The pain is excruciating and my grip loosens, allowing him to break free and swing round so that he's facing me, his hand still firmly wedged between my legs. The good news is he's let go of the girl now, and she's still moving. It's the good-looking blonde from the brothel whose name, like a lot of other things, I have forgotten, so I guess I've now returned the favour and saved her life too, at least temporarily. The bad news is pretty obvious: I'm helpless and in agony, and by the sweaty, rage-filled expression on Marco's face, I'm guessing he's not about to let me off with a kick up the backside and a firm warning. There's death in his beady black eyes.

Trying to ignore the pain, I launch a single punch that catches him on the chin. It feels like hitting stone, and the damn thing hardly moves. His death grip on my nuts does ease a little though, but before I can fully appreciate the benefits of this I see his fist coming towards my face like an express train. It seems to take a long time to make contact, and I manage to turn my head away, but the force of the blow is still immense. There's no pain – I'm producing too much adrenalin for that – only a single, explosive shock, and then I'm sent careering backwards across the room. Thankfully, Marco lets go of my balls, otherwise I'm sure I would have been leaving them behind. I hit the wall shoulder blades first, my head quickly following suit, and slide to the floor in an ungainly heap.

I'm mildly dazed, which slows my reactions. I can only watch as Marco comes towards me, lifting a leg to launch a kick that's going to be his *coup de grâce*. Fifteen years in the Parachute Regiment being bombed, stoned and shot at, and no-one's ever managed to put a mark on my face; and now, after all that, it's going to be an unfashionable tan and cream brogue doing the damage. And there's absolutely nothing I can do about it.

But the kick never comes. As I lift my hands in a feeble attempt to deflect the coming strike, Marco stumbles as the blonde jumps up from the bed and hits him with what looks like a bedside lamp. Glass shatters, and he yelps in pain. She's coughing and holding a hand to her throat, but she doesn't let this hold her back, and as Marco swings a punch in her direction she moves swiftly to one side, keeping her balance perfectly as she dodges the blow. Then, bouncing onto one foot and keeping low, she sends a vicious little karate kick into his left leg just below the knee, aiming to dislocate the joint.

Marco manages to turn his body slightly, avoiding the worst of the damage, but the kick's hurt him and there's blood running down his face from where she caught him with the lamp. And she hasn't finished yet. As he lunges for her, she stands her ground, lifts her hand, and slams a palm into the bottom of his nose.

I flinched myself. It's one of the most painful blows a fighter can deliver, and one of the most dangerous if it's done hard enough, because it can drive the bone into the brain – definitely the kind of fate someone like Marco deserves.

However, he's lucky. All he gets is a bleeding nose, but it's enough, and he really shouts this time, putting a hand over this latest injury and no doubt wondering how much it's going to cost to get it fixed. Blood seeps out rapidly from the narrow gaps between his fingers. The expression in his eyes is one of incredulity mixed with a lot of pain as he realizes that a woman half his size is taking him apart. A woman who thirty seconds earlier was pinned down and helpless on the bed.

But now he's going for something in the inside pocket of his suit, and I know it's going to be a weapon. I start to get up. The way I'm feeling I don't think I'm going to be much help, but he sees me out of the corner of his eye and it distracts him, allowing the blonde to come forward again and lash out with another kick, hitting him just below the knee.

I don't hear a crack, but it twists badly, and now Marco's deciding that whatever weapon he's carrying, it may not be enough under the current circumstances, and in one very awkward movement, he runs for the door, limping badly and making a lot of noises signifying extreme pain. The blonde grabs her shoe and something from a handbag on the floor, and a couple of seconds later I hear the front door opening and then slamming.

I realize then that somehow, yet again, I have managed to snatch defeat from the jaws of victory, and that with them both gone I'm pretty much back at square one.

I stand up, touching my cheek where Marco struck it. The skin feels tender, and it's already beginning to swell, but there's no blood, so at least I won't have to worry about changing my clothes again. There's an intense ache arrowing from my balls into my gut where Marco manhandled me, and it's that that hurts more than anything. I shake my head, trying to clear it, and start towards the bedroom door, moving faster now.

But as I come out into the hallway, there's a sudden movement to my left and I'm slammed hard against the wall. The next second, a knife blade is pushed hard against my throat.

'You know,' I say, not moving a millimetre, 'this isn't quite the thank you I'd expected for saving your neck.'

'Thank you,' she answers without moving the knife, her Eastern European accent sounding very strong. 'Now who the hell are you?'

'Someone who wants to talk to Marco.'

'What about?'

'I've been set up. I think he knows who by.'

She thinks about this for a moment, then lowers the knife. 'He's gone, but he'll be back soon, and with other people. You need to leave.'

'Well, the way you were getting on when I turned up, it looks like you shouldn't be here either. Why don't we leave together?'

She seems reluctant, so I give her what I hope is my most

trustworthy expression. 'I'm not on their side, and I'm guessing you're not either. We've at least got that in common.'

'So whose side *are* you on?'

'Right now, I'm on mine. And I've got to tell you, it's proving a pretty lonely place to be.'

She looks at me closely for a couple of seconds. Finally, she nods. 'OK, let's go. Before he comes back with reinforcements.'

I squint as we get out into the sunlight, my eyes narrowing to slits against the brightness, and I feel a banging pain in my head. I worry that the punch has done me more damage than I thought. The blonde gives me a push up the steps, telling me that we need to hurry, and I go up them as quick as I can, trying to keep my legs wide apart to lessen the pain down there.

The gate at the top is shut, but she pulls a card from her jeans and inserts it into a slot next to the lock, which releases it. That's interesting, I think, as she uses a remote control to open an Alfa Romeo parked twenty yards down the street and guides me towards it. She's got a key to this place. Marco may have been trying to kill her, but they're obviously close enough that he's given her access to his home. So why the hell am I trusting her?

But the answer to this one's easy enough. As she opens the Romeo's passenger door and I manoeuvre myself carefully into the comfort of the passenger seat, my eyes close, and for a blissful few moments I no longer care about anything. Why the hell not trust her? I think. Why the hell not?

Which, when it comes down to it, is probably the stupidest reason there is.

26

Maybe I shouldn't have moved my head out of the way of Marco's fist. If he'd caught me full on, the blow to the skull might somehow have unlocked my memory. As it is, I've just got a crashing headache and a continuing blank where yesterday was.

There's only one other time in my life when I've blanked out completely and that was years ago in a bar in Germany when a bunch of us were doing tequila slammer races. Apparently, I drank twelve in the space of half an hour – which was something of a stupid move, but one I put down to youth and peer pressure. Everyone was doing it, although maybe they weren't doing it quite as quickly as I was. I only remember downing the first two, then nothing until ten o'clock the next morning when I woke up in a pool of my own vomit with a head that made even the one I had this morning seem mild by comparison. According to my fellow drinkers, we'd visited three separate bars during what was, by all accounts, a hugely entertaining evening. I'd slow-danced with a waitress on a table in one; burned my top lip on a flaming sambuca in another; and then, some time later, just as I was putting a fresh stein of lager to my lips, I'd keeled over backwards and hit the deck like a dead man. I was picked up by four of the boys, one limb each, and carried the two hundred yards back to the barracks. On the way back, one of the four had suggested that I might be putting it on, so they decided to check whether I was genuinely unconscious by repeatedly slamming me bodily into a lamppost on the way. When I didn't flinch, even on the fourth or fifth go, they carried me the rest of the way, chucked me on my bunk, and returned to the bar to carry on where they'd left off.

The point is, I've never got that time back. That whole evening is a void, and it will be for the rest of my days. I'm thinking it's going to be the same this time round.

'Are you all right?' asks the blonde. She's looking at me with an expression that may actually be concern. That's what I'm hoping anyway.

I look at her properly for the first time. She's changed since the brothel and is now wearing a plain white T-shirt and a pair of navy blue jeans that look like they were painted on. The T-shirt's crumpled, and there's a three-inch tear running up the side stitching. There are thick red welts forming on her neck where Marco went to work, and her cheeks are flushed the colour of wine. She looks as tense as a coiled spring, and her hands are tight on the steering wheel.

I tell her I'm fine, and ask how she is.

'I'm OK,' she replies without looking at me, and gives me a thanks – a genuine one this time. 'You saved me back there.'

'Just returning the favour for earlier,' I say modestly.

'I couldn't let them kill you.'

'Why not? You must have known before what they were going to do.'

'I was made to use that stun baton on you,' she answers. 'Marco told me that if I didn't, he'd kill me.'

This time she does look at me, and I have to say that her ordeal has done nothing to obscure her looks. Straight away I'm drawn to her eyes. They're perfect ovals, the colour of polished bronze. There's something pure in them that makes me desperately want to trust what she says.

We've pulled onto the Edgware Road now, heading north in the direction of Kilburn.

'OK,' I say, nodding slowly as we stop at some red lights, 'so you were forced into attacking me?'

'Yes,' she answers, 'I was.'

'What's your name again?' I ask her.

'Alannah.'

And then I remember: that was how she introduced herself when she knocked on the door at the brothel to warn us about the fire.

'That's a nice name,' I say, 'but, you know, Alannah, I'm a little confused. You've got a key to an apartment belonging to this man Marco, and you were talking happily enough with him earlier after you'd dragged me up to that room in the brothel, which means that you work for the same outfit he does. But when my interrogator pulled a gun on me, you jumped on his back. Then a few hours later I come by and Marco's trying to kill you, and when I try to stop him and get knocked semi-conscious for my troubles, you suddenly leap into action again and do a very creditable version of the karate kid.' I sigh. 'Now you're looking at me all doe-eyed and innocent, and I've got to say it's a look that suits you very much, but it also makes me think, to use an English phrase you may not be familiar with, that there's a lot more to you than meets the eye. So, tell me, why should I trust you?'

'Well,' she answers, 'I'm a little confused as well, because you too are something of a mystery. I've never seen you before, yet you come into the club today and shoot Pero dead.'

'That was an accident. He was struggling and the gun went off by mistake.'

She raises her eyebrows sceptically. They're darker than her hair, and they stand out against the gold of her skin. 'That's not what I heard,' she says, pulling away as the traffic ahead moves. 'What I heard is that you might have information that would help them. Marco said very little about you, except that you were very dangerous, and that you had to die. That's why I helped you, because I knew what those animals were planning. But then, suddenly, you turn up out of nowhere at his place saying you've been set up and that Marco knows by who, and then insist on leaving with me. So my question is, who the hell are *you*? And since this is my car that you're in, you can tell me first.'

Her tone's firm and final. I already knew this girl had backbone, now I realize it may well be made of steel. But I've got to be careful about what I say. So I give her a basic story, tweaked just a little so that I don't incriminate myself, and leaving out the details she doesn't need to know, particularly those involving Leah. Mentioning her will only complicate matters. I tell Alannah that I'm an ex-soldier who was paid to deliver a briefcase to Marco but that he ripped me off and tried to have me killed. A friend of mine put a tracker on the case, and that's how I found the location of the brothel, but when I arrived there, I found that my friend had been murdered, and the tracker left with his body.

'Do you know anything about that?' I ask her.

She looks genuinely shocked. 'No, of course not. You're saying that someone murdered your friend out on the street?'

'They cut his throat while he was sitting in his car, no more than fifty yards from the front door of your brothel, and no more than fifteen minutes before I went inside. So, whoever did it must have been hanging around.'

Again she denies any knowledge of the killing.

'I had a gun on me,' I continue, 'just for protection, and I went inside the brothel to track down Marco. I got your man Pero to take me upstairs, we surprised Marco, and then Pero started struggling with me. The gun went off, and the rest you know.'

'What's in the briefcase?'

I think about the finger from Ferrie's apartment. 'I don't know.'

'You're just a delivery boy, right? You don't know what you're delivering and you don't care, so long as the money's right. Is that a good description?'

Her tone's surprisingly accusatory. Here I am sitting next to someone I thought was a female gangster, yet she's not acting like one. I experience a sudden, very powerful urge to tell her the truth. That I'm actually a normal hard-working guy who's got caught up in something that has nothing to do with him. But it's an urge I resist.

'Yeah,' I agree with a sigh, 'it's as good a description as any.'

'And have you got a name, Delivery Man?'

'It's Tyler.'

'Well, Mr Tyler, I might be able to help you. And you might be able to help me.'

'Really? How does that work, then?'

We've turned off the main road and are heading into an estate of cheap 1970s terraced housing built by a developer who clearly had a surplus of breeze blocks and a dearth of taste. Alannah parks outside one of them and cuts the engine.

'Come inside,' she says, 'and I'll tell you.'

I have no idea what she's going to say, nor am I much inclined to take a guess. It's been a bad day. Trusting anyone's a risk. But when you're tired and thirsty, and a beautiful blonde asks you into her house, you're really going to have to fight hard to say no. And I'm just not in the mood.

I get out of the car and follow her to the front door.

27

I follow her through the hallway and into a poky kitchen which looks out on to a postage stamp-sized back garden with a railway viaduct at the end.

'Do you want a drink?' Alannah asks, pulling an unopened bottle of white wine from the fridge.

I can think of nothing I'd like more at the moment. 'Sure,' I say, noticing that, apart from the booze, the fridge is empty.

She takes a couple of wine glasses out of a cupboard and rummages around in one of the drawers for a corkscrew. As she pours the wine and hands me a glass, a train rumbles past along the viaduct, its vibrations rattling the windows.

'Come on,' she says, and we retire to a small sitting room where the noise of the train isn't as loud.

She sits down on the sofa, and I kick off my shoes and plant myself opposite her in the room's only chair. The springs have gone on it, and I end up sinking down so low that my arse is no more than six inches above the psychedelic carpeting. I find a cushion and stick it underneath me while Alannah lights a cigarette and takes a sip of her wine. I take a big gulp of mine.

It's not particularly good stuff, but at the moment it tastes like nectar.

'Well,' I say, 'the most important thing I need to know right now is who Marco and the people he left to torture me work for?'

'The boss's name is Eddie Cosick,' she answers. 'He's what I think you call a people trafficker. He brings girls into England from the Balkan countries. He promises them a new life, with a job and money, but when they get here he puts them to work as prostitutes in clubs like the one today, and treats them as his slaves. If any of them try to escape, they're beaten so savagely that none of them attempts it a second time.'

I'm reminded of what Lucas was telling me earlier about the murders of Maxwell and Spann. The Russian businessman they'd been guarding in a Paris hotel room had apparently been heavily involved in people trafficking and had fallen out with his associates: Bosnians from the former Yugoslavia. Ferrie was very interested in those murders. Ferrie had the briefcase. Marco and his people wanted it. There's a pattern developing here.

'This guy Eddie Cosick. Is he Bosnian?'

Alannah nods, confirming the pattern. 'A Bosnian Serb. They all are.'

But this still doesn't solve the mystery of why they killed Leah, and why they're targeting me.

'You sound like you don't approve of Mr Cosick's methods,' I say, 'which makes me wonder what you were doing at the brothel today.'

She takes a deep breath and eyes me closely. 'I don't approve of his methods,' she says, 'but I think he has my sister.'

There's a pause.

'Maybe you'd better start at the beginning,' I tell her.

She takes a long, elegant draw on her cigarette. 'My sister went missing eight months ago in Belgrade. Her name is Petra and she's eighteen years old. I believe that she's been brought to London against her will and that Eddie Cosick knows where she is. That's why I've come here. To find her, and to take her home.'

'And where did you learn how to fight like that?'

'I'm a police officer.'

I raise my eyebrows. She doesn't look like any police officer I've ever had dealings with. Because of the way she's talking and the fact that she hasn't slapped on the handcuffs, I'm guessing she's not here on official business, and I'm quickly proved right.

'I'm based in Belgrade, which is how I know what happened to Petra. She became involved with the wrong people. You have to remember, Mr Tyler—'

'It's just Tyler.'

'You have to remember that our country is very poor. My sister and I come from a village where the only industry is farming. Seven years ago, when I was also eighteen, I moved to the city. I could have become involved with the wrong people too. Belgrade has many of them. But instead I worked as a waitress to raise enough money to go to college, and after that I got a job in the police force. As soon as Petra reached sixteen she wanted to come and join me. She hated village life, but I told her she had to wait until she was eighteen to make the decision. As a police officer, I've seen what can happen to girls when they reach the city. The brothels are full of them.'

She sighs wearily, and stubs out her cigarette.

'But Petra's always been an impatient girl and she decided to come anyway. One day, she turned up at my apartment, begging to stay. I couldn't let her. It would have been unfair on our parents, so I drove her home, even though she cried the whole way. Our parents are decent people and I knew they wouldn't punish her too severely. But a few months later, she did it a second time. My parents phoned me, terrified, telling me what had happened. By that time, she'd only been gone a day, so I waited at the apartment expecting her to turn up...' The sentence trails off, and Alannah looks thoughtful.

'Except she didn't. Not that day, nor the next. I reported her missing with my colleagues. Because I was a police officer, I had more influence than an ordinary civilian so there was more of an effort to find her by the authorities, but it made no difference. We were unsuccessful. Belgrade is a big city, and as the days passed and we heard nothing from her, I became more and more worried. I spent every waking hour searching. So did my father, who came to the city from our village for the very first time. We visited the bars, the cafés, the restaurants, even the brothels, anywhere that she could possibly have ended up, but as my colleagues lost interest, so our task became harder. I knew that Petra had been forced into prostitution. She would have been in touch otherwise. Prostitution is big business in the countries of Eastern Europe, and Serbia is no exception. But the people who run this business are very powerful, and I couldn't make them talk to me. Soon, my father had to return to the village to support the rest of the family. But I kept looking. If I pulled someone in for a crime, any crime, I would show them a picture of Petra and ask if they'd seen her. I'd make out that they would be treated more leniently if they had information. But no-one did. Or at least no-one admitted it, anyway. It was difficult to tell for sure because no-one wants to cross the people running the sex trade.

'Finally, a month ago, I got a break. My boyfriend, Martin, arrested a man for attempted murder after a bar fight. The man worked as security in a local brothel and he was looking at a long sentence for what he'd done, but when Martin showed him Petra's photo, he could see that the man recognized her. Petra is beautiful. She has dark hair, gorgeous brown eyes and olive skin. If someone sees her, they don't forget.'

I guess most don't forget Alannah either, but I don't say anything.

'The prisoner knew something,' she continues, 'Martin was sure of it, so he told him he'd speak to the judge about lowering the charges against him if he had any information on Petra. The prisoner still denied he knew her, and Martin couldn't get him to change his mind.'

Alannah pauses again, and fixes me with a cool stare.

'But what Martin couldn't achieve, I could. I managed to get access to him in his cell, and I told him that he was going to help. At first, he laughed and called me a foolish woman, dismissing me with a wave of his hand, and telling me to get back to the kitchen stove.'

Her voice hardens. 'That was a big mistake. After five minutes, when he was writhing in a pool of his own vomit, he got the message and admitted that he had indeed seen Petra some months earlier. She had no money and had approached a friend of his looking for work. The friend worked for a people trafficker called Goran who was always interested in finding pretty young women for work in England, where he and his associates could make big money out of them, not the pittance that's available in Belgrade. So Petra was shipped off, doubtless told that at the end of her journey she'd be provided with a good job and the chance of a happy life, and that she'd have a chance to phone her family to let them know she was safe and well.'

She laughs, but the sound is devoid of humour.

'The problem we have in Belgrade is that most people have very little money, and what money there is is in the hands of the criminals, so there is a great deal of corruption. I knew who Goran was, I knew what he'd done to my sister and the fate to which he'd sent her, but he is a protected man in the city. When I tried to question him, I was warned off by my bosses, told not to interfere, even when I explained to them what had happened. In the end, I knew there was no hope of getting Goran to help me get Petra back. I also knew that if I kept trying I'd lose my job, probably even my life.

'That's when I decided to come to England and see if I had more luck here. I knew Goran worked for a Bosnian Serb called Eddie Cosick. My plan was to take what little money I had and see if I could track Cosick down and somehow buy Petra back. Martin tried to persuade me not to go. He seemed to think it was better to let things be. But I'm not like that. And I refuse to give up on my sister, because I know she's still alive and needs my help.' She balls her hand into a fist and punches her chest, fixing me with an intense stare. 'I know it. Here, in my heart. She is alive.'

So, Alannah was determined to find her sister in the same way I was determined to find out who was behind Leah's murder. It seemed we had something in common after all.

'And have you met Eddie Cosick yet?'

She shakes her head. 'Not yet. He's surrounded by security. I was forced to take a different route. I studied what I could of his organization and found out who the people working for him were. But knowing their identities and being able to do something about it are two very different things. So, I managed to – how do you say it – ingratiate myself with one of them.'

'Marco?'

She pulls an expression of distaste. 'Yes. He is a violent pig, but he has a bit more respect for the women than any of the others. I started a relationship with him a few weeks ago. He's high up in the organization and close to Cosick so I've been try-ing to find out from him where my sister might be. But it's not been easy. Like all these guys, he's not very talkative. All he wants to do is fuck. I've got him to take me to the club on Osman Road – the one you came to today – a couple of times, and I've managed to talk to a few of the girls who work there, but I've had to be very discreet. It's dangerous to be seen asking questions, both for them and me. The girls are terrified of their bosses.

'But in the last couple of days, the atmosphere's changed. Something big has definitely been happening. Marco has been taking lots of phone calls and disappearing for meetings. He won't tell me what it's all about, and I've hardly seen him all day. So, because the attention of everybody has been elsewhere, I decided to go to the club on my own this afternoon. I know the door staff and they work for Marco, so they let me in. They don't like me, and I knew I was taking a risk hanging round, asking questions, especially with Marco not there, but I've been feeling desperate. My money's running out. London's an extremely expensive city. Even a dump like this costs a lot to rent.

'I'd been there about an hour, talking to the barman and a couple of the girls, when I was told by Pero that Marco was back and he wanted to talk to me urgently. When I got up to his office, he shut the door and started to slap me around, asking me what I thought I was doing coming here on my own. Then he knocked me to the ground and demanded to know who I was working for.'

I nod slowly, adopting a sympathetic pose, though Marco obviously hadn't hit her very hard, because there wasn't a mark on her when we'd first met out in that hallway. I ask her if she saw the burgundy briefcase while she was there.

'No, there was no briefcase.'

'And what about other people? Who was with Marco?'

'Only Radovan and Alexander, the two men who were ordered to kill you.'

'I'm trying to work out who killed my friend, Snowy,' I explain. 'His throat was cut. There would almost certainly have been some blood on the perpetrator.'

'There was no blood on anyone when I saw them.'

'How long were you with the three of them before I came in?'

She shrugs. 'Only a few minutes. Three or four at most.'

I make some rough calculations. It seems extremely likely that Snowy's killer was Radovan, the same man who'd murdered Leah. He'd probably cleaned himself up by the time Alannah saw him. But I wonder why she never saw the briefcase.

'I heard the struggle outside in the hallway,' she continues, 'and the shot. And then Marco came running back in, telling us all that Pero was dead and a man with a gun was outside. Everyone went for their weapons, but then Marco made me go out there with the baton. He said he knew who you were and that you wouldn't shoot a lady.'

'He's right.'

'That's lucky, because he would, and he had a gun pointing at me when I went out to you.'

'Well, I guess you're forgiven, then. But what I don't understand is why Marco was trying to kill you in the flat just now.'

'Because I fucked up,' she answers evenly. 'He was still very angry when we left the brothel.'

'Hold on,' I interrupt, still slightly confused. 'When you left the brothel, he definitely wasn't carrying the briefcase?'

She shakes her head. 'No. I told you, I didn't see the briefcase.'

So now I'm wondering what the hell happened to it? Surely Marco wouldn't have left it behind. Not if it was that valuable. Which means someone else took it. But who?

'Anyway, Marco was still angry with me, but he was also in a hurry. He had to go somewhere urgently – he wouldn't say where – and he told me to go back to his flat to wait for him. As he left, I made an excuse and went back inside the building. I couldn't stand the idea of you being tortured to death in there. Radovan and Alexander are animals. I've heard what they've done to some of the girls who've tried to escape. I wanted to do something that would stop them but which wouldn't blow my cover, and I didn't have much time to think.'

'So you set the fire.'

She nods. 'It was a stupid move.'

'Not the best,' I admit, 'but at least it worked.'

'I knew the building was alarmed so I used some petrol to start a small fire in a room at the back that's used by the security. The problem was it spread a lot faster than I was expecting. I think everyone got out OK, because the alarms went off straight away. I dialled the police and the emergency services, but I thought that Radovan and Alexander might leave you to burn, so I came up to see if I could set you free.'

'You did that just for me?'

'I knew we'd be able to get out onto the roof from where they were holding you, but I didn't expect Radovan and Alexander still to be there.'

'You still risked your neck,' I say. 'You know, I'm touched. Thank you.'

As I speak, I look at her and notice once again how pretty she is. I tell myself to be careful. Her story seems plausible enough, but if there's one thing I've learned today, it's that people aren't always what they seem.

'It still doesn't explain why Marco attacked you at the flat, though,' I add.

'I think someone from the brothel must have seen me go back in there. Maybe someone even saw me start the fire. I don't know for sure. But after I got out of there, I came back here and changed and showered. I wasn't sure what to do about Marco.

He'd attacked me already so I knew it was dangerous to stay with him, but he was my only hope of finding Petra, which is why I still went to his place to wait for him, like he'd told me to.

'When he turned up, not long before you arrived, he was acting friendly, but as soon as I went into the bedroom to get something, he hit me over the back of the head and jumped on top of me like a man possessed, calling me a traitor once again and demanding to know who I worked for. I knew that this time he really meant me harm, so I tried to fight him off. Then you arrived.'

She smiles, showing perfect white teeth. I smile back.

'This guy, Eddie Cosick. I need to speak to him.'

'I know how to find him,' she says, 'but I want you to do something for me as well. Will you help me find my sister?'

'And how do you think I'm going to be able to do that?'

'Now that I have lost any chance of finding Petra through Marco, you're my best hope. I can see you know how to defend yourself. I want you to get to Cosick. But I don't want you to kill him.'

'I'm not planning to,' I tell her, thinking that on the two occasions she's seen me I've made a real pig's ear of defending myself. 'I just want some answers.'

'Cosick has lots of women working as his slaves, but I doubt if any of them look like Petra. I want you to show him her photograph, and find out where she is. Then I want you to call and tell me, and while you wait with him, I'll go and get her.'

Somehow, I don't think it'll be as easy as that.

'And what do you propose we do about his security?'

'His security will be less now. He had only a few men he trusted to guard him. One was Radovan, another was Pero, and they're both dead. He still has others, of course, but they will be spread more thinly. It'll be a risk, but a man like you will be able to manage it.'

As she says this, she slowly uncrosses her long legs and leans forward, her gaze drawing me in. I know it's a deliberate move on her part, a combination of flattery and sexual allure to get me to do what she wants. I sit back and think about what she's saying. Is she just being naive and clutching at straws, or does she have some other agenda?

'Do you want some more wine?' she asks, standing up.

My glass is empty. Hers is still half-full.

She's smiling at me now, and there's confidence in her expression. And something else, too. It's a promise of more to come than simply wine, and even in my state, I know I'm not imagining it. The warning bells in my head suddenly get a lot louder. I'm reminded of something my mother once told me after my father sold his lucrative printing business and ran away with his secretary. 'Women have power,' she said. 'They can make men do anything. Their secret is they always let the man think he's in charge. He never is, and he never will be.' Not exactly original, but wise words all the same, and I feel I really ought to be taking note of them.

But none of this stops me from returning her smile again and telling her that, sure, I'd love a top-up.

My head aches, and even now the adrenalin continues to pump through me. It's been a brutal day, a series of violent snapshots, each following the other so quickly that they almost blend into one: the shock of waking up this morning beside the woman I loved (still love), and seeing what they'd done to her body; the bloodbath at Ferrie's place, and the subsequent chase; finding Snowy with his throat cut and his blood all over the car I'd sold to him only a few months before; the terrible pleasure that coursed through me when I held down Radovan's mask-clad face on the hotplate in the brothel. And now, after all that, I find myself drinking wine in a rundown shithole of a house with a beautiful woman who may or may not be lying to me about who she really is, knowing that very soon I could be making love to her.

And it's still not even dark.

28

When Alannah comes back into the room with the wine, I get to my feet and take the glass from her proffered hand, my fingers gently touching hers. Neither of us moves. We stare at each other in utter silence. Her pale lips part a little, and I can see the tips of her gleaming white teeth. I can hear her breathing. It's soft, but just a little bit faster than it was before. The marks on her neck are dark and uneven. I touch the skin lightly and she lets slip a tiny gasp.

'Does it hurt?' I ask her.

'No,' she whispers throatily.

The wine's making me light-headed, and my troubles seem to evaporate. The whole world has been reduced to this one room and the woman with the long blonde hair and golden skin who stands in front of me. For these few liberating moments, nothing else matters.

I take a single gulp of the wine, put it down on the table, and touch my lips to hers. Her hand reaches behind my neck and pulls me into a tight embrace. We kiss hard, passionately, our bodies intertwined. She tastes of cinnamon. I cup one small, round breast and knead it lightly, pushing myself up against her, my breath coming in ragged, urgent gasps. She moans, and uses her other hand to pull my shirt loose from my jeans, her fingers running across my stomach and chest.

'Let's go to bed,' she whispers.

I don't resist as she leads me up the stairs and into a tiny bedroom with bare walls and unpolished floorboards. She unbuttons my shirt and rips it off, her mouth locked on mine, before pulling away and pausing simply to gaze at me. Her lips are parted and drawn back in a voluptuous smile, and tresses of blonde hair have fallen loose across her face. It's a look of undisguised lust, and every part of my body responds to it. I want this woman desperately.

I grind my pelvis against hers, my hands gripping her hips. The feeling is so intense it's as if it's taken on a life of its own, become almost unstoppable.

And yet something does stop me.

Leah.

A flashback from this morning invades my consciousness: of her, cold and lifeless on the bed, butchered like an animal. I can hear her cries on the DVD as, terrified and helpless, she awaits her bloody fate. And then, suddenly, I picture her as I knew her in happier times – laughing, vibrant and alive. The woman I was falling in love with. And I know I can't do this. Not today. Maybe not for a long time. And certainly not while the bastard who ordered her murder is still at large.

I let go of Alannah.

'I want you, Tyler,' she says huskily, taking my right hand by the wrist and guiding it towards her midriff.

'I want you too,' I say, but I'm no longer seeing her. In my mind's eye, I'm seeing Leah dying, and I wonder, with a sense of panic, whether this image will appear for the rest of my days whenever I'm intimate with another woman. I look Alannah in the eye. 'But I can't do this.'

She seems surprised, and I'm guessing rejection isn't something she's used to. She lets go of my hand, and it drops to my side.

'I'm sorry,' I tell her, feeling vaguely embarrassed.

'What's wrong? Are you OK?'

I turn away from her gaze. 'I'm fine. It's just that there's some-one else, that's all.'

'Oh,' she says. 'OK. I'm sorry, I didn't realize.'

'It's all right. Don't worry about it. I got caught up in things myself.'

Alannah walks round to the other side of the double bed and pulls a fresh pack of cigarettes from an open carton on the floor. She lights one and turns my way.

'You're something of an enigma, Mr Tyler,' she tells me. 'In my experience, faithful, romantic men are rare. Especially those who operate on the wrong side of the law.'

'Someone's got to be the standard bearer for fidelity,' I tell her with a small smile.

She manages an even smaller one in return and sits down on the bed, taking a drag on the cigarette and blowing out a thin line of smoke towards the cracked, nicotine-stained ceiling. Outside the window, another commuter train comes rattling past.

I lean down and pick up my shirt from the floor, and she asks me where I got my scars.

'It's a long story,' I answer.

'Are you in a hurry to go anywhere?'

At some point soon I'm going to have to pay a visit to Eddie Cosick, but I'm tired, and it's been a long day. I need to rest. 'Not particularly,' I answer, pulling the shirt back on.

'Then why don't you tell me it? Get the wine from downstairs and come and sit with me.' She gives me a coy look. 'I won't bite. I promise.'

It's a foolish move, I know, but the bed looks a lot more comfortable than the chair with the springless springs in her living room, so I do as she asks, returning with the glasses and handing one to her.

'Cheers,' she says, giving my glass a little clink.

'Cheers,' I answer, making myself comfortable on the bed, conscious of her closeness.

'It's a pity we had to meet under such circumstances.'

I'm thinking it's a pity we had to meet at all, but I don't say anything. She asks me once again about the scars, and I tell her the story of the day my APC was bombed in South Armagh. Despite what I said, it doesn't take long at all, because I still don't like talking about it. It may have been ten years ago, but the memories remain as raw as ever. I'm wondering whether in the future it'll be the same with the memories of today.

Alannah listens in silence, and when I'm finished she exhales loudly. 'That's some tale. And was it the end of your career in the army?'

'No, they couldn't get rid of me that easily. I was in hospital for three weeks, and on sick leave for eight weeks after that, but I went back and stayed for another six years.'

'Why?'

'Because I wasn't sure what else to do, I suppose. But it was never really the same after that. You know, I'd lost two friends dead, and then I lost a lot of others.'

'Really? Were you bombed again?'

'No. In a way, it was worse than that.'

She leans forward on one elbow, looking enthralled. 'Tell me about it.'

I feel a flicker of concern, knowing I shouldn't be letting on too much about myself. But she already knows my name, and one of my tales about service in Northern Ireland, so I conclude that there doesn't seem much harm in adding another to the mix.

'Well, the way we were ambushed caused a lot of anger in the unit,' I explain. 'The thing is, Northern Ireland was a really frustrating place to serve. You knew who the enemy were. You knew them by name – the gunmen, the bombers, all of them – but there was nothing you could do about it.'

She looks puzzled. 'What do you mean?'

'I mean, it wasn't like a proper war, and that was the problem. Our regiment, the Paras, were trained as shock troops. We were meant to fight in proper wars, but Northern Ireland wasn't like that. There, we were just surrogate police officers. It didn't matter if you knew someone was IRA, you had to wait until they actually tried to kill you before you could fight back; and even then, because they used roadside bombs and snipers, you never really got the chance actually to take them on. So, when the guys from our unit heard that the RUC knew the identities of the people who'd attacked us but didn't have enough evidence to bring charges, everything just spilled over.

'There was a pub about half a mile away from where the bomb went off which was a well-known haunt for IRA sympathisers, and the bomber was one of the regulars. So one night not long afterwards, the remaining members of our unit led by our OC, Major Ryan, raided the place. It was meant to be an official operation to gather evidence about IRA activities, but the whole thing degenerated into a brawl. I don't know how it started. I think one of the customers started getting really irate, demanding to know on what grounds the place was being searched – that sort of thing. Apparently, he got hit in the face with a rifle butt, and then everything just kicked off. I think a lot of the guys in the unit had been looking for just this sort of excuse to come down hard, but the problem was they came down too hard, and they started laying into everyone, including the man they reckoned was the bomber. From what I heard, they spread-eagled him face down on the floor of the pub, with one man sitting on his legs, another on his back, and a man holding each of his arms, and then smashed his fingers one by one with their rifle butts. Then they took it in turns to stamp on his hands until they were pretty sure everything was broken, before picking him up and chucking him over the bar and into all the spirit bottles.

'Before they left, they warned their victims not to say anything, otherwise they'd be back, but something like that was never going to stay quiet. If nothing else, it was a tremendous propaganda coup for the IRA: civilians beaten and savaged by the Paras as they enjoyed an evening out. Apparently, four or five people required hospital treatment, with the bomber the most seriously injured. In no time this huge political firestorm broke out, and the barracks were swarming with military police and army investigators. The whole unit was suspended from duty, and a major inquiry began to root out those responsible.

'All this time, I was in a hospital bed on the mainland. The first I heard about what happened was on the news. It wasn't the lead story, thank God, but it was big news, and they kept it going for a week. In the end, five guys from the unit got court-martialled, and they all ended up serving long prison sentences. They were all people I knew well. Friends of mine. No-one from the other side ever got charged with the attack on our patrol. I'll leave it to you to decide whether or not justice was done, but like I said, serving in the army was never quite the same after that.'

'And what's happened to those five men now?'

Once again, Maxwell and Spann, the bodyguards apparently killed by the Vampire in a Paris hotel room, spring to mind.

'Two of them are dead. The others have just got on with their lives. We don't really keep in touch any more.'

'So you're not working on behalf of any of them today, then?'

'Why would I be?' I ask, wondering suddenly why she's asking such probing questions.

'No particular reason,' she answers with a shrug. 'You just said you were hired by someone to deliver the briefcase to Marco. Since you're an ex-soldier, I thought you might work with your former colleagues. How did you find Marco's flat today, by the way? Because it's not registered in his name.'

'Detective work,' I answer, thinking that she's just turned things round quite smoothly.

'A man of many talents,' she says, getting up from the bed and going over to a chest of drawers on the other side of the room.

She hunts around in one of the drawers, then returns with a photograph. Clambering onto the bed, she hands it to me. It's a black and white six-by-four showing an attractive dark-haired young woman in her late teens. The girl is smiling self-consciously at the camera, showing a row of white teeth. It looks like she's wearing a school uniform. She's pretty, but not striking, and looks nothing like Alannah.

'Your sister?' I ask.

She nods. 'You must find out where she is, Tyler. Do you promise me you'll do that?'

She moves in close, and I can feel her warm breath on my face. I notice a cute smattering of faint freckles running along the bridge of her nose. They're almost invisible against the backdrop of her golden skin. Once again I'm reminded of Leah, and I move away a little.

'I'll see what I can do, I promise you that. Have you got one of Cosick?'

She shakes her head. 'He doesn't like to be photographed, but he's in his middle fifties, completely bald, and quite short and fat.'

'He sounds lovely.'

'He also has a scar about an inch long on his chin where some-one tried to stab him once.'

'And where does he live?'

'A place called Notting Hill. Not far from here. If you go there tonight, I may be able to help you break in. I've learned how to get into places from some of the criminals I've arrested.'

'You know quite a lot, don't you?' I say. 'At the moment I'm unarmed, so how am I going to get any answers out of Cosick?'

'You could take a knife. I'm sure if you put it to his throat it would jog his memory.'

I nod slowly. 'I'm sure it would. Anyway, if you think you can break into his place, why haven't you done it already?'

'I told you. Because Cosick has a lot of security. Or he did, anyway. And up until now I've been on my own.'

I don't say anything, and she looks at me with just a hint of accusation.

'Are you going to go?'

'I'll visit Cosick, yes. And I'll find out what happened to your sister too, if I can. But I'm not going to go tonight.'

'If you don't, I will.'

'Don't be foolish, Alannah.'

'I'm not being foolish, Tyler. I want to find my sister, and I'm running out of time.'

We sit there staring at each other for a couple of seconds, the earlier desire replaced now by a mutual mistrust. I fully intend to visit Eddie Cosick tonight, but I don't want her to know about it. You see, I'm beginning to get a bad feeling about Alannah. I get the distinct impression she's trying to manipulate me, and I don't like it.

'I need to think things through,' I tell her, at last.

She sighs and gets up from the bed again. 'I'm going to take a shower, OK?'

'Sure,' I say, watching her leave the room.

For the next few minutes I lie on the bed, not moving. I'm tired, and I could almost go to sleep, but I'm uneasy. I suddenly don't like the fact that Alannah's out of sight. I remember her telling me she showered this afternoon, after she left the brothel. Maybe she's just a very clean person, I tell myself, but I'm not convinced.

Something's wrong.

And then it hits me.

When we were driving here in her Alfa Romeo and we introduced ourselves, I said my name was Tyler and she immediately referred to me as Mr Tyler. Now, if she'd just arrived in the UK for the first time, she wouldn't know that Tyler wasn't an obvious Christian name, would she? So there'd be no reason for her to put a 'Mr' in front of it. Which suggests she's pretty familiar with the culture here. Which also means she could have been here a lot longer than a few weeks.

It's something small, insignificant perhaps, but then I think about the way she speaks. Her knowledge of English isn't just good, it's fantastic. She even uses colloquialisms. And she didn't ask me who the RUC were when I was telling her the story of the court martial . . . It all points to the fact that she's a lot more clued up about things than she's letting on. For all I know, she may not even come from Serbia, although I've got to say the accent seems pretty authentic. But I'm certain she's not who she says she is, which means that I'm taking a big risk staying here. I'm going to have to move, because if she's lying, she's lying for a reason, and whatever that reason is, it's not going to be good for me.

I slide off the bed, moving as quietly as possible, and tiptoe from the room. The door to the bathroom's shut, and I step over and put my ear against it. I can hear the hiss of the shower but nothing else.

I creep down the stairs. It's dusk now, and as I step into the living room, looking round for my clothes, I see that the street lights have already come on.

I see something else as well. Figures on the other side of the street, three or four of them, dressed in bulky, dark clothing, moving rapidly and purposefully across my field of vision. I can just make out the fact that they are white males, and that they look like they're here on business, before they temporarily disappear from view. And I say temporarily, because if I'm not very much mistaken, these men are coming here.

And shoeless and unarmed is really no way to meet them.

29

There's movement outside the front door, and hushed voices, and then a face appears at the living-room window. I duck down fast behind the threadbare chair I was sitting on earlier and tug on one of my grimy Timberlands. I grab the other one and sneak a peak over the chair. The face has gone so I pull on the other Timberland and half-creep, half-run out into the hallway.

I can see the figures bunched up behind the patterned glass of Alannah's front door, but I'm hoping they can't see me, although that quickly turns out to be irrelevant because a split second later I hear the telltale bang and angry splintering of wood that tells me I'm not the only person who's got access to an Enforcer today. It's a cheap house made with cheap materials, so it's really no surprise that the lock gives straight away and the door flies open in one sudden movement, hitting the wall with an angry clap that sounds like a gunshot.

Ten feet separates me from the intruders; maybe twelve separates me from the back door. I turn to run, but then I think of Alannah. Can I really simply run out the back door and leave her here? I know she's been bullshitting me, but that doesn't matter. Earlier today, she saved my life. No question. And what if these guys are after her, not me?

With this in mind, I decide that rather than take route one out of here I'm going to be chivalrous, and I turn and run up the stairs, taking them two and three at a time. I hear the sound of footsteps in the hallway behind me, but no-one speaks, and that's what's really worrying, because it means they want to make as little noise as possible, and there's only one reason for that. They're here to kill.

I run onto the landing, keep going, and launch a flying karate kick at the bathroom door. It opens just as easily as the front door and makes pretty much the same noise.

The room's dark. And empty. The shower's going, but there's no-one in it.

'Oy, stop!' yells someone from the bottom of the stairs as I turn round and make a dash for the bedroom, the accent as cockney as jellied eel and Jack the Ripper, most definitely not Eastern European. 'Police!'

Jesus, what the hell are *they* doing here?

I run through the bedroom, fling open the window, and clamber out.

They're coming up the stairs fast, but the garden's empty, and for the second time today I slide down a wall until I'm hanging by my fingers, then jump the rest of the way, landing on my feet and rolling over. As I get up, I can hear the angry tugs of some-one trying, without success, to open the back door, and I realize that if I'd gone that way I'd have been trapped, so clearly an element of chivalry pays.

I don't look back but keep running towards the seemingly impenetrable mess of brambles at the end of Alannah's garden. I charge straight through them, ignoring the scratches and the sound of the cotton of Lucas's polo shirt tearing. A set of rusty iron railings appears out of nowhere, and I vault over them, getting a faceful of brambles in the process.

I land on a narrow footpath that runs parallel to a high mesh fence topped with barbed wire marking the border of railway property. The fence is covered in tangled foliage and a sign says KEEP OUT in bold lettering with a picture of a menacing black skull on each side of the wording. There's no immediately obvious way in, so it becomes a choice of left or right.

Unfortunately, the choice is made for me when I hear the unmistakable sound of dogs barking – big dogs, too – followed a second later by the rapid tattoo of paws on concrete. Getting closer.

I just have time to bemoan the fact that even my favourite animals have now joined the ranks of my enemies, then I'm off in the opposite direction, knowing there's no way I'm going to outrun them. I run across the road the viaduct crosses and keep going along the footpath on the other side. It begins to rise steadily, which does not bode well, and I can hear the barking getting closer, partly drowned out by the sound of an oncoming train. Through the mesh in the fence I can see that it's a slow-moving freight pulling cart after cart filled with building aggregates. The path's getting pretty steep now and my lungs feel like they're burning up. I'm fast over short distances, even uphill, but I'm not going to be able to keep up this pace for much longer.

There are two young kids, barely ten, messing about with what looks like an old fridge on the strip of wasteground that runs alongside the track. They are doubtless up to no good, but I don't care about that. What I want to know is how the hell they got in there.

And then I see it, about ten yards further on. A small, kid-sized hole at the bottom of the fence. I force myself to slow down, the patter of angry paws right behind me, then at the last second I do a hard turn and dive bodily through the hole, scrambling to my feet on the other side and running wildly for the track. The freight train's almost passed now, but even above the steady, rhythmic clatter of its wheels I can hear the excited panting of a dog. He's feet away and gaining, and I know there's no way he's not going to get me.

As I reach the raised shingle on which the track sits, he lunges. His teeth get an iron grip on my leg, but I've still got just that little bit of momentum, and as the final cart passes directly in front of me I jump skywards, getting one flailing arm on the cart's lip, and a foot on the buffer. I swing round so that I'm hanging on to the rear of the train, and the dog, a big Alsatian, swings with me. But the thing is, he wasn't expecting this and I was, and he just keeps on going, releasing his death grip at the same time. He flies off, does a very effective rolling landing, then jumps to his paws and stands there with his tongue lolling out, watching me disappear slowly into the distance.

I look towards the fence and catch sight of several men running on the other side of it. They stop as they see me come trundling past at a leisurely twenty miles an hour or so, which is when I see that they're in uniform. I can't resist giving them a little wave, and then they're gone, as the train goes over the viaduct and starts to turn a corner.

Once I get my breath back, I decide that it's surprisingly relaxing hanging on to the back of a train on a warm summer's evening, with the breeze in your hair. Darkness is falling fast and a three-quarter moon the colour of melted butter sits high in the darkening sky. There are no stars, the haze of neon lights that spreads for miles around smothering them like a blanket, but there's something beautiful about the way the city seems to come to life at night, and something exhilarating too about outrunning people who want to do you harm. It seems right now that the whole world seems to want to do me harm, yet in those moments I feel the best I've felt all day.

But I've got another mystery on my hands now, because it's obvious that Alannah didn't call people to come and kill me. She called the police to come and arrest me instead. Which leaves two very important questions.

Number one: Why?

Number two: Just who exactly is she working for?

30

I'm on a quiet street in Kilburn roughly a mile or so from where I grabbed a lift on the train, and a few hundred yards from where I jumped off it. As I walk along it, Lucas's torn shirt flapping in the breeze, I review my options.

Time is not on my side. It's twenty to nine. Lucas dropped me at Holloway Road tube more than two hours ago. He will have spoken to the police by now, and after what I'm sure he's said, they're going to be looking for me with some urgency. So I really am going to need to make Eddie Cosick's acquaintance soon. In other words, tonight. The address book I discovered at Ferrie's place is still in the pocket of my jeans, thank God, and it seems that Ferrie knew about Cosick too, because when I look the name up I get an address in W8, which tallies with Alannah's description of it as being in Notting Hill.

But as I walk, I consider for the first time the possibility of handing myself in and actually telling the police the truth, the rationale being that they're going to catch me eventually so it would be better to pre-empt them. But I swiftly discount this. I'm too heavily implicated in the events of today: the shootings at

Ferrie's place and the chaos at the brothel. As well as this, there's still the possibility that there are copies of the DVD out there linking me to Leah's murder.

At the moment, visiting Cosick is my only option. It's extremely risky, but there's nothing I can do about that. I do, however, have a real stumbling block. I'm unarmed. Which means I'm going to have to speak to Lucas. I genuinely don't want to drag him back into this, but I can't see how I can avoid it.

I use the mobile he supplied me with to make the call. He answers on the first ring, as if he's been sitting there waiting for me.

'The police have only just gone,' he informs me. 'I was going to phone you. I'm sorry, Tyler, I had to tell them that we were doing the job today on your behalf.' He sounds genuinely gutted.

'Don't worry,' I tell him, 'I know you had no choice. How much information did you give them?'

'I tried to keep it to a minimum. I said you approached us out of the blue this afternoon about a job. You wanting a track on a briefcase. You didn't tell me what was in it, and I didn't ask, because I trust you. I gave Snowy the task of following the case, and told him to keep me posted with progress calls every fifteen minutes. We got two, then they stopped. Me and you parted company, and I got on with some other work, namely a job in Islington, assuming that Snowy would phone me back. I was getting worried but obviously didn't think it would be anything too serious, so didn't bother reporting it, and then, bang, the next thing I know, the police are on the phone announcing that he's dead.'

'Won't they know you were talking to him on your mobile shortly before he died?'

'Sure, but when they triangulate my location, they'll see that I was in Islington just like I said, a good two miles away from where they discovered Snowy.'

'So you're in the clear, right?'

'The only possible concern is if someone saw me pick you up after the brothel fire, and can place me at the scene, but I'm hoping I'll be all right. There are no public CCTV cameras on that street. I checked.'

'Did they ask you anything about the fire?'

'No, I think they believed my story. There was no reason not to. But obviously they want to speak to you. They said that if you made contact with me, I was to call them straight away.'

'Thanks, Lucas.'

'No problem, but we must be getting near quits by now.'

'Yeah, about that . . .'

'Shit. Now what?'

'I've got the name of another man. The big boss. I've got an address, too. I hate to do this, Lucas, but I need one of those guns you were talking about.'

'You're not going to pay him a visit?'

'At the moment I can't see any other way.'

He sighs. 'Which means I'm going to have to come with you, doesn't it?'

'Of course it doesn't. I've already told you, you've done your bit.'

'I can't let you go there alone. If anything happened to you, I wouldn't be able to forgive myself.'

I try to protest, but he tells me not to bother.

'I'm coming, and that's it. Where are you now?'

'I'm in Kilburn. A place called Heaver Street.'

'I'll come straight over. I should be there in about half an hour.'

'Before you do, can you run a background check on this guy?

His name's Eddie Cosick. I need to know what we're up against.'

'Sure. So make it forty-five.'

'Fine. And one other thing. Can you bring me over another shirt? I had a little accident with the other one.'

'I'll be sending you a bill for this,' he tells me with just a hint of exasperation, then hangs up.

There's an old-fashioned street corner pub opposite me. The door's open, and I can hear the buzz of conversation from inside. A noticeboard out the front says that they do good food. They're hardly likely to say any different, of course, but all the activity of the past few hours has given me something of an appetite.

I step inside, figuring I've earned a break.

31

When I step out of the pub pretty much exactly forty-five minutes later, having eaten a high-quality chilli con carne with garlic bread and a mixed leaf salad, washed down with a pint of orange juice and lemonade, Lucas is just pulling up in his BMW.

I jump inside.

'You've been in the pub?' says Lucas, his tone incredulous. He's wearing a black sweater and dark jeans, along with a pair of leather gloves. With his chiselled good looks, he reminds me a little of the Milk Tray man.

'Don't worry,' I answer, 'I haven't been drinking.'

'But in that shirt? The thing's in pieces. Here, I've brought you this.'

He reaches down and produces a sweater similar to the one he's wearing, and a navy Fosters baseball cap. I put them both on as he pulls away and thank him once again for coming. He tells me that that's what friends are for, although I think he's gone well above and beyond the call of duty on that particular score.

I give him Eddie Cosick's address, and he feeds it into the car's GPS system.

'Did you find out anything about him?' I ask.

'A little. Like a lot of these guys he tries to keep a low profile, but I talked to a police contact, and it seems he's got his fingers in a lot of very illegal pies, not just people trafficking and prostitution. There's heroin and arms smuggling as well. And if you cross him, you pay for it. Last year, one of his people stole some money from the organization. The story goes they fed the guy feet first through an industrial mincer. Turned him into sausage meat.'

I think about my chilli con carne. It's not a pleasant thought.

'But there's nothing that might suggest what's in that case I was delivering?'

He shakes his head. 'Everything I found out about him is supposition. Cosick doesn't get close to the coalface, and he's got no convictions. I can't get hold of a photo of him either.'

'It's all right,' I say, 'I know what he looks like.' Although I wonder if I actually do, since I've only got Alannah's word for that. 'What about the guns?' I ask after a pause.

'We've got a slight problem there,' Lucas tells me. 'I've brought them with me, but they're not loaded. I thought I had bullets somewhere, but I don't, and the ones that were in there originally are rusted to shit. We'll look the part, but we'd better hope that no-one tries to call our bluff.'

'It's the way I want it anyway,' I answer. 'I don't want to have to shoot anyone else.'

Although, I have to admit, I'd feel a lot better knowing I had a fully functioning weapon if the bullets do start flying. My gut feeling is they won't. We're going to the guy's house, after all, and no-one wants their humble abode turned into a shooting gallery. But if nothing else, the experiences I've had today have taught me that you should never, ever bet against things going wrong.

'So, what's the plan?' Lucas asks.

'We go in nice and quiet, guns drawn, round up Cosick and any security he's got, secure them, and then I ask the questions.'

'That's it? Jesus, Tyler, you like to keep it simple, don't you?'

'Can you think of something better?'

'Not off the top of my head,' he admits, 'but then you didn't ask me to come up with anything, did you? And if Eddie Cosick is the guy who's behind Leah and Snowy's killings, and if he's the one who set you up, what are you going to do about it?'

'I'm going to ask him why.'

He doesn't try to argue. 'OK. Then what?'

'I'm going to make sure I'm in possession of all the evidence against me.'

'OK. Let's say Cosick tells you why, and gives you all the evidence he's got linking you to the murder. What do you do, then?'

'I get him to tell me where the briefcase is. We know it contains something extremely valuable to him, so I'm sure he's still going to be in possession of it. I take it off him—'

'He's not going to want to give it up.'

'He'll give it up with a gun against his head. Then I'll hide it somewhere, and since it's something that's obviously incriminating to him, I'll put an anonymous call in to the cops. And then that'll be it. Job done.'

Lucas nods, not looking too sure, and we fall silent as we drive through Kilburn and down into Paddington before passing into the fashionable enclaves of Kensington and Notting Hill. The streets here are wide and brightly lit, and crowded with the young and the loaded who've come to play among the pavement cafés and wine bars, and enjoy this last, balmy burst of summer.

The atmosphere on the streets may be easy-going and vibrant, but in the car we're both tense as we prepare for the coming operation. We're going into the unknown. All we can predict for certain is that it's going to be dangerous. An attacking military force should always have a numerical superiority over the force it's attacking, but with only two of us involved, that's almost certainly not going to be the case. If anything, we're going to be outnumbered, so the scope for things to go wrong is immense.

When Lucas picked me up, he was making jokes and seemed fairly laid back, but as we get nearer to our destination I see that this was nothing more than an act. He chain-smokes cigarettes in short, angry drags, and sweat glistens on his forehead. I'm glad he's with me, but his presence emphasizes my own selfishness in involving him in someone else's battle. I know he doesn't want to be here, and I can't blame him. His army days were a long, long time ago, and since then he's grown to enjoy the good life of decent money and easy work. An op like this is going to be a major shock to his system and he's had very little time to prepare himself.

I want to tell him that everything's going to be fine, but I don't want to make it sound like I doubt his mental strength. Instead, I think about Eddie Cosick and what he has against me. Maybe I've crossed him somehow without knowing it. Maybe Leah was his mistress, and he found out I'd slept with her and wanted to get his revenge.

For a split second, I think I may be on to something here. But then I realize that it leaves too many unanswered questions. The first and most obvious is how on earth would he have found out? And why would he have gone to such elaborate lengths to set me up, leaving me very much alive in the process? It would have been vastly easier simply to send someone round to the show-room and blow my head off. Job done, honour restored. There's no way he would have decided that as part of his revenge I should be made to go and pick up a briefcase containing something so valuable to him that he's willing to pay a hundred and fifty grand for it.

No, there's some other reason he's using me. I just can't see what it is.

And I've got to admit that I'm nervous too. It's not just that Cosick may not supply the answers I need; this time, I may not even get out of there alive. Since waking up this morning, I've ridden my luck. I could have been the first out of the kitchen door back at the house where I picked up the case and taken Sellman's bullet, but I wasn't. I could have been arrested afterwards, but somehow I managed to escape. If I hadn't taken the flick knife from Dracula in the brothel ... In all these things, the dice have rolled my way. At some point, and probability tells me it'll be soon, this luck is going to stop.

And you know what? I really don't want to die. Today's been a strange day. In most ways it's been awful. But I've felt something I haven't felt since the best of my army days. I've felt alive. I've been thrown into conflict after conflict, found myself alone in the middle of a minefield, and walked right through it. In other words, I have survived. And now I want to make it to the other side so that I can turn round and say, 'I've won.'

But I'm terrified that it's not going to happen.

32

We're almost there now. As Lucas turns off Holland Park Avenue and into a quiet street lined with mature cypress trees that runs parallel to the western side of Holland Park, the GPS system tells us that Eddie Cosick lives down here somewhere.

I look round with a combination of admiration and jealousy. Cosick has clearly done well for himself. The houses here are grand Edwardian villas of whitewashed stone that loom into the night sky. Only the truly rich have a chance of living here, and the truly rich know it, surrounding their homes with high walls and elaborate security systems to keep out those of lesser means. Cosick's own place, a detached, three-storey corner property, is no exception, set back from the street behind wrought-iron gates and a high wall that borders the entire property. There are two cars visible in the gravel driveway, a bright red Audi convertible with its top down, and a Jaguar XJS, both of which are illuminated by the twin lamps on either side of the front door. A single light shines dimly on the first floor behind drawn curtains.

'Well,' says Lucas, 'it looks like he's in.' He tries to sound casual, but I can hear his nervousness.

He indicates, and takes the first right, parking several hundred yards up the road, well away from Cosick's place, between two immense four-wheel-drives. He chucks the latest cigarette he's been smoking out of the window and cuts the engine.

'You OK?' I ask.

He manages a weak smile. 'No worse than foot patrol on the Falls Road.'

'Exactly. We've done it all before. Things that would scare the shit out of most people. And we've always survived.'

He looks a little more confident now. 'When this is over, you're going to buy me a nice big drink, right?'

'Count on it,' I tell him. 'Have you got the guns?'

He reaches down behind his seat, which is the place where he seems to keep everything bar the kitchen sink, and retrieves a Tesco bag.

'Have you still got the gloves I gave you earlier?'

I nod, take them out of my back pocket and pull them on, while Lucas reaches into the bag and removes a package wrapped in white cloth. He hands it to me, I unwrap it, and a well-kept, recently cleaned long-barrelled Browning pistol stares back at me. I place it in the waistband of my jeans as Lucas takes out his weapon, a silver Walther PPK, and stuffs it in his own waistband.

'You might want this,' he says, reaching into the glove compartment and producing a couple of black balaclavas.

'I don't think there's much point in me covering up,' I tell him. 'I have a strong feeling Eddie Cosick knows exactly who I am.'

'If you leave him alive, Tyler, he's going to come looking for you.'

I've thought about this. 'If Cosick's the man responsible for

Leah and Snowy's murder, then I'm going to make sure that one way or another he's brought to justice for it. He's certainly not going to be roaming the streets planning revenge.'

'You're going to need to be careful.'

'I will be,' I say, opening the door. 'Come on, let's go.'

He stuffs his balaclava in his jeans and follows me down the road.

The street's quiet now, and bathed in dark shadows. The only people I can see are a middle-aged couple thirty yards ahead of us, out for a night-time stroll. They hold hands, heads almost touching as they talk, oblivious to the world around them. Their intimacy makes me jealous, and reminds me what my life was like yesterday, and what it definitely won't be like tomorrow.

A light breeze, still warm, rustles through the branches of the cypress trees, and from somewhere over in Holland Park the faint strains of jazz music reach my ears. My heart beats hard in my chest, and I glance at Lucas. His jaw is set hard, his blue eyes narrowed in concentration. He's scared, but I can see that finally he's ready.

The wall bordering Eddie Cosick's back garden is a good ten feet high, and curved at the top. There are no railings, making it useful only for keeping out the casual intruder. This is a bad move, and it surprises me, given the circles he moves in, but some people think it's never going to happen to them, and most of the time they're wrong. Tonight, he definitely is.

I take one quick look behind me to confirm there's no-one watching and ask Lucas to give me a lift. He grabs my foot in both hands and yanks it upwards, like he's tossing the caber. His strength surprises me, and he gives me real momentum. I jump, arms outstretched, grab hold of the top of the wall and haul myself up in one movement. I find myself looking into a well-kept garden, lined with interesting vegetation, including pampas grass and a dwarf palm tree, and with a covered swimming pool at one end. The garden's empty, so I lie across the top of the wall, gripping the brickwork between my thighs, and stretch out an arm for Lucas to grab hold of.

'You've put on weight,' I whisper as I struggle to pull him level.

'No,' he whispers back, 'you're just getting old.'

We slide down the other side, using a rose bush as cover, and land on a brick path that runs along the edge of the lawn. I draw my gun, and Lucas puts on his balaclava and draws his. He looks sinister in the darkness, like an executioner, and it's disconcerting no longer to be able to see his face.

We make our way along the path, with me leading, until we come to the edge of a paved patio bordered on three sides by sweet-smelling lavender plants. There's a wrought-iron table and six matching chairs in the centre of it. Two of the chairs are at an angle, and on the table there are two half-full wine glasses and an open bottle of white in a cooler, as well as a jug of water with lemon slices bobbing in it. Clearly, Cosick is not expecting visitors, but then why would he be? He's got his briefcase back. He may have had a brothel burned down in the process, but I don't suppose he cares too much about that. It doesn't look like he's short of a few bob. And as for losing a couple of men . . . I'm sure they're not going to be too difficult to replace.

A pair of French windows leads into the house. They are slightly ajar, and the room beyond them is dark. We creep across the flagstones and I open them further, stepping inside. I'm in a spacious drawing room with polished teak flooring and what look in the gloom like expensive paintings on the walls. The door at the end of the room is open, and I can hear music. It's not loud, but I recognize it as the classic 1980s anthem 'The Power of Love' by Huey Lewis and the News. I've always liked this song. It reminds me of when I was a kid in the summer of 1985 when Live Aid and bad haircuts ruled the day. When the song ends, it is followed by 'Heart and Soul', another Huey Lewis number from later on that year, which I always thought was underrated. Eddie Cosick is obviously a fan. He's listening to their greatest hits.

I turn round, and Lucas nods to let me know that everything's OK. Then I start forward again, the gun raised in front of me.

We slip into a windowless entrance hall with a high vaulted ceiling dominated by a crystal chandelier. The hall is empty and dark. To my left, a wide, richly carpeted staircase with banisters on either side runs up to the next floor. Huey's deep, macho warbling is coming from up there, and it's where the only light in the house is on. Directly ahead of me the front door is closed, as are all the doors off the entrance hall. There is no sound nor sign of activity coming from beyond them.

'Looks like whoever was here might have left in a hurry,' Lucas whispers, his eyes shining like sapphires behind the mask.

'Why would they leave?'

'Shit, Tyler, I don't know.' He hisses these last words, but his voice sounds artificially loud in the stillness of the hallway.

Slowly, I start up the staircase, my legs feeling heavy. The Browning's stretched out in front of me, but if this is a trap and someone appears from nowhere, gun blazing, it's going to be next to useless. Feeling increasingly tense, I glance round at Lucas. He's following three steps behind, but like me, he's looking backwards to check that the ground floor remains clear – acting point, like he used to do in Belfast and Crossmaglen when we were out on patrol.

Above me, a long balcony stretches the length of the floor. There are three doors visible, and unlike the ones downstairs, they are all open. It's from the middle one that the light and music are emanating, the light casting an all too faint glow. My grip on the gun tightens, and I put a little more pressure on the trigger. It's an utterly reflexive move, based on years of experience as a combat soldier. I shift the barrel in a low arc, watching for any movement.

A stair creaks; a long, low whine.

I keep going, my attention drawn to something on the carpet at the top of the staircase, partially obscured by the angle I'm viewing it from.

It's an unfashionable cream and tan brogue, the toe end sticking through a gap in the balcony's banister, and it's attached to a leg.

I clench my teeth. There can't be two people known to Eddie Cosick with this kind of bad taste, so it has to be the shoe that nearly kicked my face in earlier this evening, the one that belongs to Marco.

My heart is beating loud in my chest. I remember Sellman and his friends feigning death this morning to catch Ferrie and me off guard.

If this is an ambush, I'm dead. No question.

As the staircase swings round ninety degrees, I see more of Marco, still wearing that same dark suit, sprawled out on the carpet directly in front of me. He's lying on his front, one arm dangling over the top stair, his head and shoulders hidden by the retaining wall at the end of the balcony. Behind me, I hear Lucas curse as he too catches sight of the body.

I reach the final step and stop only inches from Marco. I count to three in my head, listening for a sound that may indicate that someone is just out of sight, waiting to put a bullet in me.

This is the problem with house clearances. There are always so many ambush points.

As I wait, my eyes move in the opposite direction, which is

when I catch sight of the guy who was with Marco in the café in King's Cross this afternoon – the shifty little bastard with the Mac 10. He's lying on his back, his head and shoulders propped up against the doorframe of one of the unlit rooms. He's got the very same Mac 10 in his left hand now, and he's staring at me.

At least it looks like he's staring; in reality, he isn't actually seeing anything. A deep, curved gash like a grinning mouth crosses his throat from ear to ear, from which a curtain of blood has cascaded down onto his suit, drenching it. There are even flecks on the pale hand that still clutches the weapon he never got a chance to use.

'Heart and Soul' finishes playing on the stereo, and I know I will never be able to listen to that song again because I will always associate it with the ice-cold cloud of fear that's creeping up my spine.

The CD ends, and silence envelops everything.

As I step over Marco's body and his head and shoulders became visible, I see that he also managed to pull his gun and that it lies a few inches clear of one of his outstretched arms. It doesn't take a detective to work out that he died the same way as his friend. Although his face is pushed into the carpet, a large pool of blood has formed round his neck, and I can see each ragged edge of the wound he's suffered.

I swing my gun round, looking up and down the empty hall. I'm reminded again of Ferrie's grim story this morning concerning the deaths of my two former comrades, Maxwell and Spann. Two rigorously trained soldiers who'd been taken out without a chance to fire their weapons, their throats cut, just like this.

'It's the same guy who killed Snowy,' says Lucas, who has now reached the top of the stairs.

He's right. So, the killer Ferrie described as the Vampire isn't dead, after all.

I don't say anything. The room with the light on is beckoning me like a beacon, and I walk towards the half-open door, moving with slow, silent steps.

'Careful, Tyler,' Lucas whispers, and I turn and face him. He hasn't moved, and in his dark clothing and balaclava, he's almost invisible in the gloom. 'These guys haven't been dead long. Someone could still be here.'

It's a fact I'm brutally aware of. I listen for anything out of place before pushing the door fully open with one hand and lifting my unloaded gun with the other.

Slowly, ever so slowly, I look inside.

He's been strapped with masking tape to a chair facing the door, his head slumped forward so that I can't pick out his features. The chair belongs to a dressing table covered in bottles of perfume and other feminine accoutrements, all of which appear to be untouched. There are no signs of a struggle. He's dressed in pale linen trousers and a peach-coloured, short-sleeved shirt that's heavily bloodstained. On his feet are the kind of expensive tasselled loafers so beloved of certain middle-aged men who always seem to wear them without socks, as this man is doing. He has thick-set, hairy arms, a fat belly, and a large, completely bald head. Straight away, I know this is Eddie Cosick. And there is little doubt that he too is dead.

I'm too late again. It seems that wherever I turn, I run into brick walls. Cosick is the end of the trail for me. I have nowhere else to go.

I step inside and see that this is the master bedroom, a huge room done out tastefully in various pastel shades. A pine-coloured stereo unit sitting on top of an antique chest of drawers was the source of Huey Lewis's greatest hits.

I stop in front of the body and lift the head up by the hair. The shock hits me hard. Someone has really gone to town on Eddie Cosick. The top half of his right ear is missing where it's been sliced away – and the hair surrounding it is sticky with congealing blood. But this pales into insignificance when compared to the sight of his right eyeball, still attached to a thick thread of muscle tissue, which hangs down bulbous and glassy over his cheek. I'm reminded of my own situation in the brothel only a few hours earlier, and know full well that this could have been me.

But it's not that which is keeping me frozen to the spot as I stare down at the ravaged face. It's the fact that I recognize him.

It's been a long time, and in the intervening period he's lost all his hair and added a fair amount of weight, but even after what's been done to his face, there's no mistake. This is the man I used to know as Colonel Stanic back in Bosnia, a commander of the local Serb militia based near us in the east of the country. I only ever came face to face with him twice, while accompanying our senior officers to meetings with him and his people, and we never spoke. Occasionally I saw him pass in a convoy of open-top jeeps while I was out on patrol, and I remember that even though his forces were meant to be hostile to our presence, he had this habit of standing up in his vehicle and saluting us, as if he had to prove that he was a proper soldier.

His presence here is no coincidence, I'm sure of that. Yet I still don't know what it's got to do with me. I was just one of several hundred troops who operated in his little fiefdom many years ago. He wouldn't remember me from Adam.

It looks like methodical work, so whoever was torturing him wanted information, and was prepared to take him apart step by step in the pursuit of answers. There's a deep cut about three quarters of an inch long just beneath his left eye, where it appears his torturer was about to make an effort to gouge out this one too. Finger-like tears of blood have run down from the wound and stained his cheek. I wonder if this is about the briefcase. Was someone trying to get him to reveal its location? Incredibly, the evidence suggests he was holding out even after they'd taken out his eye.

I let go of his head and take a step back, focusing my attention on the peach-coloured shirt. A long, thin blood trail runs down its side from a darker spot further up. Cause of death is a single stab wound to the heart. Blood is still bubbling from the spot, which means that the fatal blow was delivered recently. Very recently.

I can hear movement behind me. Lucas is coming into the room.

And in that one split second everything comes together and I realize that I've been set up again. Whoever killed these three men was expecting me to come here. And only two people in the world could possibly have known I was coming. One was Alannah. The other was Lucas.

But Alannah didn't know I had Eddie Cosick's address.

Which leaves my best friend. The man who's life I saved. Who served with me in Bosnia, and who also came into contact with the man who changed his name to Eddie Cosick. Who knows all about the scars on my back. Who seems to have plenty of money for a lowly PI dealing with divorce cases and the occasional missing person. Who wasn't expecting my visit this afternoon. Who had no choice but to pretend to help me when I turned up out of the blue, but who has in fact provided me with very little that I can usefully use. I knew about Iain Ferrie anyway, and it was only a matter of time before I got his full name. And the finger . . . The finger could so easily have been a plant to throw me off the scent.

I feel an ominous sense of dread as I realize that Lucas has now supplied me with a gun containing no ammunition, while his is almost certainly loaded.

There's movement behind my back and I swing round fast as a fresh injection of adrenalin courses through me.

Lucas is standing in the doorway, his Walther PPK pointed straight at me.

33

He stares at me for what feels like an eternity, then his gun arm wobbles and the PPK drops to the floor, hitting the thick carpet with barely a noise. His mouth opens, but only blood comes out, a thick rivulet that runs down his chin. He stumbles, and I see that he's clutching his side with one hand, and that his shirt's wet.

'Oh Jesus.'

He bangs into the wall, bounces off it, and falls to his knees. Horrified, I watch as my friend of close to twenty years rolls over onto his side and begins to convulse. His right foot lashes out like a whip and hits the door with a bang.

This is the moment the spell's broken and the realization finally hits me that the Vampire is here right now, possibly only feet away. He has a knife, I have an unloaded gun. He's extremely proficient with his weapon, mine is useful only as a blunt instrument.

But I'm not going to stand here waiting to die.

Turning the Browning round in my hand so that I can use it as a bludgeon, I run forward, jumping over Lucas, and do a diving roll onto the balcony, sliding along the carpet on my back, weapon held ready to throw, until the banister stops my momentum.

There's no-one here. Not in front or behind. The balcony's empty.

I remember Ferrie's words. *He's invisible, like something out of a nightmare.*

I jump up, trying to ignore the sight of Lucas's twitching, and kick open the adjacent door. I count to two and do another rolling dive inside, hurtling along the carpet before jumping up again, the gun held in my right hand like a tomahawk. I know I'm taking a huge risk, but rage and frustration drive me on. This is my last chance to confront the bastard who's eluded me all day.

The room, though, is dark and empty. An unmade bed faces an open bay window that lets in the faint sounds of normality from the outside world: the low hum of traffic; the sound of a piano playing in the jazz concert in the park. Such a huge contrast to the nightmarish charnelhouse I'm in now.

I retrace my steps, coming back out onto the balcony. Lucas is barely moving. I run over to the door on the other side of the room to where Eddie Cosick still sits. The killer must have been behind one of these two doors. There is no other way he would have been able to ambush Lucas, not in the few seconds he had. Lucas was good, too. A bit out of practice, but still not the kind of guy to have been surprised easily.

I kick open the door. Another darkened room, the window open at the far end.

Then I stop dead. Something is playing a tune in my pocket. It's not the phone Lucas gave me earlier; that's now on vibrate. I suddenly realize that I'm still carrying the mobile my black-mailer gave me, and I haven't turned the damn thing off. I rummage around in my front right pocket, pull out the phone, and the tinny noise of the 'Funeral March' fills the silence. The screen says 'Anonymous Call'. I almost don't answer, but in the end my curiosity's too great.

'Yeah?' I say, my eyes darting round the emptiness of the room.

'You're looking in the wrong place,' states the robotic voice. The tone is calm and mocking.

I stride back onto the balcony. 'Where the fuck are you?'

'Somewhere you're never going to find me. Give up, Tyler. I've got the briefcase. It's over.'

Anger surges through me as I think about what this bastard's done.

'I'm going to get you for this.'

'No,' says the voice, with complete confidence, 'you're not. Goodbye, Tyler.'

'Who are you?' I shout as my frustration finally boils over. 'Who the fuck are you?'

But the connection's broken. I'm venting my rage at nothing.

Slowly, still shocked, I replace the phone in my pocket, knowing that, possibly for the first time in my life, I am completely out of my league. Then I remember Lucas.

The gun's no use to me – not that it ever was – and I throw it down on the carpet and run back to where he fell. He's on his back now. Choking noises come from deep within his throat, and I can see that his blood is everywhere.

'You're going to be all right, mate,' I whisper, turning him onto his side.

He coughs weakly. I put my hand in his mouth to clear the airway, and pull out a lump of thick red drool. He shivers, and his eyes roll back in his head.

'Come on, Lucas,' I hiss, feeling for a pulse, 'don't die on me.'

It takes me a couple of seconds to locate one, and when I do, it's faint and very slow. His blood pressure is falling and his heart is beginning to shut down. My hand moves across to the spot where the knife was shoved into him. The blade went between two of the upper ribs and has almost certainly pierced the heart. He's dying. My friend, Lucas, is dying.

I shove my fingers into the wound to try to stem the flow of the blood, and talk in his ear. But I know it's all over, and I feel sick in the knowledge that I'm the one who dragged him into this. Worse still, in those final moments I doubted his motives, believing him to be part of the conspiracy that's been targeting me.

I know I have to do something. On the battlefield, a soldier is expected to do everything he can to evacuate a wounded comrade, even if his injuries are such that it looks like he may not make it. I'm in no position to administer first aid, so if there is a chance of saving Lucas, I have to call an ambulance. I owe it to him. But I can't stay here. Not in a house full of corpses; not after everything else that's happened today. Now more than ever, I need to find the bastard behind this.

Lucas coughs again. More blood runs from the corner of his mouth and drips onto the carpet. He has only minutes to live, maybe not even that. I remove my fingers from the wound and grab a pillow from the double bed. I pull off the cover and push the material into the wound, trying to block the flow of blood. It's basic, but it'll have to do. I reach into my pocket for one of the mobiles, then realize that it's not a good idea to give the police something to trace. I recall seeing a telephone handset on a table in the entrance hall near the front door, so I get to my feet, run downstairs, and race over to it, dialling 999.

When it's picked up at the other end, I shout 'Ambulance!', trying to disguise my voice, knowing that they record all incoming calls. I'm immediately reconnected, and I shout it again, giving Cosick's address and stating that a man's been severely injured. The female operator starts to ask me about the injuries, so I lay the handset down on the table, knowing I've done enough to get them to send someone here urgently.

I can hear her saying 'Hello? Hello?' repeatedly as I take another look up at the balcony where Lucas lies bleeding. I don't want to leave him, I really don't, because I know he wouldn't leave me. Whatever it cost him.

So, knowing I'm being a total fool, I run back up the stairs and across the balcony to where he lies. But as I lean down, I can see that his sapphire-blue eyes are wide open and he's no longer breathing. It's too late. My friend is dead, and I don't even have time to mourn him.

'I'm sorry, mate,' I whisper. 'I really am.'

I touch his forehead, then slowly and very carefully I close his eyes, unable to meet their still, dead gaze.

I can't believe he's gone. This morning I lost my lover. Now I've lost my best friend. I am utterly alone in the world, standing in a silent house of corpses. Yet I know that if I've got any hope of avenging them, I have to move.

I wrench myself away from Lucas and, ignoring the aching in my legs, run down the stairs a second time, then through the house and onto the patio with its empty table and half-full bottle of wine. I spot a wheelbarrow next to a flower bed a few yards further up the garden path, and I use it as a springboard to jump to the top of the wall. Hauling myself up and over, I land on the pavement and walk swiftly away, keeping in the shadows of the cypress trees, and trying to look as natural and inconspicuous as possible.

I've just left a slaughterhouse. In minutes, this place is going to be crawling with cops. They'll be hunting for witnesses, anyone who's seen anything or anyone suspicious, and I don't want them to remember me.

I steal a look behind me. The street's empty. Everything's quiet.

Too quiet. Even the sound of jazz from the park seems to have faded away.

I hear something. The scrape of a shoe on concrete. It comes from the other side of the road, and it stops as quickly as it began.

I stop too, tensing, ready to run.

There's movement coming from behind the cars opposite me, figures appearing like silent wraiths.

And then suddenly the whole street explodes into life. Car headlights come on; men in caps appear from every direction; there are shouts from a dozen different voices to my left and right, from the cars that are disgorging men in caps with big guns, even from among the cypress trees. They're all shouting the same thing: 'Armed police! Put your hands in the air!'

I count six men approaching me in a tight semi-circle, all of them in two-handed shooting poses. Two hold MP5 carbines, the others have pistols, and I know that these guys haven't just turned up. They've been here a while. They were waiting for me to come out.

As other men move in on me from either side, still barking terse orders, and cuff my hands behind my back, I think again that only two people knew I was coming here tonight. Lucas is dead. I smelled his blood. I felt the terrible knife wound he'd suffered.

Which leaves Alannah.

34

It's 10.05 p.m. and I'm in a holding cell at Paddington Green, the most secure police station in London, and probably the whole of the UK. It's where they bring terrorist suspects for questioning, safe in the knowledge that there's going to be no dramatic rescue attempt by their comrades in Al Qaeda. You don't get out of here unless they let you, and even if I had the energy, I wouldn't attempt it. I've been in close proximity to more violent death today than at any time since the killing fields of Sierra Leone, and it's going to take a Byzantine effort of persuasion to prove to the police that I'm a victim in all this as well.

I'm lying on the bunk staring at the ceiling. It's hot in here, and even though the cell itself is modern and clean, there's still an underlying smell of stale sweat. The sweater I was wearing has been taken away for tests, and I'm in a T-shirt they've given me which is wet and clammy and sticking to my back. They've also removed my belt, even the laces from my Timberlands. I'm left here feeling like the low-life criminal they think I am.

I think of the people I care about who've had their lives snuffed out so horrifically today – Leah, Snowy, Lucas . . . The brutal yet straightforward truth is that they died because of their relationship with me. I am the target in all this. All three of them were simply collateral damage, killed because they were in the way or, like Leah, were expendable.

But why have I been targeted? It's the one question that keeps cropping up. Slowly but surely, I'm beginning to think it must be something to do with my past, something that happened in my army days. The presence in London of Eddie Cosick, the man I used to know as Colonel Stanic, and the fact that he seems to be the man Iain Ferrie, a former colleague, was blackmailing, makes it too much of a coincidence to be otherwise. The problem is, this still doesn't help me because I didn't really know either man, and therefore have no idea why they would have chosen to involve me in their business deal.

I wonder about Alannah. She claimed to be a Serbian police-woman looking for her sister. She even showed me a photograph of her, and seemed genuinely concerned. Yet it looks certain that she betrayed me to the police, first at her house, then at Cosick's place. They can't have been responding to my 999 call. It was too fast. I know Lucas didn't call them, and I didn't. That only leaves her. She must have been there. Watching the place. Working with someone to set me up.

A thought strikes me then. There is still a main player out there, someone else involved in this. This person wanted the briefcase, and it looks like he now has it. So maybe it was him, not Cosick, who was being blackmailed. For some reason he wanted Cosick dead, but, more importantly, he wants to keep me alive. And there can only be one reason for that: so that I carry the can for everything that's happened today.

Alannah must be working for the main player. It's why she rescued me from the brothel. It's why she tried to get me to go to Cosick's place, knowing that the police would arrest me there. It's why, when I didn't bite, she called them to her house.

According to Ferrie, the person he was blackmailing hired a mysterious contract killer known as the Vampire to secure the briefcase. This Vampire must have been at the brothel today, and Marco and Mac 10 man must have delivered the briefcase to him there. He must then have discovered the tracking device, and guessed that someone had followed and was probably close by. In a remarkable show of brazenness, he'd then tracked Snowy down, and finished him off in his customary fashion.

But then, when I spoke to Alannah, she told me she'd not seen any strangers at the brothel. She might easily have been lying, but what if she wasn't?

I try to recall what both Ferrie and Lucas said about the Maxwell and Spann murders. The Vampire got past the security cameras and caught three men, including two highly trained bodyguards, completely off guard. Just like Cosick and his men were caught off guard tonight. Ferrie spoke about him with awe. A shadowy killer who leaves no trail, as if he's invisible.

But maybe everyone's looking at this the wrong way. What if the Vampire managed to get close to his victims because there was something about him that made them let their guard down, that made them think he wasn't dangerous, that made detectives scouring any CCTV footage discount him out of hand? In other words, what if he wasn't a 'he' at all? What if 'he' was a 'she'? An attractive young woman with blonde hair and golden skin, who looked the very antithesis of everyone's idea of a contract killer?

So, no, Alannah wasn't lying about not seeing the Vampire back at the brothel.

She wasn't lying because *she* is the Vampire.

35

The more I think about it, the more I'm convinced I'm right about Alannah. But that leaves me no further forward. I still have a mountain to climb in terms of convincing the police of my innocence, and, if anything, it's now got a little bit higher.

There are, however, two factors running in my favour. Firstly, I am actually innocent, and I hope that that's going to count for something. Secondly, and possibly more importantly, I have secured extremely good legal representation in the form of my ex-wife, Adine.

I first met Adine at something most law-abiding citizens won't ever have come across. It's called an acquittal party, which is exactly what it says it is. It was four years back. A guy from our old unit named Harry Foxley had just been found not guilty of GBH for his part in a fight that had left two men seriously injured, one of them with a fractured skull.

To be fair, it wasn't Harry's fault. He was walking home from a friend's house late one night when a gang of about half a dozen drunken teenagers decided to pick a fight with him. Harry's only a little guy, barely five seven, and I suppose in the dim light, and from their position across the road, he must have made a tempting target. They started throwing abuse at him, and when he ignored them and carried on walking, they took this as a sign of cowardice. Hyped up with bravado and booze, they crossed the road and began following him, still keeping up the steady stream of abuse.

It was a very bad move. Some of the hardest people I've ever met have been little guys, and Harry's no exception. He has the lean, wiry build of a champion flyweight, and there isn't an ounce of fat or spare flesh on him. At least there wasn't then. Things may have changed, although somehow I doubt it. He smoked like a chimney and drank like a fish but possessed reserves of stamina that would put most men to shame. He was the battalion's arm wrestling champion three years running, beating men twice his size, and although he wasn't the kind of man to look for trouble, he wasn't the sort to shirk it either. So when his tormentors had worked themselves up sufficiently to launch an attack, they got one hell of a lot more than they bargained for.

Harry knocked the leader out with a single left hook, then went charging into the others, fists flying, spreading immediate panic among their number as they realized belatedly that this was going to be no walkover. One made the mistake of pulling a knife. Harry broke his wrist, then his jaw, before slamming him head-first into a brick wall. The others ran for it.

Unfortunately, the first guy he'd punched cracked his skull as he hit the pavement and spent the next six weeks in a coma, and it was alleged by one of the gang that Harry had kicked him while he lay on the ground unconscious, which is something I know he wouldn't have done.

The police, though, took a different view. Harry was one of the five men from our unit court-martialled and imprisoned for their part in the revenge attack at the pub in Crossmaglen, and he'd only just come off parole, so their decision to charge him with two counts of GBH may well have been coloured by what they perceived as his history of violent behaviour.

I didn't attend the trial, but it lasted more than a week, and I know from what I read and heard that the prosecution lawyers attempted a serious character assassination on Harry, dredging up the worst aspects of his past to bolster their arguments. However, both they and the police should have realized that in these violent days in which we live, juries tend to sympathize with individuals who are the victims of unprovoked gang attacks, and feel that they should have the right to fight back, even if the damage they inflict is pretty serious. So it was no real surprise to anyone with an ounce of common sense that Harry was acquitted on both charges.

The story, then, had a happy ending, and a party was held in a pub in the West End to celebrate. I was on leave at the time and was back in London. I can't remember now who called to tell me about it, but I ended up going anyway. I hadn't seen the guys for a long time so I thought it would be nice to catch up.

When I got there, the place was packed. Harry was holding court to a crowd at the bar where he was giving a blow-by-blow account of the events of the fateful night and looking none the worse for his ordeal. There were quite a few faces from the past, including, as I recall, Maxwell and Spann, but it was a dark-haired woman about my age, wearing a two-piece business suit and thick-rimmed black glasses, who caught my attention. She was slim and very pale-skinned, with a look you might call severely pretty, like one of those sexy secretaries who can suddenly transform themselves into a completely different woman with a quick flick of the hair and a dumping of the specs. She was standing on the periphery, nursing a glass of white wine in both hands, and looking out of place amid the revelry as she spoke with Maxwell, who'd never been one of the world's great conversationalists. I joined them and introduced myself, and pretty soon Maxwell melted away and it was just her and me.

It turned out that Adine King was Harry's solicitor. She'd been involved in his case from the start and had been with him during all the initial police interviews. We got talking, I turned on the charm, and I ended up taking her to dinner that very night at an Italian restaurant in Soho.

I don't know if you'd ever have called it a match made in heaven. We got on well enough, but we were hardly well suited. She was a well-educated member of the legal profession with a well-to-do stockbroker for a father (her mother had died when she was young) and a sister who was high up in some government department. I was still a career soldier – and not exactly a high-ranking one either – on a soldier's wage. But somehow the relationship grew. I think that at the time we were both looking for someone to settle down with. She was thirty-two and about a year earlier had come out of a long-term relationship with a City lawyer who was meant to have been 'the one', but hadn't been. Her job didn't exactly throw up many potential suitors, and her biological clock was ticking. She wanted to start a family, and I guess I was in the right place at the right time. I also liked the idea of the pitter-patter of tiny feet running around the place. Why not? I come from a big family, I didn't want to grow old alone, and I didn't meet that many eligible women in my job either.

So we got engaged. Her old man was mortified. Her sister, who was married to a director of some hotshot company dealing with internet security, was equally gobsmacked, and neither of them was backwards in telling her so. But of course this just served to spur Adine on. Like a lot of people, she didn't like being told what to do, or who she should be seeing, and we just grew closer.

She wanted me to move in to her flashy apartment in Muswell Hill, and she also wanted me to leave the army.

The thing was, at the time I was in love. I'd been a soldier for fifteen years and I'd come into some money too, the result of an aunt dying, so I figured now was the time to make a break. I'd always been interested in cars, so I put all my money into buying a BMW franchise, supplemented by some cash from the bank and even Adine's reluctant (although loaded) father.

And the rest should have been history, but life, of course, never works that simply. I did leave the army and I did move in with her, and at first things went well, but it wasn't long before they began to go downhill. We were both working long hours – me learning how to run a business from scratch (something the army gives you no preparation for), she trying to establish herself in her profession. We were trying for a baby as well, but that wasn't proving very successful either.

The truth is, by the time we got married – on one of those two-week deals in Barbados, with only a few close family present – our best days were already behind us. I was hoping the honeymoon might turn things round and signal some sort of improvement. After all, it's difficult to have too much of a bad time when the sun's shining and the palm trees are shimmering in a gentle tropical breeze. But somehow we managed it, spending most of the trip arguing. I can't even remember what it was we argued about. It was just niggling little disagreements, the kind couples have when each partner realizes that he or she's with the wrong person.

We limped along for another six months, but the faultlines in our relationship – work pressures and the failure to conceive – kept growing, and one day, after yet another explosive argument that had come out of nowhere and drained both of us, she asked me, very calmly but very firmly, to leave.

For some reason, even then her request came as a shock. You see, a small part of me still hoped that somehow we could make it work, that the stresses would fade with time, that she'd fall pregnant and everything would be OK again.

In the end, when it came to it, I didn't want to go, and I asked her to reconsider. But Adine had made up her mind. 'I don't love you any more,' she said quietly. She'd never said that before, even during our worst arguments, and I knew from the resigned tone in her voice that she meant it.

And that was that. Full of regret for what might have been, and wondering if there was anything I could have done differently, I packed my bags and left the flat that afternoon. I never went back.

We kept in touch, though, and through our break-up and subsequent divorce our relationship remained amicable. I think that, in the long run, parting was the right choice for both of us, because our bond just wasn't strong enough, but occasionally I do regret the fact that in the interim Adine hasn't had the family she wanted so much, and that I haven't either.

I haven't seen her for close to six months, but as soon as I was booked in here, I knew who I was going to put my one phone call through to. She's always been a damn good lawyer, and that's exactly what I need. Well, that's not quite right. I need a miracle, but in the absence of one, she'll have to do.

The cell door's unlocked, and I'm told by a bored-looking uniformed cop with dyed black hair that my brief's arrived. I get up from the bunk and follow the cop and his equally bored-looking colleague through a set of featureless and largely empty corridors that remind me of a hospital. I guess if I worked in surroundings like this, I wouldn't be full of the joys of spring either.

Surprisingly, there doesn't seem to be much in the way of

security round here, but then there doesn't really need to be. I'm in the holding area beneath the main part of the station, and there's no way out except through a series of electronically operated doors that eventually take you into the station proper, and straight into the arms of God knows how many other cops. Once you're down here, there really is no way out.

We reach a door, and the cop with the dyed hair knocks twice, opening it at the same time. 'Your client,' he announces curtly, then moves aside to let me through.

Adine stands up from behind a table as the door closes behind me. She's wearing a black cocktail dress with a very light cashmere cardigan of the same colour over it. Her hair's loose and longer than the last time I saw her, reaching down to her shoulders, and she's got her contacts in rather than her glasses, a look that shows off the contrast between her jet-black eyebrows and the pale translucent blue of her eyes. In short, she looks stunning. I find it difficult not to fall in love with her all over again.

'Well, it looks like you've really done it this time, Tyler,' she says with a weary sigh that seems to last for several seconds, immediately shattering the illusion.

'Hello, Adine. Nice to see you again too.'

'I had to leave a meal in the Ivy for this, you know.' She gestures towards the room's only other chair. 'I'm only doing this because I'd feel guilty if I didn't help.'

I sit down, noticing that she's wearing scarlet varnish on her fingernails. It must have been a hot date. She never wore it for me. Amazingly, even after everything else, I feel the vague stirrings of jealousy.

'You're in a lot of trouble,' she states with numbing honesty.

'I know.'

'You'd better tell me what happened.'

So I do, for the third time today, only this time I start from the beginning and I don't leave anything out, except for my theory that Alannah is the Vampire, because, for all that I'm convinced by it, that's all it is, a theory, with nothing to back it up. I don't need to muddy the waters any more than they've been muddied already.

Adine listens in silence, making notes on a pad in front of her, and when I finish she sighs again and looks at me with a combination of pity and incredulity. 'And that's the absolute truth?'

I nod. 'Yeah, it is.'

There's a long pause. I don't know what else to say. I've laid my situation on the line, and hearing the details out loud doesn't make me feel any more optimistic that I'm going to extricate myself from the pit I'm in. By the look on Adine's face, she shares this view. After a long time, during which she makes further notes, she finally speaks.

'It's a particularly lurid story,' she says, her voice laced with tacit disapproval.

'It's not good,' I admit.

'And I'm sorry about Lucas. I always liked him.' She speaks the words in a matter-of-fact manner, but that's always been her way, and I know she does feel sorry about it.

'It's my fault,' I say. 'If I hadn't turned up at his door today, then he and Snowy would still be alive.'

'But you did, and it's done now. Don't beat yourself up about it.'

No-one could ever call Adine sentimental. But she's also right. I've got to think about myself. There'll be time for grieving later.

'And you can't tell the police what you've just told me, either.'

'Why not? It's the truth.'

'It may be the truth, but if that's what you tell them, there's no way they'll release you.'

'You always told me that you have to represent a client on the basis of what he or she tells you. That you can't lie on their behalf.'

'Look, Tyler, you've just incriminated yourself in a total of four murders. And that was *before* you turned up at a house full of corpses.'

'Three were self-defence,' I protest, 'and one was an accident. If the guy hadn't struggled . . .'

'While you were holding a gun to his head, remember that.' She sighs. 'The point is, no-one's going to believe that you were totally justified in killing four people. I'm not asking you to lie, it's just important we minimize the details we give the police. Now, cast your mind back to this morning. When you were chased by the police from the house where you picked up the briefcase, did any of them get a good look at you?'

I shake my head. 'I don't think so. I kept my head down and it all happened very quickly. I also wore gloves while I was in the house, so I don't think my fingerprints'll be there.'

'Good. Is there anything that might connect the events there to the rest of the events today?'

'Not as far as I know.'

'Right, let's not mention it, then.'

'Are you sure?'

'Listen, Tyler, if you want me to represent you, you're going to have to do what I say. Understand?'

'OK.'

'Can you remember anything at all about last night?'

I shake my head. It remains as blank as ever.

'We're going to have to get you tested for drugs. I want to know what you were dosed with.'

'Whatever it was, it was strong.'

'If we get bail, which I have to say at the moment I doubt in the extreme, I'm going to arrange for you to undergo hypnosis. It's important that we find out anything that might give us a clue as to who was behind this.'

'I know.'

'And you've got absolutely no idea who it might be?'

'I've thought about it all day, but I still don't know.'

'Might it be something to do with your past?'

'That's what I've been thinking. That it's got something to do with my army days.'

'Is there anything that happened that might have pissed someone off?'

'That's the problem. I can't think of anything specific. I served in plenty of war zones but I was just one of many soldiers. There's no reason why anyone would have picked me out for revenge. And why wait this long? I left the army getting close to four years ago; these days I'm just a middle-of-the-road car salesman. I'm not interesting enough to upset anyone that much.'

Adine sighs. 'Unless we find out who might have a reason for setting you up, the attention of the police is always going to keep coming back to you.'

'But there's no motive for me killing any of these people.'

'That's as may be, but be under no illusions, Tyler. The police'll be under huge pressure to get convictions for these killings. The Met have one of the lowest clear-up rates for murder in the country. They're not going to want it to go any lower, and with you, they've at least got a decent suspect. You were arrested leaving a house where four people were murdered. The fact that you made the nine-nine-nine call from within the property places you there at about the time of the murders.'

'But the fact that I made that call should count in my favour,' I say hopefully.

'Get real, Tyler. That's no defence.' She underlines something in her notes, her eyebrows furrowed in concentration, then puts the pen down and gives me a stern look. 'No, what we've got to do is make you look like an innocent in all this, which is not going to be easy. The important thing is that you don't mention anything about the killings this morning at the house where you picked up the briefcase, or the dead girl you woke up next to this morning. I'm hoping that the person who set you up for her murder has kept his side of the bargain and given you all the evidence, rather than keep anything back to give to the police.'

'The problem is, it looks as though he's trying to get me to take the rap for everything, so why wouldn't he have sent another copy of the DVD to the police?'

'Because,' she says, 'if someone hands in that DVD anonymously and then phones to say that the killer in the film is you, it might have the opposite effect to what's intended. In other words, it might make the police suspect that you are being set up. If I were him, I'd think it was far easier just to leave things as they are. I mean, your situation is hardly a positive one.'

I concede her point. 'All right, then. What *do* I tell them?'

'As little as possible. The fact that Lucas has already talked to the police about his colleague's murder means you're going to have to admit to knowing about that. But we don't necessarily have to give the same version of events.'

I'm getting an uneasy feeling now. 'What do you mean?'

'You told me that Lucas told the detectives investigating his colleague's—'

'Snowy. His name's Snowy.'

'All right, Snowy.' She seems to find it difficult to say the name. 'You said that Lucas told the detectives that you approached him this afternoon to ask him to put a track on a briefcase, and that Snowy was the person who actually tracked it, but the two of you lost contact with him.' She pauses for a moment to consult her notes – not, I suspect, that she needs them. Adine's always had a photographic memory. 'You and Lucas parted company, and then the next thing Lucas knew the police were on the line telling him that his colleague was dead.'

'That's about right.'

'So we simply turn it around. You didn't approach Lucas about the case, he approached you. He said he was putting a track on the case and he might need your help dealing with the people who were going to be receiving it. As he was an old friend of yours from the army, you reluctantly said yes.'

'You *are* asking me to lie.'

'No, Tyler,' she says, folding her hands on the desk, 'what I'm trying to do is save you from going to prison for a long time. Now, we either do things my way or you're on your own.'

She pauses, waiting for me to contradict her. I don't, and she takes this as tacit acceptance of her plan.

'You might have been seen by someone near Snowy's body, so I think we should tell the truth here. Having reluctantly said yes, you and Lucas were also tracking the case, and discovered the tracker and Snowy's corpse at the same time. And it was then that you realized you were involved in something far more dangerous than you'd anticipated.' She stops. 'Did anyone see you go into the brothel?'

'No. I got in round the back, and I was wearing different clothes to the ones I was arrested in.'

'What about leaving?'

'There were a lot of people out watching the fire, but I was smoke-blackened, bleeding and all sorts. I doubt if anyone would be able to pick me out in an ID parade.'

'That's good,' she says, nodding slowly. 'When you and Lucas found Snowy, Lucas panicked. So did you. The two of you parted company, with Lucas apologizing for getting you involved.'

I'm beginning to feel sick. After everything that's happened, this feels like the final act of betrayal.

But Adine's on a roll. 'You didn't hear from him again until earlier this evening,' she says, 'when he told you that he intended to go to the house of the man he believed had had Snowy killed, and he wanted your help in case things went wrong. He identified the man as a gangster called Eddie Cosick. You were kept in the dark about what Lucas's involvement with Cosick was, and you tried to dissuade him from going, particularly when he suggested taking guns, but again you felt that you couldn't say no. You bitterly regret the fact that you accompanied him to Mr Cosick's house, but in your defence you say that you insisted the guns you took were for show only, and were unloaded. Are you getting all this?'

I'm having difficulty keeping up with the lengths Adine is willing to go to get me off the hook, but I reply that, yes, I am getting it all.

She reminds me that I have to remember every single word. 'Make one mistake in the story and they'll be on to you immediately. They're trained to pick up any inconsistencies.'

'I know. I was trained in anti-interrogation techniques myself.'

'Good,' she says with a cool smile. 'So, when you turned up, going in through an open door at the rear of the property, you discovered the bodies of three men who Lucas identified as Cosick and his bodyguards. But while you were in the room with Cosick, an unidentified assailant stabbed Lucas and escaped before you could either see or apprehend him. You immediately dialled nine-nine-nine to summon assistance and made strenuous but ultimately unsuccessful efforts to save Lucas. Only when you were sure he was dead did you leave the scene, the way you came in, afraid of being caught with the bodies, and that's when you were apprehended by the police. Which is exactly what happened, isn't it?'

'Yeah,' I sigh, 'that's what happened.'

'Good. Now we've got a plausible story.'

She makes me go through it again twice, and when I finish successfully for the second time she looks satisfied and vaguely pleased with herself.

'I think we might be able to get you out of this,' she says. 'There's still a long way to go, but at least we're on the right track.'

I tell her that's good, remembering that years ago Adine once told me she'd wanted to become a lawyer because she had a keen interest in the pursuit of justice. Those were her exact words: a keen interest in the pursuit of justice. I realize, somewhat belatedly, that she must have been bullshitting.

'OK,' she says, standing up with her notebook, 'I think we're ready to face the music.'

36

Two detectives are doing the questioning, although a camera mounted on the wall suggests that other people are probably watching and listening in. They sit at the opposite end of a formica table to Adine and me. The senior of the two, who introduces himself as DI Mike Bolt of the National Crime Squad, is tall and broad-shouldered with short, neatly cropped hair that's undergoing the transformation from blond to grey. He's a good-looking guy in his late thirties, with a lean, angular face and twinkling blue eyes that look like they don't miss much. He also has a deep S-shaped scar on his chin, and two more on his left cheek, giving him the appearance of a vaguely glamorous soap opera gangster. His colleague, DS Mo Khan, a little Asian guy with a barrel body and a very big head, is about the same age, possibly a year or two older, and from the beginning, his dark, heavily lidded eyes watch me with a constant mild scepticism.

They start off by asking me to tell them in my own words what happened at the Cosick house. I tell them the truth, and they appear to accept it. They then ask me to describe my day, and I'm momentarily caught out. I wasn't at the showroom today, so

I can't say that. I can't tell them anything that can be proved wrong.

Adine buys me breathing space by intervening and asking, with a nicely refined tone of incredulity, what relevance this could possibly have.

'We're just trying to build up a picture,' Bolt answers, smiling affably at Adine, as if butter wouldn't melt in his mouth.

By this time, I've got a story. It's not a very good one, but it'll have to do. Trying to do my own line in affable, I explain that I wasn't feeling too great this morning, so I stayed in bed. I'd recovered by lunchtime, and that was when I got a call from my old army colleague and friend Lucas, saying he needed help. From there, I keep to the story I agreed with Adine, finishing up with me back at Cosick's place. It all sounds quite believable to my ears, and again, both men appear to accept it, although there's still a faint light of scepticism in DS Khan's eyes.

'Did Mr Lukersson tell you what was in the case?' asks Bolt.

'No.'

'You didn't ask?'

'I did. He told me it was best I didn't know.'

'And you accepted that?'

'I didn't like it, but yes, I accepted it. The thing is, Lucas was a very good friend of mine. I trusted him not to get me involved in something that would get me into a lot of trouble.'

The lie comes easily, and I experience a nasty twinge of guilt at the extent of my betrayal. I wish I wasn't doing this.

Bolt nods sympathetically. He looks like he understands, but I'm not fooled for a moment.

'And what was Mr Lukersson's relationship with Eddie Cosick?' he asks.

'He was very vague. I got the feeling that they must have had some kind of business dealing.'

'But Mr Lukersson was a private detective,' says Mo Khan, leaning forward in his seat. 'What kind of business dealing could he have had with a Bosnian gangster?'

'I don't know.'

Bolt looks puzzled. 'And you didn't ask any of these kinds of questions when you discovered the body of Ben Mason, the man you describe as Snowy? When clearly you must have realized that Mr Lukersson was involving you in something that *was* going to get you into a huge amount of trouble?'

'Yes I did, but Lucas was panicking. He said he had to get out of there. I tried to talk to him, but he left in a hurry.'

'How did he leave?'

'In his car.'

'You didn't go with him?'

I know what they're doing because I've told them this already. They want to lull me into a false sense of security, then trip me up. I'm ready for them, though, and once again I answer the question, telling them that I left on foot.

'Which way did you go?' asks Mo.

I give Adine's high-heeled, black leather court shoe a barely perceptible tap under the table – a sign we've agreed to use when I need a couple of seconds to think.

'Why's this relevant, DS Khan?' she asks.

'We're trying to build up a picture, Ms King,' he says, giving the same stock answer as Bolt did earlier. He pronounces the Ms mzzz, then looks at me.

I have to be careful here. It's got to be a route they can't check easily.

'I walked,' I answer, 'up the Kingsland Road. I got a cab near the top and got it to drop me off home.'

'What were you wearing?'

'Sorry?'

'What were you wearing today when you left the scene of Ben Mason's murder?'

'A pair of jeans and a shirt,' I answer casually.

Khan asks me to describe the shirt, and I tell him it was white, which might have been true when I went into the brothel but definitely wasn't by the time I came out.

'And you didn't see Lucas again until when?'

'When he picked me up to go to Eddie Cosick's house.'

'And you still didn't ask him about the contents of the case, or his relationship with Mr Cosick?'

Khan's tone is perfectly reasonable, but I know he's beginning to lay on the pressure. I force myself to remain calm, but it's difficult. I'm exhausted. The anti-interrogation techniques I've been taught don't help because I'm not trying to withhold information. Quite the reverse. I want to appear to be co-operative.

'I asked,' I say, sounding weary, 'but he still wouldn't tell me. He kept saying it was best I didn't know, and he was acting very tense.'

'And you still went with him?'

I nod. 'Yes, I still went with him.'

And so it goes on. A slow, torturous process of answering one set of questions, moving on to answer another set, then going back over something else. It's nothing like the movies or the TV, where the interrogations tend to be fast and dramatic. It's more like a very long and very dull game of chess. The advantage I have is that they don't really have any idea what's going on. The murders of Snowy and Cosick and his crew, and even the brothel fire, don't make any obvious sense, so it's difficult for them to theorize. They can only look at the facts. I was at both murder scenes, but there's nothing to suggest that I was actually responsible for them. There was some blood on the sweater I was wearing when I was arrested, which came from Lucas, but

257

nowhere near enough for me to have tortured Cosick and cut the throats of his two bodyguards. And there's no motive whatsoever for me doing the same to Snowy. So, in the end, what have they actually got?

Not a lot.

But the point is, they know something's wrong.

When they start to go through the events at Cosick's house for something like the fourth time, Adine finally grows weary. 'My client's already answered these questions numerous times, detective inspector, and he's been an extremely co-operative witness, so can we just move on, or better still, release him on bail so that he can go home and get some sleep?'

Bolt smiles patiently, fixing her with piercing eyes. 'As you'll appreciate, Miss King, we just want to make sure we've got everything right. This is a large-scale murder inquiry, and Mr Tyler is the only person who knows what went on who's still alive. It's essential that we cover every possible angle.'

'As far as I can see, that particular angle's been well and truly covered.'

The smile hardens a little, and he turns back to me.

'Now, Mr Tyler, if we can just go back to the Ben Mason murder scene . . .'

I sigh. 'Yes?'

'You saw Mr Lukersson drive away?'

'I've already told you I did.'

'Which direction did he go?'

'On to the Kingsland Road, and he indicated left, which means he went north.'

'Can you remember what time that was?'

I shrug. 'Three o'clockish?'

'But you can't remember for sure?'

'No.'

'You said earlier that Mr Lukersson spoke to Mr Mason on the phone about fifteen minutes before you discovered the body. Is that right?'

Be careful, I tell myself. They're planning something here, I can feel it.

'That's right.'

'And you were with the body for how long?'

'Not long at all. A couple of minutes at most.'

'And then Mr Lukersson left?'

'Yes.'

'OK, so he left about twenty minutes after the phone call. Now, we've recovered the mobile phone we believe Mr Lukersson used to make that call, and the time it was made was 14.33, so it's fair to say he left about 14.53 or thereabouts?'

I can feel Adine tensing beside me – or am I just imagining it?

'I guess that'd be fair,' I answer slowly.

'The reason I ask is because Mr Lukersson's car was spotted by two separate witnesses parked up on the bridge over Kingsland Road less than a hundred metres from where Mr Mason's body was found, at 15.40.'

I don't panic. 'Maybe I've got my timings wrong.'

'Both witnesses also saw Mr Lukersson standing outside his car and then helping a second man into it before driving away.'

My heart starts to hammer, and it's with supreme difficulty that I assume a posture of total innocence.

'What's this got to do with me, officer?'

'That man was wearing the same clothes you said you were wearing.'

'There must be a mistake.'

'So, you're saying you left before the fire started,' says DS Khan quickly.

'Yes.'

Bang. Wrong answer.

And Bolt and Khan know it.

'I'm sorry,' I say before anyone else has a chance to speak, rubbing my eyes at the same time, 'I'm obviously tired. What fire?'

Is it enough? The room goes silent once again.

Bolt touches his ear and turns away from me. I realize then that he's wearing an earpiece, and someone's speaking into it. Someone who's watching the proceedings. Bolt's face tenses in concentration. A deep, furrowed V appears on his brow.

Seizing her chance, Adine demands bail once again, reminding them that I've been an extremely co-operative witness.

Bolt ignores her. 'Interview terminated, 11.27 p.m.,' he states curtly, and he and DS Khan stand up. 'We'll be talking again soon,' he tells me.

37

Adine sighs. We're in the room where I met her earlier. It's close to midnight, and she looks tired. There are dark patches under her eyes, a sharp contrast to her ivory skin, and I'm sure she wishes she'd never answered my earlier phone call. I can't blame her. This isn't how I like spending my Friday nights, either.

'They're going to keep you in for a while yet,' she says.

'On what grounds? I've answered their questions.'

'You have, but unfortunately they don't believe you.' She rubs her neck wearily, and once again I notice her polished fingernails. 'There isn't any hard evidence against you, but there are inconsistencies in your story.'

'Well, it wasn't my story. It was yours.'

'Don't start blaming me, Tyler,' she says icily. 'It's you who's admitted to being in a house with four bodies, and discovering another in a car five miles away, all within the space of six hours. I'm just having to make the best of a very bad deal, and without any preparation either. I'd already done a nine-hour day today before you called.' She glares at me.

'I'm sorry, Adine. I'm just stressed, that's all. And pretty exhausted.'

'OK.' Her expression softens, and I remember briefly how much I once cared for her. 'Whoever's story it is it has weaknesses. They can't believe that you accompanied Lucas to Cosick's house without knowing what his relationship with Cosick was, and without having some idea of the contents of the briefcase. That's not to say that they think you actually committed any of the murders, but they're sure you're holding something back from them.'

'But they can only hold me for so long, right? Forty-eight hours or something?'

'Without charges, yes, but they can apply to a magistrate for an extension on that. And they can also charge you with something else.'

'Like what?'

'Burglary. Possession of an unlicensed firearm.'

'It wasn't loaded.'

'That doesn't matter. The point is that you went to someone's house armed with a handgun, fully prepared to threaten them with violence. That'll be enough to keep you in custody. Potentially for weeks.' She must see the look of abject defeat on my face because she continues quickly, 'I mean, obviously I'll try my best to get them to grant you bail, but it might take time, and it also depends on how they get on with the rest of their enquiries.'

'And whether they find out about my involvement with Leah, or the killings at Ferrie's place this morning.'

She nods slowly. 'Yes, there is the possibility of that putting a spanner in the works.'

Which strikes me as something of an understatement. If they find out my involvement in either of those two incidents, my situation's going to take a dramatic turn for the worse. Not for the first time today, I wonder if I was wrong not to tell the police the whole truth, and whether, by extension, I have been badly advised by the woman sitting opposite me.

There's a knock on the door. Adine stands up, looking puzzled, and goes over to answer it. She speaks briefly to the person on the other side of the door, but I can't hear what he or she's saying. Then she turns to me.

'I'll be back in a few minutes.'

While she's gone, I pace the room like a caged animal. I think about Alannah and her role in this, but I can't even mention her name to the police without further incriminating myself. And if she is this mysterious contract killer, Alannah won't be her real name, and her address in Kilburn will almost certainly throw up no clues. She will have left no trace of her existence. Just as Leah didn't. She will have simply disappeared into thin air, and without Lucas to help me find her, I'll be clutching uselessly at shadows.

Lucas. My old friend. His death has hit me hard, perhaps even harder than Leah's. It's left me with an empty feeling in my gut. I'm depressed and I'm tired. Worse still, I'm alone.

The door opens, and Adine re-enters the room. I try to read the expression on her face. It's not easy, but I get the feeling it's bad news.

She stops in front of me, sighs audibly and says, 'I can't believe it.'

'What?'

'All the time I've known you, Tyler, you've always managed to land on your feet.'

I think about my current predicament. 'I wouldn't go that far.'

'I would,' she says, an uncertain smile spreading across her rouged lips. 'They're releasing you on bail.'

Saturday

38

It's still warm when we walk out of the front entrance of the station, and the sounds of the city feel sharp and clear in my ears after my period of incarceration.

'I don't know how we managed it,' says Adine, and there's an element of disbelief in her voice as well as pride.

'It must be your talents as a lawyer,' I tell her.

'Maybe,' she says, looking at me, 'but I'd watch yourself, Tyler. We need to find out who's behind this, but don't go doing anything stupid like taking the law into your own hands. The important thing for now is just to stay out of trouble.'

I smile. I'm so relieved at leaving custody that I feel light-headed suddenly. 'Don't worry about me, Adine. I'll be on my best behaviour.'

'And don't forget, you have to report back here at nine o'clock Monday morning. It's almost certain that they're going to want to question you again. If that happens, call me and don't say a word until I get here. In the meantime, I'll send you a bill.'

'I don't get it free?' I say, grinning. 'Not even for old times' sake?'

'I'm doing it for old times' sake,' she answers, without smiling, 'but the old times weren't so good that you can avoid paying for my services. I've got a lot better things to do with my life now than spend it bailing out ex-husbands who've got themselves into trouble.' She looks at her watch. 'Well, it's a quarter past twelve, so I don't think there's much point in resurrecting my date. Do you need a lift somewhere?'

'Would you mind driving me home?' The thing I need most is sleep.

Adine's driving an Audi A4 convertible. I ask her what happened to the BMW she received as part of our divorce settlement.

'I fancied a change,' she says as we drive onto the Marylebone Road heading east.

'Removing all traces of me, eh?'

She gives me a sideways look. 'Don't flatter yourself, Tyler. I moved on a long time ago.'

'Thanks,' I say, staring out of the window, caught out by the barbed nature of her words.

'Oh, stop feeling so bloody sorry for yourself,' she snaps. 'You moved on while we were still married. It was like living with a ghost.'

'What the hell's that supposed to mean?'

'You know exactly what it means. Perhaps if you took more notice of what goes on around you, things wouldn't be so bad. The problem with you is you're so damn selfish. You pick people up and you drop them. You fall in love with every girl who walks into your life.'

'That's not true.'

'Yes it is. You fall in love, and then the love just fades because basically you can't handle it. I don't know if it was the army that did it, the fact that you were always moving on from one posting to another, but it turned you into a really, really difficult person to relate to.'

I feel a sense of déjà vu. This argument has blown up out of nowhere, just as they used to when we were married. The lights of the city pass intermittently across her face, giving me glimpses of what I see as a hard, triumphant expression, and I feel a surge of bitterness.

'You weren't exactly easy yourself,' I say, my voice loud in the confines of the car. 'All you've ever cared about is your bloody work. Nothing else.'

Immediately, I regret my words. I know I'm being massively unfair on her, particularly given the way she was there for me tonight, but it's too late.

The car stops at traffic lights, and she turns furiously in her seat. 'You bastard. You're so damn holier than thou, aren't you? Why don't you try looking in the mirror for once? Go on, try it. Because if you like what you see, you'll be the only one who does.' She shakes her head with a potent combination of rage and pity. 'You know how much you always talked about all that camaraderie in the army, about how you made those friendships for life? How you'd do anything for your mates? Well, tell me, Tyler, how many times did you visit your so-called brothers in arms when they were in prison? Even though they were only there because they were trying to avenge what happened to you. How many times, eh? In three, four years? None. That's how fucking many.'

She stops as suddenly as she began, and an oppressive silence falls in the car. I never realized how strongly she felt. It's a real surprise.

Unfortunately, it's not as much of a surprise as the revelation that she knows I never visited any of the five men court-martialled for the pub attack.

You see, I never told her this. In fact, quite the reverse. I lied to her when she asked me about it once, saying I'd visited all of them at least once, and in some cases more than once, and the reason I'd lied was to alleviate the guilt I felt for not having done so.

In all the time we were married, I never kept in touch with any of those five men. The last I saw of Harry Foxley was at his acquittal party. I think, in fact, it was the last time I saw any of them.

So, how the hell does she know?

The lights turn green, and Adine pulls away.

'I didn't tell you I never went to visit those guys,' I say eventually, without looking at her.

There's another long pause.

'I know you didn't,' she says quietly. Her earlier anger's evaporated.

'How do you know, Adine? Who told you I never went to see them?'

'Harry Foxley.'

'But you haven't seen Harry—' I begin, but even before I finish the sentence I know I'm almost certainly wrong.

'I'm sorry, Tyler. I didn't want you to find out this way.'

We may have been separated for more than two years, but it's still a body blow to hear those words. For a moment I even forget all my current woes. Instead, I remember that at one time I had honestly loved Adine, and that the real tragedy was that she didn't think I had. Even now, it's hard to think of someone else with her, particularly someone I once knew.

'Were you seeing him when you were seeing me?' I ask.

She shakes her head. 'No, I would never have done that.'

'So, it was afterwards?'

'Yes. He called me up out of the blue. He said he'd heard that we'd split up and he asked me out for dinner. We went out a couple of times and, you know, one thing led to another.'

'Yeah, I know. And not content with sleeping with my wife, the bastard took the time to badmouth me for not bringing him flowers and chocolate in the glasshouse.'

'I was your ex-wife at the time, and no, it wasn't like that. He wasn't badmouthing you.'

'Wasn't he?'

'No.'

I ask the all-important question, my voice quiet. 'Are you still seeing him?'

Her response surprises me. She lets out a derisive snort, and says, 'That's what I mean, Tyler. You just drift through life. You don't see anything you don't want to see, do you?'

'What do you mean?'

'Harry Foxley died two months ago. He took an overdose of barbiturates.' She looks at me incredulously. 'All your supposed camaraderie, and you didn't even know about it.'

I'm momentarily stunned into silence. It's as if this day is a constant stream of unpleasant surprises. Nothing is what it seems. No-one is who you think they are. I'm finding out things about people I'd rather not know. And none more so, it seems, than myself.

So, Harry's dead now. Added to the deaths of Maxwell and Spann, it means that of the five men court-martialled and imprisoned for the pub attack in 1996, only two are still alive.

And it's them I start to think about now.

39

We don't really talk much for the rest of the journey. In the end, there's not a lot else to say. Thankfully, the traffic's sparse and it's relatively quick. When Adine finally pulls up outside my house, it's a quarter to one.

She stifles another yawn, and looks at me. There's sadness in her eyes. It's an awkward moment which I do my best to soften by placing a hand on her arm.

'Thanks for tonight. I really appreciate it.'

She responds with a small nod. 'I'm sorry about what I said. I'm tired, that's all. It's been a long day.'

'I know, I understand. Why didn't you tell me about Harry dying?'

'I didn't want you to know that I knew about it. Harry and I hadn't been seeing each other for a while, and I thought if I said anything to you, you might suspect what had been going on. I also assumed someone else had told you.'

'No,' I say wearily, 'no-one did. Did you go to the funeral?'

She nods. 'It was quite a small affair.'

I wonder why he killed himself, but I don't ask any more

questions. Instead, I lean over to kiss her, but she deftly turns a cheek and I end up missing her altogether. It seems an apt way to say goodbye.

Coming back to my dark, empty house feels strange after the frenetic events of the day. I'm tired but awake, wired almost. I know I won't sleep well tonight. There's half a bottle of red wine in the kitchen from a couple of nights ago. I take out the metal stopper and pour myself a glass, thinking how different my life was when I first opened it. But even then there was a storm brewing, a storm so strong it's almost swept me away.

Slowly, I'm beginning to piece together what I think might have happened. There are still huge unanswered questions, but for the first time I have a strong idea who may be able to answer them. Finding the people I need to talk to is going to be no easy matter though, and I wish Lucas was here to help. Then I think back to what Adine said about me picking people up and dropping them later, and I wish I'd taken issue with her on this, because I was never that way with Lucas. He was my best friend. No-one can take that away, and when I have the time, I'm going to mourn him properly. But not yet.

I take a long gulp of wine. It's a light Rioja, and it goes down well. I also pour myself a pint glass of water and drink half of it before retiring to the lounge. I need to sit down and recharge my batteries.

It strikes me that at no point today have I watched the news to find out how the mayhem I've been involved in has been reported, so I collapse onto the sofa and switch on the TV. Sky News is doing a sports round-up, so I use Sky Plus to bring up a recording of the latest headlines. I join it in the middle of a feature on the brothel fire. There's aerial footage of the building as it burns, thick cloying smoke taking up much of the screen. The commentator says that four people were taken to hospital suffering from smoke inhalation and that firefighters and investigators are currently sifting through the wreckage to see if there are any bodies inside. He adds that police are still not confirming any connection between the fire and the discovery of the body of a man who'd been stabbed to death fifty yards away.

The next story centres on some supermodel having been filmed snorting cocaine, which doesn't seem like news to me, but then what the hell do I know? She's followed by a piece on a spaniel called Egremont who can apparently do simple arithmetic by barking the total of two added numbers. Egremont's shown successfully adding two and three, and then the music comes on to signal the end of the headlines and the recording loops back to the beginning.

I'm still trying to work out how the dog's owner first realized he could add up when an image appears on the screen that causes me to choke on my wine.

It's a close-up shot taken by a CCTV camera. And the person in it is me.

It's not a perfect picture, thank God. I'm running, which blurs the image very slightly, and looking down and away from the camera so that my face is partially obscured, but it's clear enough for anyone who knows me. The commentator says that police are anxious to trace the man in the image in connection with the deaths of four men in a shooting incident in east London earlier today. I am, apparently, armed and extremely dangerous and should not be approached by members of the public. My picture disappears from the screen to be replaced by daylight footage of the house where I met Iain Ferrie. Scene-of-crime tape surrounds it, and white-overalled SOCO officers can be seen going in and out of the front door while a uniformed officer stands guard outside.

I don't wait around for the next story. I suspect it'll be the Eddie Cosick murders, but that's not important now. What's important is that I get the hell out of here, because every moment I remain makes my capture more likely. I can only assume that the police who were interviewing me tonight haven't seen this CCTV image, otherwise there's no way they'd have let me go. But that's not going to remain the case for long.

I have no grand strategy for a way out of this, certainly no chance of a long-term escape. But I have two key advantages. One, I don't give up. And two, for the moment at least, I'm free. If I keep moving, I'm going to make it hard for them.

I drain my glass and stand up. Not for the first time in the past twelve hours, it's time to start running.

40

The mobile phones I was carrying when I was arrested have been kept by the police for further analysis, so I use the landline to phone the local taxi firm, who've always been a reliable outfit. The controller says he'll have a cab with me in five minutes.

I run up the stairs, grab a change of clothes and a few toiletries, and thrust them into an overnight bag. I put on an old black leather jacket and a cap to act as camouflage, and arm myself with a large buck knife and a can of pepper spray, both of which I keep in a drawer by the bed in case of unwelcome night-time visitors (even my quiet area of London can be a dangerous place). I hide them both in the inside pockets of the jacket, knowing they're not going to be a great deal of use to me, but they're better than nothing. By this time I can hear the sound of a car stopping in front of my house. I poke my head out of the window and feel a surge of relief as I see it's the taxi. Bang on time.

I'm out the front door quickly and straight into the back of the cab. I give the driver the address of my showroom, and he pulls away without speaking. I wonder when I'll see my house again, or indeed if I ever will. Whether Adine gave me sensible advice or not, now that the police can connect me with yet more killings, convincing them of my innocence will be even harder. Just the fact that I keep popping up at all the murder scenes is way too coincidental.

The journey to the showroom takes under ten minutes at this time of night. It's not safe here either, but I'm not going to be stopping long. I just need a car, then I'll be off again.

I get out and pay the driver, giving him a couple of quid as a tip, then unlock the heavy steel gates and go inside. I hurry through the car park, past the cheaper models we sell, and open up the office.

Immediately I know that something's wrong.

There's no telltale beep to warn me to switch off the alarm, and I always set the alarm when I leave the office. Without exception. In the nearly four years I've run this franchise, I have never forgotten to switch it on. Why would I? In this room are the keys to every vehicle in the place, and that's getting on for a million pounds' worth of stock – a fact I never let slip from my mind.

I switch on the light and look around. The office is tidy, looking much the same as it does when I enter it each morning. Nothing appears to be missing, and everything's in its proper place. The drawers on the desk are all locked, and there's been no attempt to force them, and the strongbox beneath the desk, which contains all the keys to the cars in the showroom, is untouched. But somebody's been here. I'm sure of that.

There are no signs of forced entry, so whoever it was used keys. There are only two showroom keyholders in the world. One is me. The other is my brother, John, who lives in Kent. He hasn't been here. He would have told me. And even though much of the rest of the world seems to be on my back today, I'm not going to count him among that number. He's a quantity surveyor, for Christ's sake, and married with three young kids.

So that only leaves me. I own two sets of keys. One set I keep hidden in a false wall at home, the other I carry with me, and they're the ones I've just opened up with now. I can't be sure I didn't come here on Thursday, but if I did, I would have re-set the alarm. That leaves only one possibility: someone stole my keys when I was drugged. It was someone good as well, because not only did he let himself in, he also disabled a complicated (not to mention expensive) alarm system. Unable to re-set the alarm without the code, he simply locked up, came back and replaced the keys.

But what was he looking for?

The light's flashing on the desk phone. Not surprisingly, I've got messages. I put them on. There are twelve messages from Friday, but all are from existing clients or potential clients, and nothing's out of the ordinary. There's also a message from Thursday, timed at 5.03 p.m., from a private seller with a second-hand model he wants to get rid of. So, I must have left early. Perhaps to meet Leah. Or someone else.

I remember the number I wrote down when I was in Lucas's apartment earlier. Dorriel Graham, IT security consultant, the hacker guy Lucas claimed could find anyone. I put it in my wallet, and I'm hoping it's still there now.

It is. The folded slip of paper pokes out from one of the sleeves, and I remove it. I want him to find two people for me, but I'm also wondering if he can do something else as well.

I pick up the desk phone and dial. He answers after three rings, his voice a slow yet breathless drawl, as if the very act of speaking is an effort.

'Yes.'

'I was given your name by Martin Lukersson.'

'I know no-one of that name. I think you've got the wrong number.'

'You're Dorriel Graham?'

'Sorry,' he says, not sounding it at all, 'I don't know a Dorriel Graham either. Goodbye.'

'Please, listen. This is a quick job. It'll take you ten minutes and I'll pay you five hundred pounds.'

There's a pause.

'Lukersson should be more careful who he gives out my number to.'

'I need addresses for two people, and I need them urgently. Like now.'

'I don't like being woken up.'

'No-one does. But this is worth five hundred pounds.'

'Five hundred pounds isn't that much money,' he says, sounding bored.

'It's for ten minutes' work,' I remind him, my voice hardening.

'Do you have a credit card?'

'Visa.'

'Give me the card number, the expiry date, your name as it appears on the card, and the three-digit security code on the reverse. Now.'

It's not a great idea to be doling out my credit card details to a man I don't know, but right now that's the least of my worries. I give him the details, and wait impatiently while he writes them down.

'And what are the names of the people whose addresses you want?'

I tell him, and he writes this information down as well.

'Your card's authorized the payment of five hundred pounds. I'll phone you back when I have the information.'

'Can you also do something else?'

'What?'

'If I give you a landline number, can you get me an itemized list of the calls that have been received on it in the last two days, with the names of the callers and the times they called?'

'That'll take hours and cost you a lot more than five hundred pounds.'

I make a quick calculation. 'How about if you can just get me the numbers for Thursday afternoon? Say, between midday and 5.04 p.m.?'

'I can get you the numbers and the times, not the names. What's the landline number, and who's the account with?'

I give him my office number. I know it's a long shot, but I'm hoping that whoever I met last night left a message on the phone, which they then broke in here to delete.

'It might take a bit more time, and it'll cost another five hundred pounds.'

I tell him that's fine.

He hangs up, and I'm left waiting. In the distance I can hear the sound of a siren, and I tense. I really don't want to hang around here much longer. It's way too dangerous, but without a mobile phone, I can't move. I open up the strongbox, find the keys to an old BMW 5-Series in the car park, and put them in my pocket. Even now I'm loath to take one of the better cars, just in case I crash it.

The siren's getting closer, and it's been joined by another one coming from the south. Waiting here's too much of a risk. I rip the phone out of its socket so that Dorriel Graham doesn't end up talking to the police rather than me, and run out of the office and over to the car, switching off the alarm en route. The sirens are louder out here, both only a matter of seconds away.

I jump in the 5-Series, flick on the lights and fire up the engine. There's not a lot of room to get out, so I back straight into the car behind, which thankfully is an ancient 3-Series that's on the market for less than two grand, then turn the wheel hard right and tear off in a screech of tyres, going straight through the half-open gates with only a couple of inches of room on either side, and out onto the road, turning south and taking the first left. I've left the car lot completely open, but I'm figuring the police'll be there very soon and will be able to secure the place. And if not . . . Well, frankly, that's the least of my worries.

I drive for about fifteen minutes, heading in a northerly direction, until I pass one of those rare sights these days: a phonebox. It's on the forecourt of a twenty-four-hour petrol station, and I use it to call Dorriel Graham.

This time he answers on the first ring.

'It's me. Have you got what I want?'

The moment of truth.

'Yes, I do,' he answers in his bored monotone, and gives me two addresses. One is in Fife, the other in Hertfordshire. He also gives me their home phone numbers.

I write the information down while keeping the receiver propped in the crook of my neck.

'I also have a print-out of the calls received by the landline number you gave me. Where do you want me to send it to?'

'I'm on the move at the moment. Are there many of them?'

'Between midday and 5.04 p.m., there are thirteen.'

There were twelve messages, so that sounds about right. I get him to read them out. They're a mixture of landlines and mobiles, and one of the landlines is from out of town, and immediately familiar.

And that's because I've just written it down. It's the number belonging to the address in Hertfordshire.

I feel a numb sense of shock, even though I shouldn't really. He's certainly intelligent enough to have pulled this off. It's just that I really hadn't wanted it to be him. Not after everything we've been through together. I was hoping it would be Rafo, the Fijian now living in Fife, who'd served six years for his part in the pub attack.

Not my mentor. My commanding officer.

Major Leo Ryan.

41

It's 2.30 a.m. on Saturday morning. Dark clouds are scudding across the sky, and it's starting to rain – the heavy, soaking drops you get in the tropics. The initial shock I felt has already metamorphosed into different emotions. First, sadness, that someone I respected so much and for so long could hate me enough to have put me through this. And there's an acute sense of anticipation, too. At last, I think I know the identity of the man behind Leah's death, and that of so many others. He will have all the answers I'm looking for.

What happens after I've heard those answers is something I'm still trying not to think about.

Thick walls of pine trees line both sides of the road. I am in the countryside on the Hertfordshire/Essex border, very close, I'm sure, to where I woke up this morning. Beside me on the passenger seat is the road atlas I bought from the petrol station next to the payphone. I am only fifteen minutes away from the junction of the M11 I joined when I drove back to London sixteen hours and a lifetime back.

I slow down as a turning appears up ahead. I can see a sign

on the grassy bank. It says PRIVATE ROAD – NO ACCESS, and then beneath it there's a second sign of varnished wood saying ORCHARD COTTAGE. As I take the turning, I see that it's little more than a track, leading deeper into the pines. I drive down it about twenty yards before parking the car up on the verge and killing the lights. I get out of the car, noticing that the rain's getting heavier now, and look into the darkness ahead. I can see no sign of human habitation, but I know that Orchard Cottage is down here somewhere.

I start walking down the track, keeping to the edge of the tree-line, breathing in the cool, moist air, enjoying the feel of the rain on my head. I feel alive again, out here among the pines. The surroundings remind me of Bosnia and Kosovo, places where, whatever anyone says, I genuinely did experience camaraderie. I love the open air, and I realize how much I miss nature's vast, majestic expanses now that I live in the city. It's why I dread the prospect of incarceration so much. I make a vow as I walk: I am not going down for this. One way or another, this has to end tonight.

As a soldier, you have to learn to manage your fear of death. Some do it by finding God; the majority manage simply by thinking that it won't happen to them. That's not as hard as you may think on a battlefield. You factor in that a few will die, but you also play the percentage game, which means that probability-wise you'll survive. That goes out the window when you're on your own, though, and for much of today that's the way it's been. I had Lucas with me for a while, but now he's gone, and once again it's just me. Armed only with some spray and a glorified pen knife. But I do have the one commodity all soldiers need: surprise. No-one will be expecting me.

The track bends round to the right, and I can see a faint light flickering through the trees. I'm getting close. With a growing, almost tangible sense of anticipation, I pull off the track and fight my way through a thick set of brambles, moving deeper into the woodland. I walk in a steady south-westerly arc, taking my time. The pine trees seem to close in on me, their branches intertwining to plunge me into a darkness that would be absolute were it not for the light of the cottage. Around me, there is dead silence. It amplifies my own sounds as the twigs break beneath my feet. I've been trained in the art of moving silently, but it's been one hell of a long time since I practised it.

A break in the trees appears in front of me. I stop when I reach it, and look out. I'm facing an overgrown rear garden that leads up a hill into further woodland. The garden belongs to a two-storey house with latticed windows which sits in a dip down to my left. Lights illuminate both floors.

Orchard Cottage.

This is the place I want.

I remove the lid from the pepper spray in my jacket pocket and undo the strap on the sheath containing the buck knife, then move swiftly across the lawn towards the cottage. When I reach the back door I try it more out of hope than expectation, and am surprised to find it's unlocked. Very slowly, very quietly, I open it up and step inside.

I'm in a darkened hallway with a stone floor. It smells vaguely of dogs. Pairs of walking boots are lined up against one wall, and various coats hang from hooks above them. From further down the hallway I can hear the loud ticking of a grandfather clock. It's all so frighteningly normal.

I unsheathe my knife and creep further into the house, past the staircase and towards a partly open door out of which a thin shard of light is escaping. I can hear movement coming from inside. It sounds like someone's shuffling papers.

I stop by the door and wait, planning my next move. From

what I can hear, the distance from the door to my target is at least six feet, probably more. He may be armed, so I'm going to have to move very fast to incapacitate him. The major's an experienced operative, one of the best. This is not going to be easy, and this time if I make a mistake, I know it'll be my last.

I reach for the handle, but as I do, I hear a chair scrape on the carpet and somebody standing up. Whoever it is is walking towards the door. I step back into the shadows, and as he emerges, I grab him from behind in a headlock, pulling him back towards me. I can feel him beginning to resist so I press the knife hard against his throat.

'Hello, sir,' I say, 'long time no speak. Please don't make any sudden moves, otherwise I'll have to kill you.'

He's no fool, and remains stock still. I can't see his face, so I don't know what his expression is. I'm hoping it's shock. But he lets slip a deep, throaty chuckle, and I know then that he's the one who's been tormenting me on the phone today; that his is the voice beneath the suppressor.

'I didn't expect you to make it here, Tyler,' says Major Ryan in his gruff, educated tones. 'But then perhaps I should have done. You've done well today. Better than I anticipated.'

I pat him down and discover a pistol in a waist holster, underneath the waterproof mac he's wearing. The mac's wet to the touch, so I know he's been outside recently.

'Why don't you tell me exactly what you *were* anticipating?' I suggest, removing the pistol. It's a brand-new Heckler & Koch. 'In fact, why don't you tell me everything?'

'I think you've been through enough to deserve an explanation,' he admits.

'I know I have,' I say, turning him round and walking him back into his study – a spacious, traditionally decorated room with mahogany furniture, and bookshelves lining the walls. I give him a shove towards the leather chair next to his huge, spotlessly clean desk, then I point the gun at him and ask the question I've been waiting to ask all day: 'Why did you do it?'

The major makes himself comfortable. I haven't seen him in years. Not since the court martial. Considering that his unblemished twenty-year career was ruined when they threw him out of the army, and he spent at least five years behind bars, he looks damn well for it. He's dressed like a country gent in a lincoln green waterproof mac, tweed trousers and burgundy brogues. His hard, pockmarked features are heavily tanned, and he wears a confident half-smile as he meets my eye.

'You were expendable, Tyler. That's why.'

'But I never did anything to you,' I tell him.

The major's expression hardens. 'No, but you never did anything for us, either.'

'What do you mean?' I demand, although I think I already know the answer.

'We sacrificed our careers for you when you were hit by that bomb.'

'I didn't ask you to.'

'I know you didn't. But you could have shown some appreciation. We lost everything. Not you. You bounced back, Tyler. You rejoined the army. You carried on your career like nothing had happened. And did you ever think about us?'

'I did,' I protest. 'I thought about you a lot. All of you.' But I know my words sound hollow.

He shakes his head. 'I don't think so. You were always an individual, Tyler, never a true team player. Yet it was you, the least deserving, who seemed always to be the most successful. You left the army, ran a thriving business, took Harry Foxley's woman—'

'Don't be daft. She was never his woman.'

The major sighs, concedes the point. 'Do you know what annoyed me about you, Tyler? The fact that you never paid for anything. You enjoyed an easy, good life and you never paid a price for it. Until today. Now you have. It will have made you a better man.'

'And that's it . . . just because I didn't do things entirely your way, and I've been reasonably successful, you put me through all this?'

'Don't flatter yourself, Tyler. It wasn't revenge. We needed you today, that's all. It was just that no-one was too worried about what happened to you afterwards.'

I take a deep breath. It's difficult to believe I'm hearing this. That people I cared about have hated me for so long.

'Why don't you start from the beginning?' I ask him. 'What is the relevance of the briefcase I picked up, and what the hell does it contain?'

'The briefcase contains materials a number of people, some very high up, are extremely keen to avoid being made public, because those materials could help to convict them of some truly horrible crimes.'

I think again of the finger. 'Go on.'

'These materials were gathered by an individual who was blackmailing several men. One of those men was Eddie Cosick.'

'Don't you mean Colonel Stanic?'

A half-smile forms on Ryan's granite features. 'Yes, Colonel Stanic. I was hoping you wouldn't get to him, because I knew then that you'd make the connection.'

'So, what was Stanic to you?'

'He was a business associate of mine.'

'You don't hang around with very nice people, major.'

He glares at me. 'Let me tell you something, Tyler. When I left prison, I had nothing. My wife had left me. I had no money, no pension. I needed to survive. I'd always had a good working relationship with Stanic, so I made contact with him again, and helped him move his operations to the UK. I had help from others as well. Men like Foxley, Maxwell and Spann. We got a good business going, and as a result I've made back some of the money that was taken from me.'

'It looks like you've done very well,' I tell him, looking round the room. Nothing in here's cheap.

'It's nothing less than I deserve,' he says firmly. 'After the way the establishment betrayed me.'

The major was always a ruthless man. I notice now an arrogance to him that I've never really seen before, or perhaps it's something I've simply forgotten over time.

'You said you knew the real identity of the blackmailer,' he says. 'What was his name?'

'Iain Ferrie,' I tell him.

The major raises his eyebrows. 'I recognize that name. He served in the regiment, didn't he?'

'That's right.'

'Ah, so that's how you knew him.' He nods slowly, pondering this information. 'What a coincidence.'

'Ferrie told me that the case contained something terrible, something I never wanted to see. So, what exactly was the kind of business you were in?'

The major's half-smile returns. 'I thought Mr Stanic and I were in the same business – smuggling contraband, drugs, weapons, occasionally people – but it turns out that our businesses were actually diverging. You see, Mr Stanic made a lot of money from prostitution in this country, which was an area of the business that we – and by "we" I mean my former army colleagues and me – weren't involved in. However, he discovered what you might term a niche in the market.'

'What do you mean?'

'Some of his customers had rather bizarre tastes. They liked to do more than simply have sex with the girls. In some cases, they liked to beat and torture them. Even in a couple of cases, kill them.'

'Jesus, you're joking.'

'You were a soldier, Tyler. You saw what people are capable of doing. Sometimes even for pleasure. No, I'm not joking.'

There doesn't seem much that I can say to that, and I tell him to continue.

'I never knew about this side of Cosick's business,' he says. 'If I had, I wouldn't have approved. But someone else did. The blackmailer. Our old colleague, Ferrie. I'm not sure how he found out about what was going on, but he did. And he gained evidence of what was happening as well, and, more importantly, who was involved. My understanding was that he was black-mailing several customers, and those customers, terrified of exposure, contacted Stanic. Stanic tried to deal with matters him-self since, as you can imagine, he wasn't keen on anyone else finding out what he was up to. I believe he set up a rendezvous with Ferrie to hand over a payment in exchange for the evidence in the briefcase, and then tried to have Ferrie killed. But when that failed, and Ferrie began demanding even more money, Stanic called on my expertise.

'We knew that Ferrie wouldn't trust any of Stanic's men turn-ing up again to make the exchange, so we needed to bring in someone new. Someone gullible enough to fall for our set-up, and who could be trusted to follow instructions without running away with the money. Who could take all the risks without ever being able to point the finger at the people who sent him. Who was resourceful, brave and able to fight his way out of any trouble. And who, of course, was utterly expendable.' He stares me right in the eye as he speaks. 'That was you, Tyler. That was you.'

I feel like I've been kicked in the face. 'And you murdered Leah? Just to make sure I did what I was told?'

'It was unfortunate,' he says sharply, 'but, we thought, necessary. She was collateral damage.'

I think of Leah, the woman who for three short weeks I'd cared so much about, then of Major Ryan's cold, pitiless description of her. Collateral damage. She was nothing to him. I wonder how he could have become so twisted in his outlook on life. I feel the rage building within me. I want to tear this bastard apart, beat his head against the wall and make him suffer just a little of what Leah and Lucas suffered, but I force myself to keep calm. When I have the answers I still need, I'll take my revenge. Because I'm going to kill him for this, even if it has to be in cold blood.

I think about asking whether my relationship with Leah was a set-up, whether she too had been working for my enemies, but this is one answer I can't bring myself to hear. Better simply to leave the memories as they are.

'So, tell me,' I say, still trying to put all the pieces together, 'if Colonel Stanic was your business partner, why did you kill him?'

'Because the two of us had very different ideas about what we wanted done with the contents of the case. He, of course, wanted them destroyed, because they incriminated him and his so-called "special" customers. But I didn't. I wanted them made public.'

'Why?' I ask, frowning.

'Why do you think? These customers are high-ranking members of the establishment. There are the names of judges in that case. Of politicians. The very people who destroyed the careers of good men, men whose boots those bastards weren't fit to lick. I fought for this country for more than twenty years, in every war they sent me to. I followed every order I was given, but the one time, the one solitary time I asked them for support, they hung my men and me out to dry to appease a bunch of bombers and thugs. And they weren't content simply to wreck our careers, they had to grind our noses in the dirt as well, trying us by media, then throwing us in prison like common criminals.' His face darkens as he speaks, the bitterness coming off him in waves. 'Some of the men never got over it. Foxley, for one. He worked with me after he came out of prison, but he never got over the betrayal. He committed suicide, you know.'

'I know.'

'Do you? I'm surprised. You never went to the funeral, or even sent a card.'

'I'm sorry about that,' I say quietly. 'I wish I had done.'

'You're a fool, Tyler,' he says almost wearily. 'You deserted your comrades, and now you're paying the price.'

'It's no reason to put me through this. You're just using it as an excuse. You would have used me anyway, if you thought it was convenient.'

He shakes his head vehemently. 'No, never. I'm always loyal to those who are loyal to me.'

And what's so tragic is that I see he really means it, too. He genuinely thinks that he's acting from some kind of moral high ground. I look at him with a mixture of anger and pity, unable to equate the commanding officer I respected so much with the deluded ruthlessness of the man sitting before me now.

'You know, Major, whatever's been done to you in the past can never begin to justify what you've done today. You're a monster.'

'I'm no monster,' he snarls, and starts to get up from the chair.

'Stay where you are or I'll take your kneecap off.'

He sits back down, his expression hard and soulless. 'You can't call me a monster. The monsters are Stanic's perverted clients, and I can use them to bring down every one of those hypocritical bastards in the liberal establishment.' He spits out these last words, and a fleck of saliva lands on his chin. 'I want to throw their whole order into chaos,' he continues, his eyes alive with a fanaticism that fascinates and terrifies me. 'Bring the government to its knees and consign every one of the cowardly incompetents who run it to the dustbin of history.'

He pauses, calming down now.

'But Stanic was only ever interested in making money. He would never have agreed to the case's contents being made public, so he had to go. My plan initially was to get the code for the case from Ferrie and then put in an anonymous call to the police, so that when you delivered it to Stanic's men, they could intercept it and I could deal with Stanic separately. End of story. However, without the code, I wasn't able to do that.'

'So, you were never going to keep your side of the bargain with me. I was going to be arrested along with Stanic's men?'

'I couldn't risk leaving you at liberty. You were always resourceful enough to have worked things out if I had. As you have done.' He looks at me with an expression of admiration. 'I'm impressed.'

'I wish I could say the same, Major. Now, tell me, where's the case?'

'It's near here,' he answers.

'Why haven't you handed it in yet?'

'Because it's been booby-trapped, and I didn't trust the police not to destroy it in a controlled explosion rather than defuse the bomb. But now it's open, I will make sure the contents are delivered to them anonymously.'

'How did you open it?'

'I know a thing or two about explosives. I defused it myself. It wasn't easy – Ferrie did a good job with it – but I'm a determined man.'

'So am I,' I say evenly, 'and I've come a long way today. I think it's time you took me to it.'

'I don't think so,' he answers, meeting my gaze.

A cold yet ferociously intense rage rises in me. 'You know, Major, I once looked up to you, but that was a long time ago. Never again. You're nothing but a cold-hearted abomination, whatever you may think, and you're responsible for the murder of the two people I really cared about. So, if you don't do exactly what I say, I'll put a bullet in both your kneecaps and walk behind you while you crawl to wherever the case is.'

'I don't think you'll shoot me,' he says, but the confidence in his voice is belied by the lines of tension appearing on his face.

I keep the gun steady. 'I'll count to five. Then I'll fire.'

His hands grip the side of the chair. 'You think you can take me?'

'I've taken everyone else today.'

The major smiles grimly, and the tension dissipates. 'That's true,' he says, 'All right then. I'll show you it.'

As he gets up, I stand to one side. 'After you,' I tell him, 'and no tricks.'

'I don't need tricks,' he answers, leaning down beside the desk.

When his hand comes back into view, it's holding the burgundy briefcase. Straight away I notice that the red light next to the locking mechanism which signalled that the bomb was armed is no longer flashing. So, he has defused it.

I feel a nerve-jangling sense of anticipation. 'Open it.'

He looks at me, and there's something mocking in his expression. 'Are you sure you want to see?'

'Yes.'

He clicks open the locks.

I can hear my heart beating.

And then he flings it open with a flourish and steps aside, and I'm standing there, staring at something that even now I find hard to comprehend.

A jigsaw of human pieces, all wrapped tightly in clingfilm, tumbles out of the case's interior. I see a whole hand; five toes still attached to a piece of the foot; I may even have caught a glimpse of a perfectly skinned human face, I am not entirely sure. I don't really want to know. There are bones, too, faded and yellowing with age: part of a femur, some ribs . . . And photographs, poking out from underneath. I can see only part of one. It's of a young woman, and I gasp as I recognize the face from the picture Alannah showed me, of the woman she claimed was her sister, Petra.

And as I look from it to the major I see something in his eyes, and I recognize it immediately as a bright, malevolent triumph, as if he's just proved to me that the world is a far more evil, depraved place than I ever could have imagined, and that there are indeed monsters out there even greater than him.

I don't know what to say. Feeling faint, I take a step back, my gaze dragged back to the case and its terrible contents.

And it's then that I hear a noise behind me and feel the cool touch of the razor against my neck.

42

I'm pulled back into the darkness of the hallway, the grip tight around my neck, the blade pushing into my flesh. I can't see my captor, but I know it's a woman. I can smell her scent. So I was right about Alannah, I think, without any degree of satisfaction.

The major closes the case and stands in the middle of his study, looking at me. Surprisingly, his expression is one of sympathy.

'I'm sorry it had to come to this, Tyler. Now, drop the gun.'

He's still in my line of fire and I keep the gun pointed at him, recovering now from my shock as my survival instincts kick in. I know that if I do as he tells me, I'm as good as dead.

'No.'

'She'll cut your throat, Tyler, don't think she won't.'

'I know she will, but my last movement'll be to pull the trigger. I'll take you with me, Major.'

She tries to pull me further into the hallway so he's no longer in view, and it's surprising how strong she is, but I resist, even though she ups the pressure on the razor. Any second it's going to cut the skin. I don't want to die like this; I've seen too many victims of her handiwork today. But I'm not going to

296

let the major out of my sight. My finger tenses on the trigger.

'Tell her to stop,' I hiss, conscious of the movement of my Adam's apple against the blade, 'or I'll fire.'

He nods at her, and she relaxes her grip a little.

'It seems we have – what do they call it? – a Mexican stand-off,' he says calmly. 'So, what are we going to do now?'

'Let me go and I'll walk out of here. We both want the same thing. I don't want those bastards to get away with whatever it is they've done.'

He shakes his head. 'But you won't just walk out of here, Tyler, will you? You'll come back for me. I know it.'

He glances over my shoulder, and a silent message passes between him and Alannah. I know he's telling her to take the risk and make the cut. I am a second away from death. But I can't go like this. Not with Leah and Lucas unavenged.

'Wait,' I hiss. 'There's something you should know.'

The major frowns. 'What?'

In one rapid movement, I grab the wrist holding the razor with my free hand and yank it away from my throat. Then I slam my head backwards and drive it into her face. I hear a cry, and she stumbles, but before I can get out of the way the major throws himself at me, grabbing the barrel of the gun. Instinctively, I pull the trigger, the gunshot like a whiplash in the enclosed space. His momentum sends me flying backwards, but I dive to the side to keep out of range of the razor, and we land together on the carpet, with him on top. His face is screwed up in pain, his eyes tightly shut, and he rolls off me clutching his gut where I've shot him.

A gutshot. It's one of the most painful wounds a person can endure, and it can be hours before you die. He bunches himself up into the fetal position, and lies there rocking back and forth.

For the time being he's out of action, so I turn my head in the direction of Alannah. But she's nowhere to be seen. The hallway's empty, the only sounds the major's tight, laboured breathing and the incessant ticking of the grandfather clock.

I lie there in the semi-darkness, the gun stretched out in front of me. Where the hell is she?

A door further down to my right is open. She must be in there. There wouldn't have been any time for her to get any further. I don't want to go inside. This girl's good. Too damn good. But there's no alternative.

Slowly, I get to my feet, my eyes adjusting themselves to the gloom. In the dim light provided by the major's study, I see a huge photo of him and someone else on the wall. Even in my current situation, I can't help but be drawn to the head-and-shoulders shot of the person next to him.

'Oh Jesus,' I whisper, my voice loud in the confines of the hall-way.

The person smiling back at me from the picture is a young woman I can only assume is the major's daughter.

And it's not Alannah, it's Leah Torness.

43

She comes out of the door like a wraith, dressed in black, the blood running from her nose like melted tar where I struck her with my head. No longer the sweet young thing with the smile and the button nose from the supermarket, but a pale-faced killer with a gaze of stone.

I am still reeling from the shock. So the video I saw was a complete fake, and now the final pieces of the jigsaw puzzle are coming together. It was Leah I must have met on Thursday evening, who managed to lure me here for the set-up, although she took a risk calling me from her father's landline. And God knows which poor Eastern European sex slave I woke up beside the following morning, but the reason her head was missing is simple enough: so that I'd go to my grave thinking that the woman I loved was dead.

And that woman is here now and as I stare at her, still trying to come to terms with what I'm seeing, her right arm flashes up like a striking snake, the movement so swift it's almost a blur, and this time there's no razor in it but a pistol with silencer attached. I know Leah's going to fire, but, even with the gun pointed at me, I've been hit so hard by the huge and terrible extent of her betrayal that I'm unable to react. Only yesterday I loved this woman. She was the one I genuinely wanted to build a future with. And all the time, all the time ... The lie simply refuses to sink in.

But my hesitation's a mistake, because Leah Torness's eyes are utterly devoid of mercy. I see the flash of light, and the shot hisses out of the silencer. I'm knocked sideways and sent spinning. I stumble into the major's body, hit the wall and collapse to the floor, dropping my gun in the process. I've been hit in the shoulder.

The pain is like nothing I've ever experienced. It feels like someone's poured petrol into the wound and set it on fire. I grit my teeth and shut my eyes. I've lost. After coming so close, I've finally lost.

When I open them again, Leah is bent down beside the major. 'It's OK,' I hear her whisper, her voice suddenly full of emotion, reminding me of how she used to talk to me. 'We'll get you help.'

Then she stands above me, the silencer pointing down towards my face. The end of it is barely three feet away.

My mouth goes dry. The pain is roaring through me in waves. After everything I've been through, I have no energy left to fear my fate. When she pulls the trigger again, it'll all be over. I'll be joining Lucas, Ferrie, Snowy and so many other comrades from down the years.

'My father always said you were a good soldier, Tyler, which is why you'll die quickly.'

'Why?' I whisper, and I'm not asking the reason she's going to kill me. That part feels strangely irrelevant. What I want to know is why did she pretend to share so much with me? Why did she let me make love to her? Why did she tear me apart when I'd never done a thing to deserve it? But she doesn't answer, maybe because she can't, and I know it's the end.

I clench my teeth and tense, waiting for the inevitable impact, determined not to close my eyes. Making her watch me in these last seconds, and hunting desperately for any tiny chink of emotion in her eyes to show that somewhere deep down she feels a twinge of regret about what she has to do . . . but there's nothing.

Nothing at all.

The front door flies off its hinges and lands with a crash on the carpet, and a blinding white light like a lightning strike fills the room. Leah's eyes widen and she stumbles, dazed by the flash grenade, before regaining her footing and staring at the door.

There follows a shout that for the first time actually fills me with relief. 'Armed police! Drop your weapon!'

'Drop your weapon! Drop it now!'

The silencer's still pointed at my face. Is she going to pull the trigger? One last, murderous act of defiance?

But no. In one movement, she swings the gun away from me towards the door, the idea of surrender as alien to her as it was to her father.

This time, however, her luck finally runs out. Two angry bursts of automatic weapon fire shatter the silence, and Leah disappears from view. Just like that. Gone in an instant.

Again, there's that long second of silence when everyone stops to draw breath, and then the shouting and activity start as people pour into the hallway.

Someone leans over me, his face close. 'You're going to be all right, mate,' he says, but the pain is so intense I'm not sure I believe him. He moves aside and calls for medical help. 'This one's been shot as well,' I hear him shout. 'Shoulder wound.'

I no longer care. I'm beginning to black out now, and I'd welcome unconsciousness with open arms if only I could lift them. But my whole body feels like lead. People move across my vision, but they seem to blur into one another like watercolours in the rain. Only one stands out. She has long blonde hair. I squint, try to concentrate my gaze, anxious to see if it's her or not. It's difficult to tell. She has her back to me. And it's too late. I'm going. Going . . .

Gone.

One week later

44

DI Mike Bolt comes to see me again. I wouldn't say we'd become friends, but it's his third visit and I'm getting quite used to his company. The first time he came with his colleague, DS Mo Khan, and they questioned me under caution, the doctors apparently having said I was fit enough to be interviewed. That was four days ago. Bolt asked me if I wanted the services of a lawyer, and I knew that Adine would kill me if I didn't call her, but for some reason I honestly didn't feel I needed one. You see, I'd got to this position where I knew there was no point not telling the truth. All the lies I'd used to save myself had just made matters worse, and in the end I simply didn't have the energy to keep up the charade. It was time to lay everything on the line and throw myself at the mercy of the forces of law and order, and that's what I did. I told them the whole story as I knew it from beginning to end, adding, for what it was worth, that I was sorry I'd bullshitted them in the first place. I had to be a bit economical with the truth when it came to the fact that I'd killed four people, of course, since, self-defence or not, admitting something like that would have spelled the end for me.

Bolt said that he was pleased I'd seen sense, and he seemed it as well, but he also told me that I was under arrest on suspicion of murder, and that I couldn't leave the hospital.

This wasn't exactly news. For the whole time since I'd come out of the operating theatre, I'd been in a room on my own, well away from any of the hospital's other patients, with a police guard outside the door. Even if I'd wanted to escape, I couldn't have got very far, considering the number of tubes and wires I was hooked up to. To be honest, at no point did the thought cross my mind. I'd had enough activity and excitement to last a lifetime.

The second time, Bolt came on his own. He even brought me a box of wine gums and some grapes, which I thought was a nice gesture. He had a few points that he wanted clarifying. I gave him the information he needed, then asked him some questions of my own. I wanted to know what had happened to Leah, or Alice as her name turned out to be, and he told me that she'd died from gunshot wounds at her father's house, having never regained consciousness. The news still saddened me, but it was also as if a strange, dark chapter in my life had ended, and could now at last be put behind me.

I asked about the major as well, and Bolt answered that, like me, he was still in hospital with gunshot wounds but was going to make a full recovery. He wouldn't give me any further information, citing the fact that investigations were still ongoing, so I let it go at that. Instead we shot the breeze for a little while – about football, of all things. I was sure he was only talking to me to create some sort of camaraderie, but to be honest, I appreciated the company. Because of my situation, the number of visits I get are fairly limited, and people aren't exactly queuing up to see how I'm getting on. My brother's come once, as has my mother, and, to be fair, Adine, but that's pretty much it, and I can't help but brood over the fact that had Lucas still been alive, he would have been here for at least an hour every day, livening the place up, because he was that sort of guy. I never saw that much of him in the last couple of years of his life, maybe once every three months or so for a bite to eat and a few drinks, and I will always regret that I didn't spend more time with him towards the end.

It's a sad but undeniable fact of a soldier's life that comrades die. You're taught to grieve and then to move on. Yet I find it difficult to comprehend that last Friday morning there was a thriving private eye business in Whitechapel staffed by two good friends of mine. Then I paid them a visit, and now that business and those men are no more. It's a bitter cross to have to bear.

Maybe, just maybe, if I'd had more time for the men who'd been flung out of the army for avenging what had happened to me and the others that day in South Armagh, none of this would ever have happened. But as Bolt pointed out on his last visit two days ago, if they hadn't tried to take the law into their own hands by avenging it, none of it would have happened either. I suppose you can keep going back, can't you? If the IRA hadn't planted that bomb; if the British hadn't intervened in 1969; if Oliver Cromwell had been a nice guy ... The point is, what's done is done, and that's the end of it.

Anyway, Bolt's here now. He hasn't brought wine gums or grapes this time, but he's looking pretty happy, which I'm thinking is probably a good sign and, as he sits in the chair next to the bed, I quickly get confirmation that it is.

'We're going to be taking the police guard away from your room,' he tells me, 'so, officially, you're no longer going to be in our custody.'

I ask him if that means I can go. 'Technically, you're still under suspicion of murder, so you're going to remain on conditional bail for now, and we're keeping your passport until the situation changes. But, yes, as far as I'm concerned, you can go.'

'Thank God for that. I was never any good in hospitals.'

Bolt smiles. It's a look that suits him, even though it accentuates his scars. 'Me neither. I was in one for six weeks once.'

'Really? What happened?'

'Car accident.'

'Is that how you got the . . .?' I tap my face.

He nods.

'It must have been a bad one.'

'It was.' He clears his throat. 'I can also let you know that we've made some arrests in connection with the rape and murder of three Eastern European prostitutes. The arrested men include a government MP and a prison governor.'

'Jesus.' I shake my head. 'I thought I'd met some of the worst this world has to offer. It seems I didn't even know the half of it.'

'There are a lot of bad people out there,' he admits, 'some of them in high places. But we always get them in the end.'

I think back to the packages of decaying human flesh, and the photograph Alannah had shown me. 'And it was Ferrie's evidence, the contents of the briefcase, that led to them being arrested?'

He nods.

'How the hell did Ferrie get hold of all this stuff?'

'We believe he was already blackmailing a prominent business-man in an earlier sex abuse scandal, and that this man was also involved in the case we're investigating now. It's conjecture, but we think Ferrie was watching the guy, and that's how he found out about it. He compiled quite a dossier, which included details of burial sites, so it wouldn't have been that difficult to have recovered the body parts.'

'What good are the body parts?' I ask. 'From a blackmailer's point of view?'

'Well,' he says with a sigh, 'most importantly, they contain DNA traces and other physical evidence connecting them to the person or persons who killed them. But they can also be used to identify the victims, which is useful in building up a picture of how the whole operation worked, and who was involved in it.'

I try to make myself comfortable in the bed. My shoulder still aches intensely.

'What happens now?' I ask him.

'The arrested men are being questioned. So far, no charges have been brought, but if they are involved and we have the evidence we think can convict them, they'll be charged with murder.'

'You mean, it's not cut and dried?'

He leans forward in his seat, and speaks quietly. 'Off the record, the evidence against them is strong. That's as much as I can say.'

'And what about the major? Can you tell me what's happening with him now?'

He sits back. 'He's still in custody in hospital, and since his arrest he's refused to say a word to any of us, but his silence hasn't helped him. He's now been charged with a number of offences, including murder, so he's not going anywhere fast.'

I wonder where they've got the evidence from for charges. As far as I know, nothing implicated the major at any of the murder scenes. And with his business partner dead, there is no-one else, bar me, who can point the finger at him. And all it is is my word against his. I think again of Alannah's part in all this, but when I ask about her, I draw a blank. Bolt doesn't seem to know about her – or, more likely, he's not saying anything. So she remains, as ever, a mystery.

There's another mystery, too. 'Was Ryan really using his own daughter as a contract killer? Ferrie said she was nicknamed the Vampire.'

'I don't think we'll ever know the full story there,' he tells me. 'The thing is, you often get unsolved murders attributed to mysterious contract killers, and there's been talk in police circles in Europe of a killer known as the Vampire, but most of it stems from the triple murder in Paris, the one where your former colleagues Maxwell and Spann were murdered. Because of the way the killer got in and out so efficiently without anyone seeing him, he's now being conveniently blamed for killings all over the place, which is probably more to do with lazy police work than anything else. It's certainly possible that Alice Ryan committed the Paris killings, but there's no hard evidence to prove it. What we do know is that at the time of the Paris murders, Maxwell and Spann were under investigation by Interpol on suspicion of drug and gun smuggling, and from what we've been able to piece together, both men had ended their business relationship acrimoniously with Major Ryan and gone into partnership with the man they died alongside, so the major may have a motive for having them killed.'

I lie back in the bed and shake my head. You go through life thinking you know so much, but in fact you know nothing at all. These last few weeks have been a revelation to me, and mainly for the wrong reasons.

Bolt gets to his feet. 'You're a very lucky man, Tyler. You've come up against some very dangerous people and you're still alive.'

I don't feel very lucky, but then again, I am still here. With another couple of scars to add to my total, granted, but still here nonetheless, and largely intact. Maybe I should be thankful.

'You're still going to need to report in to us regularly, and we're going to want to speak to you again at some point, so don't go off on any long trips round the country, OK?'

'What about short ones?'

Bolt pulls a business card from his pocket and hands it to me. 'Call me if you leave town.'

'Sure.'

We say our goodbyes, and he tells me to stay out of trouble.

Fat chance of that, I think.

45

An hour later, I walk out of the hospital with my few meagre possessions in a bag and start off down the street. The heatwave's gone now, and the temperature's back to normal for early September. The sky's a gunmetal grey, and it's drizzling fine rain. I think about getting a cab home, but then decide that, having been cooped up in a hospital bed for the past week, a long walk'll probably do me a lot of good.

I haven't gone thirty yards when a car pulls up beside me and a very attractive blonde woman pokes her head out of the open window.

'Need a ride anywhere?' asks Alannah, the traces of an Eastern European accent still there, but less noticeable than before.

As usual, curiosity gets the better of me. 'You'll tell me who you really are this time?'

She smiles invitingly. 'Promise.'

The car's a Toyota Corolla, and not a particularly new one either. As I get inside, she pulls away from the kerb.

'I heard they released you.'

'You heard right,' I answer, not wanting to make it easy for her. Where Alannah's concerned, I still feel a sense of betrayal, although given the other people who've put the knife into me these past few weeks, hers is fairly small-scale.

'I also wanted to thank you properly for saving my life,' she adds.

'I actually saved it then, did I?'

'Come on, Tyler, don't be like that.'

'You'll forgive me if I'm feeling a little jaded, but I'm getting tired of being bullshitted the whole time.'

'I didn't want to have to lie to you, I promise.'

I fix her with a sceptical expression.

'What I'm going to tell you,' she says, turning my way, looking as beautiful as ever, 'I don't want repeated to anyone. Understand?'

'OK,' I answer uncertainly.

'I *am* a police officer, and I *am* from the old Yugoslavia, originally at least, but I work over here now. I can't tell you who I'm with or where I'm based, but my role's an undercover one. I infiltrated Eddie Cosick's organization to try to gather evidence on his people-trafficking business. We never realized the true extent of what he was up to, and how many other people it involved, but in the last days of the operation I did realize that something very important was happening, although when I first ran into you I still didn't know what it was. I intervened on your behalf in the brothel when I found out they were going to kill you. I was deep cover, but not so deep that I could stand by while someone was murdered.

'But the problem was that as soon as I got involved, I effectively blew my cover. When you came to Marco's flat, he genuinely was trying to kill me, so yes, you did save me. After that, though, I didn't know what to do about you. When you told me about the case I knew we needed to see it as well. I thought that if I got you to go to Cosick's house, we could use this as an excuse to raid the place. We could say we'd got an anonymous call about an intruder, go inside and recover the evidence that we could use to hold him.'

'But the girl in the photo you showed me, Petra . . .'

'No, she wasn't my sister. But Petra is her name, and her story's a true one. We were approached by her sister, who *is* a police officer in Belgrade, who told us she was missing, and about Eddie Cosick's people-smuggling operation. I thought if you showed the photo to Cosick, it would panic him.'

I think of the girl in her school uniform, smiling self-consciously at the camera, and I remember her photo from the briefcase. 'And she's one of the murder victims, isn't she?' I ask, knowing what the answer's going to be.

Alannah nods grimly. 'Yes. She is.'

We're silent for a few moments. I feel an overwhelming sadness at the thought of this young girl dying a depraved, lonely death thousands of miles from her home and family at the hands of such cold-hearted killers. The grim irony that if it hadn't been for Major Ryan they might have got away with it is not lost on me.

I look at Alannah. 'I suppose when I told you I wasn't going to go to Cosick's place, that's when you called in your colleagues to arrest me?'

She nods.

'And you called the police to Cosick's place as well?'

She nods again. 'I did.'

'How did you know I was there?'

'Technology,' she says. 'When you were back at my place, I planted a tracking device in your shoe.'

That explains a few things, not least how the police managed to turn up at Ryan's house too, but it doesn't make me feel any better. 'So you could have caught me at any time?'

'Yes, but I was ordered to let things run and see what happened. We moved in when we saw you were heading to Cosick's place, but we weren't quick enough to stop you going in, or to prevent the death of your friend.'

'I know you weren't,' I say bitterly.

The news that Lucas's death could have been avoided is a real blow. In the days since I watched him die, I've thought about him often, more often than I ever did in life. With him gone, my world's an emptier place.

'I'm sorry about that, Tyler.'

I don't acknowledge the apology. 'And what happened after I was arrested? How come I was let go again?'

'I had nothing to do with that. But again, the idea was to let you run and see what you turned up. There was a feeling you knew more about things than you were letting on, and you were followed discreetly, from a distance. Unfortunately, we lost the signal on the tracker when you entered the woodland around Leo Ryan's house, and it took some time to locate you.'

'By which time I could have been killed.'

I look out of the window at the ordinary people passing on the pavement outside as they go about their ordinary lives, and I hear Alannah apologizing again.

'OK. Well, I guess the apology's accepted,' I say at last. 'And thanks for helping me back at the brothel.'

She smiles, showing gleaming white teeth, then her expression becomes more serious. 'Listen, Tyler . . .' She pauses a moment, and I try to read whatever's behind her dark eyes. 'When I kissed you back at the safehouse, I wasn't putting it on, you know. That's partly why I'm here.' We're turning into my road now, only yards from home. 'I was hoping that maybe we could take things a step further. Maybe, you know, go out some time. Finish off what we started.' She comes to a halt outside the front door and looks at me expectantly, brushing a curl of blonde hair from her face.

She really is beautiful, a vision in various shades of gold.

'I don't think so,' I say with a tight smile, 'but thanks for the offer.'

I open the passenger door and get out, and as I walk to my front door, fishing in my pocket for the keys – a sadder yet wiser man than I was before all this started – I don't look back, nor do I feel even a twinge of regret.

I may be alone, but sometimes, just sometimes, that's the best thing to be.